The Valley

The Valley

BARRY PILTON

BLOOMSBURY

'Elderberry Wine', Words and Music by Elton John and Bernie Taupin
© Copyright 1973 Universal/Dick James Music Limited.
All Rights Reserved. International Copyright Secured.

First published 2005
This paperback edition published 2006

Bloomsbury Publishing Plc, 36 Soho Square, London W1D 3QY
A CIP catalogue record for this book
is available from the British Library

ISBN 0 7475 7173 2
9780747571735

All papers used by Bloomsbury Publishing are natural, recyclable
products made from wood grown in well-managed
forests. The manufacturing processes conform
to the regulations of the country of origin.

Typeset by Hewer Text Ltd, Edinburgh
Printed by Clays Ltd, St Ives plc

www.bloomsbury.com/barrypilton

For Jan

Part One

Chapter 1

'It was the trousers,' said the postman. 'When I saw the dog had got the trousers, I knew something wasn't right.'

Gareth stared gravely at the ground, tapping the tractor wheel with his boot. This was a detail he hadn't known about.

'Dog didn't want to play with them or anything, just dropped them at my feet. They were his best pair too, chapel pair.' With every farm he stopped at, the postman's account of the previous day's events improved in colour and texture. 'Dragged across the yard in the mud.'

Gareth looked up, shocked. 'What, not . . . not the ones he had on when he . . . ?'

The postman nodded grimly.

'Dear God! How did they end up in the farmyard? I mean, if he was already—'

'Yes, took us a while to work that out.' The postman was not keen to take questions, reluctant to surrender the thrust of his narrative. 'Anyhow, straightaway I said to the dog, "What is it, girl, what's up?" And she ran over to the barn. Well, I knew Hefin wasn't in the house, I'd been knocking, with a parcel. Replacement part for the generator. That's what'd brought the dog out. So I followed her over to the barn.' He paused, ostensibly for composure but betraying a gift for timing. 'And that's where I found him. Hanging.'

'Had he been dead long?'

'All night, I reckon. He was white with frost. White and stiff. Reminded me of a lynching, the way he was dangling there in the gloom.'

'Must have been one hell of a shock.'

'He's my third in two years. At least he had the consideration not to use a shotgun. Not like John Howells up at Ty Mawr. I'll never forget the state of that kitchen, it was –'

'Yes, I remember you saying.'

'Oh. Mind you, the sight of poor old Hefin, all alone, suit and tie and long johns . . . his dog whimpering under the beam. That'll stay with me a fair while.'

'Was it you cut him down?'

'No. Police did that. Did you know they got lost? 999 call and they got lost.'

'Apparently the call goes to some central computer somewhere these days.'

'Moscow.'

'I don't understand the business with the suit. Why would he get all dressed up just to . . . just to die?'

'I don't know. Last chance at some dignity, I suppose. There was sod all dignity to be had in the state of that farm. And that was the other strange thing. He'd locked the place up. Half derelict, scarcely worth anything as scrap, and he'd locked the place up. And then walked out with his best clothes on.'

There was a silence as they both reflected on this. Neither of them said it, because they were old-fashioned men, but somehow they found this the most moving aspect of all.

'And even they got ruined, by the mud. It was the belt, you see. He'd used his belt, just twine really, to . . . to loop round his neck. Jumped off the hay bales and . . . well, the jolt must have . . .' His hands depicted trousers falling from a corpse. 'That's what the police reckoned anyway,' he added, to distance himself from the charge of prurient speculation.

'A week before Harvest Festival,' sighed Gareth, and won-

4

dered about the pasture he rented from his late neighbour. 'Who'll look after the dog?'

'Jessie? Don't know. Isn't there a brother?'

'In pigs. Don't need a dog for pigs. And she's a good working bitch.'

There was another long pause. Accidentally, they had strayed off the subject of the tragedy, and they could not find a bridge back. They had covered all the 'hows?', and knew there was no need for a 'why?' The deceased had even found leaving a note to be superfluous. He was an ageing hill-sheep farmer. Period. The postman nodded at the middle distance, in a muted manly way, and restarted his engine. He still had another twenty people to tell the story to.

But he couldn't tell any of them what was really churning around in his mind. As he bumped down the potholed track back towards the valley road, he kept going over and over his interview with the new area manager.

Dafydd used to love his job. 'I'm with social services,' he would say with a laugh. And it was true: he would check whether Mrs Higgins had fallen from her walking frame, assist old Norman to water his upper row of flowering baskets, transfer home-made cakes from the Commodore's sister to the village hall, and it all came for the price of a stamp.

As for stray heifers, he'd lost count of the times his van had helped corral the randy beasts, nudging them back down lanes and on to home territory.

The first warning sign had been the pedometer from Cardiff, special delivery from headquarters. He hadn't even known what a pedometer was then. One of the young sorters, Richie, had known – and told everyone with triumphal glee – because the word had cropped up in his pub quiz. 'A mechanical instrument for counting paces and measuring distance,' he announced. And they had all laughed.

Eight cottages and three farmhouses were removed from his round as a result of that mechanical instrument. In one case, the front door was just six paces over the 'statutory maximum distance from a maintained road necessary to qualify for delivery by Royal Mail'. So the owners all had to put up mailboxes at the end of their tracks. As if they lived in Arizona and were expecting some rubbish American mailman to drive by and throw letters in their general direction. These people were old friends, lonely widows and frail, retired farmers who wanted a cheery word as much as any dull brown envelope. Of course, he ignored the ruling.

Then, after the pedometer, came an assessor. And he (or perhaps she, for there was no known sighting of the person) calculated the exact time required per property for the satisfactory delivery of mail to the rest of the valley. Dafydd was one hour fifteen minutes over target. Nor was he the sole offender.

The union promised representations. His own, somewhat petulant, proposals to the branch – that extra time be allowed for 'a savage dog situation', 'a wild bull situation', 'a fallen tree situation', 'a flood situation' and 'a thick mud situation' – were judged by more seasoned negotiators to be 'unhelpful'. Apparently, reference to these normal aspects of rural life would be considered provocative by head office. Diplomacy was to be the chosen channel.

After two months, an unofficial admission was obtained from the authorities that bad weather was 'a grey area'. But still they insisted that rounds be subject to strict timekeeping. And from then on the joy started to go from the job.

Dafydd had been among the more vociferous in mocking the unreason of modern management, but never in his daftest dreams had he considered it necessary to propose rules for a dead-body situation, with a statutory minimum time to be allowed per corpse during the course of duty.

He had stayed an hour and a half beside the frozen body of fifty-eight-year-old Hefin, late bachelor of the parish, and watched a misty-red October dawn rise over the hills. He had helped the police with their questions, and had arranged for someone to tend the sheep. As a result some letters were late.

'Do you not think ninety minutes was excessive? He had been deceased for some twelve hours, I understand. It's not as if you were applying a tourniquet.'

'I was a witness.'

'No you weren't. You found him. That's all.'

Dafydd hated the new area manager, and the fact that the man was twenty years his junior. Nor did his being an incomer from Swansea help.

'I had to give a statement.'

'Like what? "I found him"? That's three words. That take you an hour and a half, does it?'

'There were also the sheep to—'

'You're not responsible for sheep. Unless you want to pack this job in, and become a sheep farmer.'

Dafydd sensed he was close to having a noose slipped round his own neck, and knew he had to decide between silence or throwing a punch.

As he dropped to second gear for the one in six past old St Brynnach's, he still regretted he had not opted for the punch. He might have been sacked, but he would have been kept in drinks for a month. And drinking was getting to be his only pleasure of late.

Instead, he had spent the morning catalysing his resentment into a bloody-mindedness, and his provision of a news update service on the death of Hefin had already put him fifty minutes behind target. Had he been a new man, he would have claimed he was helping with the valley's grieving process. Indeed, young Ms Courtney-Stone from the converted barns, who was having rather a struggle to establish herself as a homeopathic vet, had said that dead bodies in stressful contexts could create a psychological undertow, and was firmly of the view that Dafydd should ask for counselling.

While Dafydd had no time for such nonsense, he suspected the

Post Office was probably just the sort of organisation to have a detailed policy on post-traumatic stress disorder, if only because PTSD involved jargon and sounded cutting edge. The idea did, however, offer one major attraction: if he were entitled to any protracted sick leave it would cause considerable stress to the area manager.

He was still savouring this fantasy as he accidentally scattered Marjorie Whitelaw's hens with his van. She emerged turbulently as ever from her caravan, shooing the dozen Buff Orpingtons back to the abandoned VW Beetle that served as their henhouse.

'I hear you've killed somebody else off with all these bloody bills you deliver,' she shouted, and gave a fortissimo laugh. 'Tea?'

'Why not?' He got out of the van and stretched his legs. He thought the detail of the trousers would go down well with her.

Chapter 2

'. . . £22,000.'

Stéfan hesitated. He didn't like hesitating. Dynamic, flamboyant, imperious, these were the adjectives he liked to leave in his
wake. Stinking rich was another description he didn't object to.
But not patsy, his visceral competitiveness would not allow him
to appear a patsy. And to pay a five-figure sum for what should
have been his for nothing, could have been his for nothing, put
him in patsy territory. In front of 150 strangers, soon to be
neighbours. So he hesitated.

Stéfan was, on the other hand, also prey to vanity. And buying
Lot 563 could do a great deal for his vanity. Ownership would
enable him to feel part of Britain's historic continuum, as the
toady from Sotheby's put it, in his brochure-speak. Lot 563
would also be the cultural icing on his cake. The cake was the
listed, twenty-eight room Jacobean manor house, plus land and
outbuildings, whose six-figure purchase had so recently been
sealed by his signature, complete with curlicues for the occasion.
The icing was the archives.

'Against you, at £22,000 . . .'

Or perhaps he should just bid for a giant urn, and settle for that
as his memento of the mansion's past. On all sides, the historic
contents of the estate were being murmured over. Woodwormy
dining-tables, with initials carved by generations of the gentry;
obscure statues, crapped upon by generations of the rookery;

9

monstrous tureens, made mirrorlike by generations of dutiful scullery maids. And outside, in one large sad clump, stood the old ironware of agriculture, purpose now known to but a few, and desired only by the nerdishly romantic. As Stéfan blinked about him in the fug, he found himself reflecting that he was younger, by many years, than any item in the long day's catalogue. Younger, probably, than any of the serious buyers.

A large dollop of water suddenly splashed down his neck, putting an end to this satisfying thought. Looking up, he saw a row of heavily pregnant raindrops preparing to ease themselves from the sodden canvas above his head. He made a sideways leap across the coconut matting, just missing the rump of a Sloanish lady in jodhpurs, and realised that seven hours of this upper-class clearance sale had rendered him oblivious to the rhythmic drumming of the rain upon the marquee.

Most likely the significance of the rain was lost upon him. Being as yet on little more than nodding terms with the landscape, he no doubt believed his new-found family seat was merely suffering the whims of an obsessive cloud. But the long, winding ascent from the foot of the valley up to the high moorland was more than just a scenic glory. For every two miles advanced, the rainfall increased by ten inches a year. At the first dog-leg bridge over the river, the cottage owners benefited from thirty inches' worth. Fifteen bridges and ten chapels later, the hill-sheep were splashing around in an annual ninety inches.

Crug Caradoc, ancestral home of sundry Lord-Lieutenants of the county, stood in red-creepered and decaying splendour over three-quarters of the way up the River Nant; here the steep-sided valley unexpectedly opened out on to what looked like a Swiss mountain meadow but was actually a flood plain, a fact unmentioned by estate agents. The Jacobean mansion on the Roman tump had the sessile oaks of mid-Wales for a backdrop, and in the foreground a generous terrace descended to two lakelets fed by the river and seventy-five inches of rain, jugs of which were now disturbing Stéfan.

'Any advance on £22,000 . . . ?'

He knew he was nearing the final call. Since £10,000 it had been head to head, and the bastard of it was, he knew he was up against a dealer. He had caught sight of him earlier, a cocky, unshaven little man in a hooded zip-up jumper, running suspicious fingers along the private parts of the pricier furniture and making squiggles in a small notebook. But unlike the other dealers – and there were many – he affected a public contempt for the proceedings, and indeed for most of the objects on offer. Were these trade traits of a master poker player, or just provocations of an impostor? Stéfan simply could not decide.

The rival bidder did not sound local, did not dress local . . . yet he looked local and all the locals knew him. And today the locals were out in force. They were there in deference to the occasion, to the house and to its history . . . though no chance to nose would be ignored. The farmers were the most evident – all governed, it would seem, by a nineteenth-century dress code. They gathered at the rear in woolly ranks of low-key tweed and ties and wellington boots, as if knowing by osmosis that sub-Sunday best was order of the day.

Present in equal force were the county set who, mysteriously, were never seen in public except at point-to-points or upon dismemberment of a dead relative's assets. And thus, since the owners of all large country houses in rural Wales are related, either by birth or dynastic sex, they have regular provision for recycling their furniture. Their choice of attire for this event testified that class is not dead. The gentlemen all went for the matching ensemble, with Barbour triumphant in every department except (presumably) underwear, while the ladies opted for the somebody-royal-on-horseback look, but more floral.

Stéfan's choice of clothes was, by contrast, unique. He had turned up in a white cricket sweater, white shirt and a pair of white flannels. No one quite knew why. Had he childhood memories of some dog-eared schoolbook on village life in Britain, and not fully grasped the essentials? Or had he heard the role of squire was vacant and confused it with colonial administrator? Or did he not know it was October?

These were among the questions being put to Clydog in the refreshment tent. As chief reporter, indeed only reporter, of the weekly *Mid-Walian*, he had gained what Fleet Street would call 'privileged access' on the previous day. However, his forty years of births, marriages and deaths and the occasional hay-barn fire had not honed any noted inquisitorial skills. Rather, this old sub placed his trust in more amateur arts: twice a day his portly, tweeded figure would potter round the local market town of Abernant and, just by the raising of his hat, gossip would stick to him as flies to flypaper. And then he'd be off – perhaps, if lucky, to see the breeder of prize-winning piglets.

In truth, Clydog the Knowledge was not prepared for Stéfan, or anyone foreign. He was certainly not prepared for being driven at 110 miles an hour round the bypass, or being pressed to drink a magnum of champagne – from the bottle, at the traffic lights – or being informed in a stentorian voice, during a hotel lunch, of the dimensions of his interviewee's todger.

Clydog had done his best. He had asked questions as vigorous as his heart condition would allow. But the news that 'Stéfan is a foreign name' was not much by way of a scoop. Asked where he came from, Stéfan had laughed and said 'Nowhere that you could spell!' Then added, 'Home of the Mongol hordes' before laughing again, at unreasonable length – and leaving Clydog unsure what the joke was, or what he should write. At the risk of impertinence, Clydog had tried enquiring as to his line of business. And been told rather more about property deals than he could understand, the words nightclub and import-export majoring in the monologue. Whether all this involved gangland murders and drug smuggling, Clydog was unable to say.

Clydog was unused to new money. Like all the valley, he was unused to change. For forty years he had been the chronicler of stasis. And for more than forty years he had been witness to the dynastic decline of Crug Caradoc. Yet even Clydog had not been able to predict the overthrow of Eryl, its one-time heir, whose absence from the auction spoke such volumes of bitterness; nor had he foretold the murky manoeuvrings of Trystan, who had so undeservedly inherited these spoils of the past. Spoils which he had now put under the hammer.

And when the locals tempted Clydog with a pint or two, as they did now, he could tell them little of the future either, save that the new owner from afar liked the idea of Welsh country life because 'you got more bricks for your buck'.

Back in the marquee, Stéfan had become bored with the stand-off.

'Oh fuck it!' he said, in unexpectedly plummy tones for a foreigner. Three rows of moneyed heads turned, and he boomed at full throttle, '25,000!' Then gave vent to a braying, unsubtly intimidating laugh. He knew from long experience of negotiations that a sudden leap in price was the rabbit punch, the blow that broke the spirit of the opposition.

'Twenty-five and a half,' said the auctioneer, and thirty yards away Stéfan saw a stubbly face smirk at him from beside the tent flaps.

At heart, he understood the problem. There was an inequity of benefit. He wanted the family deed boxes for sentimental reasons, to bask in their heritage. His rival wanted their contents for commercial reasons, to bask in their profits. For Stéfan the bidding was indulgence, for the dealer it was business. This was not an equal contest, it was scissors versus stone.

As he pondered on this dilemma, torn between prudence and vengeance, he was smiled at by the Sloanish lady in jodhpurs whom he had nearly upended earlier. Haughty and horsy, she too had an outfit that caused comment. With polished riding boots, breeches so tight that it seemed she enamelled her buttocks, a quilted burgundy top, a chiffon scarf, rainbow-finned glasses, and make-up in bulk, it was hard to tell if she was en route to the pony club or a fancy dress ball. One suspected that she deludedly thought herself en route to the county set.

Stéfan had watched all her own bids fail – her horse was going to be very short on equine leatherwear this winter – and assumed her smile was out of empathy. Had he asked a local, any local, he would have been advised that her smile was strongly related to his ability to lay out £25,000 on a whim. The horsewoman observed him closely through her dark-tinted lenses, and then, after injecting further warmth into her features, she took a step towards him. Had he asked a farmer, almost any farmer, Stéfan would have learnt why he made her heart beat faster. She liked a man with stabling.

His instinct said caution, he sensed neurosis, a woman who brought trouble. He smiled back.

She touched him on the cricket sweater with her crop. 'Felicity. I'm in the hunt,' she said with practised cut-glass vowels, and then moved away, leaving Stéfan to grapple with rural double meanings.

'Against you at £25,500 . . .'

He reassessed. Part of the fun of buying the house was making his townie friends pig-sick with envy, and to have rare historical documents stuck all over the bog walls would make them even pig-sicker. Nonetheless, the main game plan, as he constantly announced to everyone, including complete strangers, was to have a country estate ready for when he retired at forty, that age when all successful men retire and leave London. That was what mattered. And yet, and yet . . . Like many an outsider and exile he hankered after roots, longed to appropriate a past, and the brittle bundles illuminating the private history of this house, this seventeenth-century manor house, were not just abstractions to him. He had seen the actual documents. He had felt them. For it was he who, by chance, had first come across the archive. An archive that chronicled four centuries and seventeen generations of ownership by just one family, the Llewellyns – who, with the death of ninety-two-year-old Gwendolen, had finally come to the end of a four-hundred-year line.

He vividly remembered the perfect summer afternoon in late

August when he broke into the deserted house. The swallows were swooping through the roofless outbuildings and snatching flies just inches off the surface of the upper lake. The cattle of a tenant farmer were chomping noisily in the meadow. A pair of iridescent green dragonflies were mating on the wing in the walled garden. He had shouted 'dirty buggers!' at them, for he was a witty man, and he had listened to the echo.

He had found himself spoilt for choice of broken windows. As Clydog could have told him, it was years since the family had spent money on such trifles. Decades, even; neglect of the estate had begun before the war, when a frisky polo pony in India had bounced the colonel on his brain, and his wife had discovered drink. Thereafter, for Gwendolen, maintenance of the inheritance had come a poor second to upkeep of the cellar. Even the proceeds of a minor Van Dyck had gone on Châteauneuf-du-Pape.

Stéfan had eventually squeezed through some sort of scullery window at the back, not an easy squeeze for a man of his bulk. From there he passed through a panelled anteroom, which in turn led to a grand entrance-hall. Oak doors offered promise in every direction and, though the finest artefacts were gone, lost to folly and to family vultures, there remained pantechnicons of pickings still to be had. But it was the house itself he wanted.

This was, admittedly, not the orthodox way to view a property for sale. He had been at a weekend house-party in the borders, celebrating his twenty-seventh birthday, when he heard the tale of 'the house that time forgot', that familiar phrase of lazy journalism. Yet the account also had the tabloid lure of tragedy and treachery. Even the name Trystan, the usurper, came from the ancient word for 'tumult' and had overtones of dark Celtic deeds.

So, on impulse, Stéfan had driven alone across the moors to find this ancient manor house. As he told the other guests on his return, he had barely gone five yards up the long gravel drive before he felt the cheque of destiny in his hands.

Stéfan made his way through dusty shuttered room after dusty shuttered room; in one would be rotting carpets, in the next a fading tapestry of the Napoleonic wars, the next a shrouded four-poster bed. And everywhere a soft silence. The corpse had been gone a month, the last mourners had long left the wake, the house was now breathing to its own rhythms. He wandered from library to study to parlour, pondering on new furnishings and where to show his guitar collection to best advantage.

Eventually, he reached the attic rooms, the servants' floor. From here too he could look upon history: the peeling cottages, the overgrown grounds, the fractured glasshouse, the ruins of a tennis court that had not seen a forehand in forty years, the half-dug hole for a swimming pool never swum in.

A door was ajar on one of the small rooms. By chance he looked in. A glint of metal drew him to the broken corner cupboard. Inside was a set of World War I ammunition boxes. He dragged the top one out. And that was when he saw the photos. He was there until the light gave out.

A hundred and twelve people worked for the estate in the summer of 1897. And when the harvest was safely gathered in, every one of them – farmers, farriers, gardeners, labourers, butlers, valets, cooks, housekeepers, parlour maids, chamber-maids – had put on their one set of simple finery, and lined up in tiers on either side of seated Sir Richard and Lady Margaret, with their five children and four springer spaniels, along the terrace of Crug Caradoc. And a Mr Dai Williams, photographer of Messrs D. Williams and Sons, formerly of Llanwern, buried his head under his tripod's black cowl, fired the release, and put on record a scene of ramrod formality.

Innumerable moments of such ritual, no doubt preceded by much excitement and horseplay, charted these years of apparent plenty, years when the rump of almost every sheep in the upper valley bore the Llewellyn brand. Patriarchs and matriarchs were time and again pictured standing beside horses, and hunting dogs, and garden ornaments, and vegetable displays, and even farm implements, always in their full regalia but rarely smiling, just gazing determinedly towards posterity.

Nor was the social history confined to pictures. The same methodical mind had retained the household accounts, and their compilation surely took a heavy toll on quills.

Almost every day, a carriage went fifteen miles to the local station halt (where once, according to an overwrought diary entry, Queen Victoria herself had descended to visit a favoured MP and friend of the Llewellyns). And almost every day, at this tiny station the guard would unload a hamper from Harrods. Indeed, Harrods hamper upon Harrods hamper cascaded on this far-off family as if each day heralded a picnic for five hundred. Thanks to exemplary housekeeping, every can of consommé, every jar of caviar, every tin of shortbread, every bottle of vintage wine, was accounted for. As the family gourmandised, so their consumption was itemised, by a servant's copperplate in lined exercise books.

These same books also listed the wages of every person on the payroll. It provided an instructive juxtaposition. The annual salary of a chambermaid was entered as four shillings and sixpence . . . which put her cost for the year at less than a case of champagne. And in one month alone there were a dozen cases of champagne.

In the third ammunition box was a lifetime of diaries and correspondence. Somewhere in this torrent of words was the full story of the rise and fall of the House of Llewellyn – fierce rival for four centuries to the House of Powell in the lower valley. It seemed, however, from the briefest of samplings, that the hereditary rich adapt uncertainly to poverty. One account described the hard winter of '63. With a cavalier eccentricity, it related how a set of dining chairs had been chopped for firewood, thus keeping the family warm even as they dined off Dresden, with a Rubens on the wall.

And in the fourth and final box was the backbone of the dynasty: 400 years of legal documents. Of property rights, land purchases, farm leases, dowry demands, stock sales, court cases . . . These were the manuscripts integral to the history of the house, dating back even to the day when Crug Caradoc was built – a year when Shakespeare was in full flow. This was a fact not without relevance. For there, almost lost among the scrollwork, was a farmhouse listed as the property of Llewellyn . . . and named in the History Plays. Visited, indeed, by Hotspur. So, somewhere in all these miles of manuscripts was perhaps proof of whether Shakespeare himself ever came to the valley, and with which grand family he had stayed.

'For the last time, at £25,500 . . .'

Stéfan stiffened, bit on his lip and tried to forget that he was the prime exhibit of the day.

'Oh fuck it!' he said, even louder than before. 'I'll have a bloody swimming pool instead!' And with bad grace and in a strop, he exited into the rain.

As the hammer landed, Nico, the troublemaker with the stubble, tugged on his hood and smiled. He knew at least three buyers who would be interested in taking different parts of the collection, one of whom would pay dollars.

On that wet afternoon in the Eighties, the valley was parted from its history. And as new blood started to seep through its world, all the old certainties began to fracture.

Chapter 3

It was the bell-ringers who first noticed the problem. They were thirty-seven minutes into 'Cambridge Surprise Minor' when Mrs Hartford-Stanley felt a draught on her bottom. The night was dark and stormy and she instinctively put it down to the wind. Then, a few more changes rung, she was tugging on her sally when she felt it again – a ripple of cold air up her pleated skirt.

Being an experienced ringer, the intense concentration needed was second nature to her. Yet even as she kept her focus fixed on the intricate sequence of bells (5–6–3–4–2), somewhere far off-stage in her mind was a niggling, undefined sense of something odd. She had not heard the ancient oak door of the church creak open, nor the scurrying of dead leaves that would attend it. 4–2–6–3–5. And the echoing flagstones were sure to have registered the entrance of even the most discreet visitor. Not that a visitor was likely on so wet a night in such a distant hamlet 2–3–5–6–4. But wind there was. And then it came a third time. Like a goblin with cold breath.

In a reflex action, she turned her head, looking quickly from the bell-tower into the nave. And saw nobody. And nothing. 6–4–5—

'Oh, shoot! Shoot, shoot, shoot, shoot, shoot!'

The bells tumbled to a discordant halt.

'I'm so sorry, everybody!'

Sympathetic smiles masked the others' disappointment. No one blamed her, they had all done it in their time. Though no doubt several were not best pleased to have driven up to ten miles through falling branches and flooded lanes only to see their evening's pleasure so soon truncated.

'That's not like you, Rosemary,' said the conductor, a genial old hand in the science of ringing.

'Yes, I'm sorry, I—'

'I thought Mr Chigley's trousers had fallen down again,' said Joanne, a skittish spinster in her fifties, and giggled.

The others joined in the laughter, although old Mr Chigley, a rather lonely and overweight seed merchant, could only manage a forced smile and a beetroot blush. The night of Mr Chigley's trousers had passed into local bell-ringing legend. Halfway through a 'Kent Treble Bob Major' the top button of his corduroys had ceded victory to his stomach and slowly, inexorably, bell by bell, his trousers had descended to his ankles. Yet such was the discipline of the team that they had managed to continue ringing in full view of his underwear for nearly two minutes before a collective hysteria made progress impossible.

'No,' said Rosemary, 'I was distracted by . . .' But by what, exactly? She turned and looked behind her. Then she walked with deliberation across the floor of the old bell-tower.

'What is it?' asked the conductor.

'I'm not sure.'

She stopped, and stared intently at the ancient stone walls in front of her.

No one was to be seen, but everywhere the footprints of the diocesan surveyor were ironed in the dew on the graveyard's grass. In the high trees that framed the church, the sentinel rooks had for an hour squawked warnings of his presence. By the time the vicar hurried through the lychgate, it was a textbook autumn morning – a brilliant blue sky, a mist rising off the river, and a blood-red sun that had yet to make headway against the cold.

The vicar puffed his way down the path of yews, past the tumbled tombstones and the looted Llewellyn vault. He was a Bunteresque figure but with eyes too close together to be jolly, or indeed sexually mainstream; prematurely old at thirty-five, prematurely balding with dandruff on his cassock, he had a public persona that did much to explain the decline of the Church in Wales. As he rounded the far end of his parish church he caught sight of the surveyor on his knees.

'You can use the church for that, you know,' he quipped.

The surveyor did not look up. He had pulled back the brambles and was burrowing into the ground near the river bank. Below him a dipper bobbed uncertainly at the sound of the cleric and then flew low and fast upstream, to seek refuge under a small humpback bridge. He watched the bird go by. As a child, the surveyor had watched kingfishers and even otters along this tranquil stretch of the lower Nant.

He pushed himself up a little stiffly, and rubbed at the green smear now on both knees of his navy-blue suit. Then he held out a spadeful of earth. And slowly cascaded its contents on to the ground, an action clearly intended to be of significance.

The vicar looked blank. 'I'm not with you, Euan.'

'Come and look at this.' Euan, the older man by some twenty years, led the vicar back along the side elevation of the church. The oldest church in the valley, St Brynnach's nestled almost unnoticed in a dell, its seclusion evoking the ancients' idea of sanctuary. At its eastern end curled the river, at its western end rose the woods, and away to the south stood the mountains.

Euan came to a halt a few yards from the porch, where the great oak door opened into the nave. He stepped back and gestured towards the building. 'Norman,' he said, pointing up at the squat old tower. 'Victorian,' he said, pointing to the body of the building. 'Silurian,' he said, waving at his pile of excavated earth.

Somewhat to Euan's satisfaction, the vicar still looked blank. 'A geological term.'

'Oh.' The vicar smiled, the placebo smile that he used to stave off his parishioners and their crises. But such smiles were wasted on the surveyor, who had a brusqueness not amenable to an approach of vacuous happiness. The vicar reconsidered Euan's words. 'Are you saying there's a problem?'

'There's a problem.'

'Is it serious?'

'Put it this way, have you considered a career change?' Confident he had the vicar's attention, he moved closer to the church's stonework. 'Look, see here . . . and here . . . and here.' His finger traced a path up the joints. 'This is where the Victorian section was joined to the Norman section.' He paused. 'And now it's saying goodbye.'

As the vicar looked more closely he could discern a definite crack, which steadily widened as it rose up the building. 'Oh God in heaven . . . ! So . . . so how far will the church move?'

'Given time . . . ? To the sea.' These were the moments he cherished in his work for the diocese. Unknown to his colleagues in the religious buildings department, he had for years been a secret subscriber to atheism. And now, at a time of tighter budgets and leakier churches, his specialist field of work afforded him ever more job satisfaction. 'It's falling into the river, nave and all.'

'It must be possible to underpin it or something.'

'Normally, yes. The trouble is, Reverend, whoever built this church hadn't read their Bible.'

Again that bovine look of incomprehension crossed the vicar's face.

'The man who builds his house on sand . . . ?' offered Euan. 'That's what the Victorians did with their end of the church. It's just standing on earth. Not a rock in sight. And this lovely river is meandering closer and closer. Eating away at the house of God.'

'Oh dear . . .' As at all moments of crisis, his hand went

straight to the boiled sweets in his cassock. Just as panicky spring lambs bolt to the teat. After years in this valley, he was only too aware that the house of God was being eaten away, but up till now he had blamed it on a declining population, materialism, television, apathy and moral decay. Silurian sediment had not been a major worry. And now, in an instant, he had seen his livelihood flash before his eyes. Not that spreading divine love was anything but a thankless, dreary task. Religion was no longer the social glue of these hills. Now, to see a couple of 4 × 4s by the lychgate on a wet Sunday was cause for Hallelujahs! And that was the combined haul for two churches. All women, all moaning, all gossiping, all worrying about the Sunday joint. The menfolk stayed at home, their only chance to watch their dirty videos. They bought them from the cobbler's in Griffin Street, he knew that for a fact, from the poky annexe hidden behind that thick velvet curtain through which they kept disappearing.

'I'll put the full details in the report.'

'Oh right.' The vicar didn't want to know details, any more than he would want to pore over X-rays should he be afflicted with cancer. He just stood and stared at the crack in the church wall, sucking noisily.

'But I need to check inside first. Will the Commodore be long?'

'Who knows? Who ever knows?'

The Air Commodore was holder of the church key. Although technically this was the most minor of administrative roles, it symbolised a larger truth. His family, his aristocratic, land-owning family, had worshipped at St Brynnach's for generations and had the tombs to prove it. With the demise of the rival Llewellyns upriver, none could now refute the Powells' claim to be the valley's premier dynasty. From their Queen Anne house, whose roof could be seen across the water meadow, came a constant supply of flowers to bedeck the altar and dusters to polish the plaques. Though no formal proof existed that they were blood relatives of Jesus, the family was firmly of the view that St Brynnach's was a personal gift from a higher authority.

The two men stood a few feet apart in uneasy silence, marking time among the gravestones. Nearby lay the valley's newest grave, Hefin's headstone an interim cross of wood. The sun was edging up over the yews and had begun to cast extravagant shadows across its fresh earth. The vicar pondered his personal tragedy. He felt bitter at the injustice of geology. 'So,' he asked eventually, 'what's to be done?'

'Prayer?' suggested the surveyor.

The vicar sensibly ignored this suggestion. 'This would be the second church I've lost. I was rationalised at Nantgarreg. Three times in one month I was preaching to just the churchwarden. And then he got flu. Is it still safe?'

'This building? For the moment, yes. I wouldn't advise any rousing hymns, though.'

'Little chance of that. Mrs Skinner still plays the organ and she's eighty-nine. One wrong foot on the loud pedal and her head would explode.'

'Is the church ever full?'

'Harvest Festival, of course. Weddings. And funerals. Most of the valley comes to a funeral. Particularly when it's a farmer.'

'I'd steer clear of the altar. Especially if the nave starts to slope.'

'Good . . . morning.' The soft, nervous tones of the Air Commodore took them by surprise. He had appeared behind them, his six-feet-two-inch frame having navigated the stile in the graveyard wall. Despite looking gaunt and tired, he had walked down through the fields, down one of the myriad rights-of-way in the valley that now marked yesteryear's forgotten paths to church. Even more gaunt and tired, and defeated by the stile, was Rupert, his old black labrador.

'You . . . er . . . you wanted the . . . um . . .' Conversation with the Commodore was always difficult.

'Good of you to come, Air Commodore,' said the vicar.

'Some sort of . . . um . . . problem, my sister said.'

'That's right,' replied the surveyor.

'Mmm . . . nasty things, problems. Seen the dipper this morning?'

'Yes, indeed,' said the surveyor.

'Good. Very good.' He stared at the ground.

The Commodore had not had a good war. Invalided out was the whispered word. The exact cause of the problem was not known, but was believed to be all that noise and shouting. Always a delicate child, his life in the rural ruling classes had not prepared him for, well, for anything. A breakdown had ensued in the late 1940s. And 1950s. And, indeed, most succeeding decades. His sister Dilys – who still lived with him – was a noted hostess, and few were the guests who did not have accounts of standing alone with him in front of the hall's lifesize oil portrait of his father, unable to discover a single subject in the English language to which he would respond. This awkwardness was a misfortune compounded by his wife Josephine, who had been in bed with gin for over fifteen years.

'The key.' He held the church key out to the vicar.

It was a monstrous key, nearly a foot in length. Without a religious function, it would have constituted an offensive weapon. The vicar took it from him and creaked the oak door open, a creak given new significance by the eastward march of the nave.

Inside, at first glance, it was religion as usual. The echoing mustiness, with a hint of Brasso and fresh-cut flowers, still hung around the pews. The bell-ropes still lay looped over their hooks. The hymn numbers, testimony to the valley's farewell to Hefin, were still displayed on the board.

What was new, however, was that the secular world beyond the church was now visible from within. On the frontier between Norman and Victorian was a clear flicker of daylight – and a crack which explained why Mrs Hartford-Stanley had felt a frisson in her upper thighs for the first time in many years. The surveyor described it as a 'yawning gap' to upset the vicar further. Euan set about bridging this crack with slivers of glass so that, as they fractured, the pace of movement could be monitored. By such matter-of-fact measures did reality strike home.

The prospect of being left with a third of a church greatly disturbed the Commodore. For generations his family had had a whole church. To the Powells, the provision of spiritual welfare for their community was an historic duty, a duty exemplified by the wide range of embroidered kneelers they made available. Nor were their good works just godly. Patronage had long been in their blood, and today it was on the headed notepaper of many a local cause. Red Cross, Blue Cross, Green Cross, dogs, cats, lepers, a Powell would usually lend their name, or at least their rose garden.

This sense of duty had been passed down to the Commodore. Although he rarely spoke in whole sentences, he was often heard to mutter individual words of some length, words like obligation, responsibility, integrity – traditional words that took him back to his childhood days of Latin. (For several centuries there had been a family crest, but *necessitas non habet legem* – 'necessity has no law' – was judged to be out of tune with the times and was now kept in the stables.) The Commodore also hoped to be on a polished plaque one day, next to his ancestors, and if the church were short of a nave this would be difficult. He was therefore eager to suggest remedies for the impending crisis.

'Bring-and-buy sales.'

'Bring-and-buy sales?' queried the vicar.

'Always a great success.'

'I don't think that—'

'Tombola?'

'Yes, but—'

'Raffles?'

The vicar pressed the surveyor to hazard a guess at the cost of underpinning.

'Impossible to say,' he replied. And then said, '£25,000.' And then added, 'Plus.' For good measure.

'£25,000!' said the vicar, astonished. Extrapolating from an average collection plate of £3.50, this was not cause for optimism. '£25,000?'

The Commodore considered this new information for a while. And then cried, 'A garden fête!'

Chapter 4

'He may look like some slurping psycho out of a zombie movie,' said the estate agent, 'but he's basically harmless.'

Jane twisted herself sideways in the front passenger seat, and looked back at Mr Probert. Rob, her boyfriend, was struggling to double-declutch the old Morris 1000 Traveller from second to first, a manoeuvre he had never found necessary in England, and this had left Jane in charge of conversation. 'And he'd be our nearest neighbour?' she asked.

'He's a good field away.'

'Oh, that's all right then,' said Jane.

'His trouble is he's lonely.'

The wheels skidded briefly on wet leaves as the 1,098 cc engine over-revved up the steep lane.

'Fifty and never been kissed, I reckon!' he added. Before leaving the office, Mr Probert had decided the best sales strategy was to employ light-hearted witticisms on the subject of Glyn, the Commodore's worst tenant. In Mr Probert's attempts to sell the late Hefin's farmhouse, Glyn was having the effect of human dry rot. To date, three prospective buyers had not even made it up to the property after they had experienced the leering rustic by his farm gate.

'How d'you know we'll see him, this sexually frustrated neighbour?' asked Jane.

This was the question to evade. One always saw Glyn. Or

rather Glyn always saw one. Harmless he might be, but spy satellites could not have improved on Glyn's detection rate of strangers. And access to the empty old farmhouse on the ridge went via the entrance to his tenant smallholding.

'Oh I don't know for sure we'll see him,' Mr Probert said, with estate agent honesty. 'Though I guess when your farm's got no power or heating you do like to get out a bit!'

'Is that right?' replied Jane with exaggerated interest. Her tone immediately reminded him why this young pair was able to consider the purchase of remote Pantglas: its absence of all known amenities.

'Your turn to get mucky,' Rob said to her, bringing their car to a halt.

The single-track road, which had wound upward from the moment it left the valley bottom, had run out of tarmac.

A fork and two farm gates lay ahead, each closed. To the left, a rough track followed a stream down to a dilapidated building in a hollow. To the right, a mud slalom climbed up through a copse towards a distant meadow.

The trick, as the estate agent knew, was to leap out of the car, open the gate, race through the gate, close the gate, and leap back into the car before the arrival of Glyn. It was, however, a two-door estate car and he was in the back – along with several dozen well-squeezed tubes of oil paint, a broken oar, a joke dildo and a rich crop of unidentified animal hairs. Mr Probert was deeply regretting that he had chosen today to service the firm's Range Rover.

'Come on, prissy pants! Out!' urged Rob.

'Fuck off! I opened the last gate!'

'If I take my foot off the brake we'll roll back in the ditch.'

'It's raining.'

'It's Wales.'

'Can you fit remote controls to farm gates?' Jane asked, laughing as she forced open the rusty car door with her shoulder.

The car stood at an angle on the slope, which added gravity to the problems of exiting. To keep the door from slamming, Jane swung both legs out together, and the clammy plastic seat made her short skirt rise to the top of her thighs. As she levered her lower body out and up she saw the eager, unshaven face of Glyn arrive panting from his hovel, and felt her whim to wear knickers that morning had been wise. She squelched across the mud to tackle the gate to Pantglas, struck by the accuracy of the long-forgotten childhood word 'turnip-head'.

'Good morning, Glyn,' called Mr Probert.

'Morning to you, sir,' replied Glyn, keeping his eyes fixed on Jane's crotch.

'Hallo there!' said Rob, leaning forward to smile through the passenger door.

'How do you do, sir,' replied Glyn, keeping his eyes fixed on Jane's crotch.

'Lovely dog,' said Jane, as his border collie bounded up to join in her struggle with the latch.

'Name's Twm, miss,' replied Glyn, keeping his eyes fixed on Jane's crotch.

He leaned low over his rotting gate. A stocky figure, his clothes exuded wafts of wood smoke made malodorous by weeks of sweat and body odour. Even at ten paces one could sense that mains water played little role in his life.

Despite his enthusiasm for company he made no attempt at conversation, seeming content with the visuals of life.

'Not seen you at market lately,' said Mr Probert.

'I've had a problem with phlegm,' replied Glyn.

There was a brief pause in the interchange as he appeared about to illustrate these health problems.

Then, with a sudden tug, the latch was released. The moment he saw this, Rob revved his old banger forward – a move that played havoc with Glyn's eyeline – and bounced the gate open with his bumper. Leaving the gate to clang shut, Jane called

'Goodbye' and leapt back into the car as it yawed noisily up the track.

'Well, that's worth five thousand off at least,' she said, turning to address Mr Probert. 'After all, the risk of impregnation by an alien life form every time you go shopping, that's not exactly a plus point.'

'Oh, the view's the plus point. Eleven hundred feet. Woods and mountains in every direction. You don't get that in Leeds.'

'Manchester.'

'Right.' His patter faded. The Morris Traveller continued to jolt up the track.

Mr Probert was not happy with houses. Normally he did animals – cows, sheep, pigs, that sort of thing – and to sell those he just had to call out bids and bang a gavel. And perhaps make the occasional remark about the quality of their semen. It all happened in a huge tin shed, pungent with the odours of animal fear and piss and dung, and warmed by the packed bodies of hard-pressed farmers. It was a comforting if fetid world that he had known since schooldays – schooldays that he had shared with many of the buyers and sellers. And with whom, after the day's sales, would come the shared pints in the snug of the Market Tavern.

Of late, though, the pints had served only to drown the lament of declining profits. The market in animals was hitting hard times. So his boss had added house sales to the firm's portfolio, transactions that took place up a flight of rickety stairs, like an afterthought to the real business of the land. For valley people did not move home. They stayed put, resistant to such frivolity. But every passing decade now doubled the acreage needed for survival, and accumulating field after field had left many a farmhouse surplus to requirements. So today the homesteads were being picked off like cherries, separated from their land, parted from their purpose, and sold for the value of their views.

And were usually bought by a new breed of country-lover, with whom he had no common language.

'What's that smell?' asked Jane, sniffing the air. 'I can definitely smell something.'

'It's burning rubber!' snapped Rob, cross with her for asking, furious with himself for stalling. The second of the hairpins had been the car's undoing. Its bald tyres were a handicap even on a bypass, but this track was little more than ruts. Occasionally, a few bricks and upended slates had been stamped in to offer some grip but mostly the surface was mud and sheep shit.

After several minutes of wheelspin and smoke, the three continued on foot.

Mr Probert had decided they were bohemians. On first seeing them he had opined to the office they were hippies, a judgement based on little more than a T-shirt slogan and a packet of Rizlas. But their desire to be property owners had upgraded them to bohemian. What remained undeniable, though, was their un-worldliness. The photo of the farmhouse had undoubtedly fired their interest, yet both had failed to ask any of the normal questions about easement rights and drainage. The man, who often smiled when there appeared to be no joke, had asked about the possibility of a duck-pond. And a wind turbine. (Twice.) The woman had enquired about low-flying aircraft. Such attitudes had left Mr Probert no longer sure what constituted a good selling point.

The track wound up through a dingle of wind-stunted hazel, and crossed a rivulet that tinkled with treacherous innocence. Even in the dank dog days of autumn one could not mistake the magic of the landscape. Several times Rob stopped to stare, to admire the fungus on a rock or the ferns in the fork of a branch. This apparent sensitivity was all the more surprising for Rob had the sinewy build of a bantamweight and an inner-city stubble.

'About the only place sheep don't get, halfway up a tree,' said Mr Probert.

'Whose are the sheep?' asked Jane.

'Gareth's. Field belongs to Gareth Richards now.' He was about to add that it had always been grass-let to Gareth until the tragedy of recent events, but then realised such matters were probably best not aired.

The pair began to draw ahead of him on the long haul up, the advantage of his gumboots being offset by his paunch. Driven on by their eagerness to view, Rob and Jane were ten yards in front when they emerged beyond the tree-line.

'Jee-sus!' echoed down to him.

Followed by 'Fucking Ada!'

And a long whoop.

The stormclouds were just starting to break, and the dramatic contrasts of light and shade were racing across the meadow above them. The grassland and its battalion of mole-hills stretched some two hundred yards up towards the ridge, where yellow-ochred walls were just visible beyond a chaotic hawthorn hedge. A long slate roof was glistening in the day's first rays. A specimen pine tree towered protectively at one end. Broom and gorse and hawthorns were scattered over the surrounding hillside. And no other habitation could be seen for miles.

'The owner was a . . . er . . . a bit of an eccentric.'

'He was a lunatic!'

'How long's it been like that?'

'About . . . about thirty years, I'm told.'

'Thirty years . . . !'

'That's what he should get.'

Estate agent and clients were gathered in the farmyard, gazing at the farmhouse's most unusual feature.

The particulars described the building as a rare 150-year-old long-house. A long-house was once the most traditional of Welsh farm buildings, now much prized and protected. Long and low and narrow, they were designed to keep the elements at bay. Often, as here, the building was L-shaped, and in its lee a rectangular farmyard lay hidden from the world and the worst of the westerlies.

Along the short stroke of the L at Pantglas were the stone barns used for hay and the bric-à-brac of farming. Along the long stroke of the L were, originally, the parlour, the lounge, and the four bedrooms, each room the width of the building.

What the particulars did not mention was the combine harvester. Which was parked in the lounge. And in two of the bedrooms.

'This would presumably reduce the value somewhat?' enquired Jane.

To provide this unconventional parking space it had been necessary to demolish an external wall, two internal walls, and a ceiling of the ground floor. The result was a neat, if brutalist, excision which exposed a complete cross-section of the building's innards. Indeed, surreally on display some ten feet above the ground was an exquisitely tiled Victorian fireplace, whose fires could only be lit by ladder. The small-paned bedroom windows at the rear also remained intact, though their panoramic view could only be fully appreciated by climbing on to the combine's cab roof.

'Some of these old farmers, they were real characters,' said Mr Probert, clutching at straws. Then he added, 'It's a '57 Massey Ferguson. The old red ones are getting very rare.'

'And it's in excellent condition because it's been kept in the lounge,' observed Jane helpfully.

'That's right.' He knew for a fact it had been used last summer. 'Full working order.' Mr Probert sensed there was still some customer dissatisfaction to defuse. 'The house'll be with full vacant possession, of course.'

'But just a little short on walls.'

In truth, the combine harvester should already have gone. Somehow, though, its vintage value had fallen under the vulturine eye of Nico, the mocking dealer from the marquee. With predatory haste, he had ploughed the profits of Crug Caradoc's archives into purchasing this icon of agriculture. But, as always, there was a catch to deals with Nico. This time, it was the small matter of where to put a '57 Massey Ferguson, given that he lived in town, in a flat above his antiques shop.

And his solution was that, while he sought a collector of geriatric tractors, the two-storey vehicle would stay parked in Pantglas's lounge. Because, like many in the valley, the vendor owed Nico a favour . . . a quid pro quo for an unusual private service Nico had recently rendered him.

'Yes, but the accommodation is as advertised,' said Mr Probert, struggling on with Jane. 'Kitchen-parlour, two bedrooms, bathroom, outbuildings and lots—'

'—of potential.' She made the word sound dirty as she batted back his ace. Although Jane had a slightly dippy look to her, and it was easy to be distracted by her thighs, she was usually the more practical of the two, and busied herself putting pound signs on what Rob called his dreams.

Indeed, he had already wandered off, drawn as if by a magnet into the barns at the end of the farmyard, where he was stood gazing at some of Mr Probert's potential. 'Look at the light!' he called. 'Look at the light!'

Entry was by two vast arches, unbothered by doors, and at the rear the thick stone walls were dramatically pierced by those vertical gashes once essential to Norman bowmen. Even the farthest corners of the barns could not escape the low-angled rays of the winter sun. And if extra natural light were needed, it flooded through the patchwork of missing slates. This was a garret-in-waiting.

Rob paced it out, stepping round an abandoned milk churn and some spilt feed, and exulted in the space. The floor was flagstoned, thick, worn, uneven, original. The walls would withstand a battering ram. In the air was the smell of age, on the eye the sense of craftsmanship. Rob ran his hands along the stonework, as if savouring the unfashionable pleasure of roughness.

Here the pictures would paint themselves. The house was on a ridge, the barn was on a spur, and all Wales, it seemed, was visible. It was a landscape in thrall to the wind. The clouds swirled like an eddying sea, the grasses bent as if in prayer, and the bushes crept low for survival. But it was the trees that dared the most. Out beyond the barn against the skyline staggered a defiant row of hawthorns, distorted and deformed as they struggled to obey the laws of growth. Every shoot and every branch grew sideways, the network of twigs and foliage ballooning like a head of hair trapped in the blast of a hair-dryer. The images that came to mind were bonsai by Dalí, but Rob was no surrealist and he had his own plans for the landscape.

'*And* it comes with a house,' said Jane loudly, all too aware of his attention span.

'Oh, I'm sorry!' He turned round, squeezed her bottom. 'Let's go check out the floral wallpaper! But you must agree,' and he waved his arm at the cavernous space, 'this does beat our attic!'

She smiled. 'And when it gets dark? What are you going to use, luminous paint?'

The estate agent made a swift intervention. 'Oh the barn can easily be wired up to the generator. No problem.'

'Who wants light bulbs?' said Rob. 'I could work by hurricane lamp! Now that would be romantic. I could wear a smock and hang the lamps here, in rows!' He reached up and slapped the squat beam that ran the width of the barn, his laughter echoing off the walls.

Even Mr Probert's shaky sales sense knew not to mention that the last object to hang from that beam was the stiffening corpse of the previous owner.

The tour of the long-house made it evident that little of decorative significance had happened in the past century. There was a Rayburn whose blackened oven was testimony to pre-war roasts, an iron bath whose stain raised the possibility of a past life as a sheep dip, and a toilet whose cistern contained a dead rook. Yet the weather had by and large remained outside, although a leaking gutter had caused some of the wallpaper in the smaller bedroom to hang like a giant abscess. Elsewhere the neglect had been broadly benign. Even the ubiquitous flagstones were currently enjoying a renaissance in the glossier reaches of style magazines.

In a perverse way, Jane found such habitability almost a disappointment, a hindrance to her negotiating position.

'Be over £10,000 for mains electricity. At least that again for general modernisation. Then there's the slates off the barn. The guttering. The paintwork. The two-storey car park. The neighbour who becomes a werewolf every full moon. We'd be looking for a considerable reduction.'

'There is considerable interest.' And it was true, there was considerable interest. Mr Probert thought they were all mad. He himself had a very pleasant little bungalow, with mod cons as far the eye could see. 'What sort of reduction?'

Jane hesitated. She had yet to qualify as an acupuncturist. So a lot depended on Rob's income, which depended on Rob's sales, which depended on the quality of Rob's inspiration. And, of course, on the quantity of Rob's buyers.

'And then there's the state of the track. It's a bit of a bummer if you can only get to your house when it's dry. Must need 5,000 quids' worth of hardcore at least.'

'It's a knack, driving up it, that's all.'

Mr Probert was lying. The most powerful vehicle to attempt the climb recently had been a hearse. Despite being in immaculate working order, it had failed to get past the first hairpin. Even though at that point the coffin was empty.

'Anyway,' added Mr Probert, trying a bit of hardball, 'I'm afraid the state of the track is not really relevant to the price of the house.'

It was again Nico, ever the fixer, who had come to the aid of the corpse. He had driven secretly up to Pantglas to get the measure of the Massey Ferguson, only to find himself in the company of two undertakers and the late, stiff Hefin. Naturally, he had offered his services as a middleman. Although new to the funerary field, he possessed one great asset, that *sine qua non* of antique-dealing: a Volvo Estate – with the minor disadvantage that it was at the time full of pungently dead pheasants, who in turn stemmed from another dubious deal, this time with the Commodore's gamekeeper.

And so it came about that Hefin Phillips, aged fifty-eight, made his final journey from the farm strapped to a roof-rack. Which was a favour much appreciated by the vendor, Hefin's brother and heir – a man busy with pigs over eight miles away – who had in turn reciprocated with parking rights for the '57 Massey Ferguson.

'You see, with a rural idyll,' Mr Probert went on, 'you're up against the "second home" market. The sort of people who like skipping through grass twice a month. At premium rates.'

Jane looked across at Rob, who was making a very poor show in his role as reluctant buyer. 'Will you excuse us?' she said, and the couple went off to huddle.

Mr Probert pretended not to watch as they wandered round the wilderness that was once a vegetable garden. Some vicious gooseberry bushes and a few beanpoles strangled by convolvulus were the only remnants of self-sufficiency, but location was all. Set on a lumpy bank beyond the farmyard, it gave views to die for. East, south and west, the empty swathes of common land gave a green grandeur to the hilltops. And the only building visible in all that landscape was L-shaped Pantglas.

After three circuits they were back.

'We think the asking price is too high,' said Jane, 'given that half the house is missing.'

Mr Probert nodded, then allowed himself a smile. 'Not missing exactly. I think you'll find most of it's under the vegetable garden.'

'However, we would like to make an offer.'

'How much for?'

'£25,500?' said Jane.
'You've got yourself half a house,' said Mr Probert, smiling.
'Good?' said Jane to Rob.
'Pub?' said Rob to Jane.

Chapter 5

There used to be one public house for every two miles of the valley road, making the descent from moors to market town a long-term project. Opening hours were a matter of personal choice, a reflection of the season or insomnia, or just bloody-mindedness. Occasionally, the police would raid, but in a spirit of fair play they would usually telephone to arrange their visit. The longest opening time on record was believed to be ten days, when a blizzard on the moors obliged the trapped clientele to drink the pub dry in the interests of survival. Even the advent of the breathalyser did not immediately impinge on the pursuit of drink. At night, the serious drinker would often arrive on horseback, knowing his nag would safely return his insensate body to the appropriate family bosom.

Remoteness encouraged the more individual breed of landlord, unschooled in modern notions of public service. At the Griffin Inn, Major Watkins, rtd, would refuse to serve beer in half-pint glasses to male customers, proclaiming to all drinkers present that this nancy practice encouraged the spread of homosexuality. At the Boar's Head, Edward Mason, also retired, would refuse to serve anyone employed by the water authorities. (A five-year dispute over billing meant that even casual mention of the word 'water' could trigger a verbatim account of four court cases.) At the Red Lion, Mr G. Matthews, a retired immigration officer, lived in hope of the day when a non-white drinker would enter his premises . . . so that he could bar them. But as yet no non-white person had ever been seen in the valley.

All fell victim to that common folly of retired folk, the belief that to run a country pub was a piece of piss. And over time, the long hours and the laws of economics thinned out their numbers. And the pubs became barns. Or second homes. Or useful collections of bricks.

The pubs that stayed serving were free houses, a sure sign that the brewery chains had done their clinical sums. Three months' tourism and nine months' rain did not amount to break-even point on ploughman's lunches. So only the local landlords kept pulling the pumps. And by the Eighties, the valley choice had shrunk to two.

On the edge of the moors was Dolly. Dolly was a legend, almost as old as the century. Originally, the writing above her front door had read 'Dolly and Walter Price', and declared them joint licensees. That inscription had been a source of much pride for it made Dolly the fifth generation of her family to run the tiny alcoholic outpost. Husband Walter, however, always yearned for wider horizons. And one day in the Sixties a tour bus of lost Americans unexpectedly stopped to sample the ale. Eager to pass on knowledge of his native Wales, Walter had proposed two days of his services as a free guide. He was never heard from again.

But Dolly just kept on serving, year after year. As a watering-hole, the Wheatsheaf was in the Irish tradition: the bar was in the parlour, the pub was a private house. The domesticity of these arrangements made payment seem almost in bad taste. As Dolly aged, she moved her bed downstairs, to the room seen beyond the bar. This had the advantage that she could nap between customers, though the effect on passing trade of a pint poured by a little old lady in a nightdress was harder to determine. Nor did Armond help.

She went nowhere without Armond. The first sight any customer ever had of her, Armond would be in her arms. And always the introduction would be the same. A rendition of Greig's Piano Concerto. 'Would you like to hear Armond play?' she would ask. And then she would take the fluffy paws of her beloved Sealyham and dramatically pound them up and down the length of the bar as she 'mmm'ed the beat with her eyes tight shut.

The Wheatsheaf appealed to a rather specialist market.

The valley's one remaining hope for drinkers was the Dragon's Head. Its position was promising. Opposite the village hall in a straggling hamlet of cottages and farm-buildings, the pub had a fine view of the mountains. Eighteenth-century beams and low ceilings spoke of a rich hostelry history. And at just twenty minutes from town, it offered the prospect of a fun evening out. There was just one problem. Gwillim.

Gwillim was a farmer, a surly, brute-sized cattle farmer. His only observable pleasure in life was to block the traffic when he herded his cows for their twice-daily milking. The source of his embitterment – or at least the principal source – was his tenancy. His farm belonged to the estate, the now much-shrunk estate, of the Commodore. And, as with most tenancies, there was a small explosive device in the sub-clauses. In Gwillim's case, it had been primed nearly two centuries earlier. His farmhouse had been built on to the public house (or possibly vice versa) and those two professions had become formally intertwined in the lease. He was legally responsible for the Dragon's Head. Should he cease to be a publican he would also cease to be a farmer. And become both homeless and jobless.

He resolved this dilemma by serving beer with the worst possible grace. Sometimes he denied he had any beer to serve. Sometimes if he had beer to serve he insisted it was five minutes' walk away in the cellar. Indeed, almost anything was five minutes' walk away in the cellar. Occasionally, he did not come back. But the moment most treasured by the locals was his annual response to the mini-Eisteddfod, held opposite in the village hall. This event attracted bourgeois types from up to fifteen miles away, and afterwards their dry throats, parched by an hour of 'Land Of My Fathers', would drive them in their dozens to the Dragon's Head. The cries would go up for spritzers, and Cinzano, and whisky sour, and gin and tonics, and sherry, and sometimes, with lunatic hubris, a vodka martini straight up with an olive. The six-foot Gwillim would stand four-square, like Horatio defending the bridge, and to each cry he would bellow 'No!' The record was believed to be seventeen straight 'No's, followed by a refusal to supply free tap water.

A normal Friday lunchtime like today was an altogether quieter affair. Only those locals who had gained respect by years of dogged persistence were present. They totalled four, all men. And a dog.

By the bar stood Gareth, hill-sheep farmer of 120 acres, and Eryl, dispossessed heir of the Crug Caradoc estate; Gareth was much depressed by the height of his wife, and Eryl was much depressed by the loss of a house with twelve bedrooms. Click-clacking in the background were the dominoes of Teg and Ben the molecatchers, both in their seventies and also faced with uncertain futures. The dog was Jessie, who had passed in mysterious ways from Hefin to Gareth.

Although four was a small sample, they reasonably reflected the perennial concerns of the valley: sex, money and moles.

'About a million pound, I reckon,' said Eryl, for roughly the tenth time. He wiped some slops of bitter from the Zapata moustache that straggled mournfully over his mouth.

'Yes, about a million pound,' he repeated bitterly, 'if you add in the fishing rights and the shooting rights. And the development potential.' He said the words with saloon bar authority, his attempt at gravitas undercut by the sweatshirt with 'Boogie Baby' on it. Eryl's grasp of 'development potential' was an unexpected expertise, and in all probability did not extend as far as its correct spelling.

Since prematurely parting company with school – a minor

public school that did not take kindly to vomit on its premises – Eryl had not bothered with the irritant of a career. An old-style dropout for most of his twenties, he had now graduated to jobbing carpenter; an aspiring playboy, he was now shacked up with Bryony from the health-food shop. Both situations led to long unhappy lunch hours.

'I could be in the Riviera now. On a yacht. With my tongue down a model. If it wasn't for that fucking conman! Screwing me out of my inheritance!'

He paused, as he had paused a dozen times already that morning, in hope of a sympathetic response to his plight.

'Double six!' came the triumphant cry from the long pine table in the corner. Several dominoes were thrown angrily on the stone floor.

'No wonder he's buggered off and left the country. My lawyer says I could have sued him. It was criminal what he did.'

A million-pound lawsuit would certainly have been an unusual event in the daily life of the valley, but still Gareth said nothing. Indeed, since slouching in some twenty minutes earlier, clad in his battered, dung-smeared Barbour, Gareth had said nothing apart from 'hallo'. The scandal of the lost inheritance had made few inroads into his own unspoken thoughts. He remained preoccupied with his failure to achieve the erections expected by his young wife, but, being of the old school, felt this was a subject best not shared.

Forty-one-year-old Gareth knew he had never been the best-looking of men – like his stunted father before him, he had inherited the features of a ferret – but he had had high hopes of Moira. Times though, as even he was dimly aware, were changing. In the old days, 120 acres were enough to satisfy a woman. Now they wanted conversation. And those women who weren't obtained in-house, who came from foreign parts, had no end of oddities about them. When he and Moira first met – at a rugby international in Cardiff – he had felt a bond with her Donegal roots. It was a land with similar levels of rainfall, he had gathered, plus a shared history of sheep, and so, his shyness thus eased, he had been lured by her lilt and her hair. Only when he had got her home, some months later, with a ring on her finger, had he realised that the length of her legs could be a problem.

'After all,' Eryl went on, 'I was the nearest blood relative. Almost the only blood relative. Well, not blood. But you know what I mean.'

He meant adopted. It was scarcely a secret, his looks matched no valley profile. Although a drinker, Eryl was a rugged sort of drinker, barrel-chested with coarse blond hair tied in a dated ponytail – in another life he could have been a *Baywatch* surfer, except that he had poor skin. In this life he was a Llewellyn, but without the DNA. And now without the money.

'No, that's two quid you owe, you bastard!' Behind him, the molecatchers were getting restive. Four pints meant abuse, six pints meant punches, eight pints meant kicking, and after ten pints Teg and Ben could be relied on to provide free entertainment by fighting in a ditch. A wave of self-pity came over Eryl, and he briefly saw his future as a life in moles.

'I was in her will for twenty years.'

'Eighteen,' said Gwillim, unexpectedly appearing from the cellar. He positioned himself and his tankard on their side of the bar, not from comradeship but so that in the event of passing custom he could deny all knowledge of the landlord's whereabouts. 'Eighteen years.' In recent weeks, he had been spared few details of this beery, teary tale and its many reprises. Should there ever be – over Gwillim's dead body – a pub quiz held at the Dragon's Head, all ten rounds could be devoted to the scandal of Great-Aunt Gwendolen's will. For scandal there was.

'Eighteen, twenty, whatever. I was in her will until her marbles were got at by *him*! You knew the old lady, Gareth – bright as a button she was until she hit ninety . . . and Trystan came crawling!'

Gareth just nodded. For some time now, he had felt unable to comment with confidence on women of any age. And that was the key word: confidence. No man can be confident in life when his head only comes up to his wife's neck. And they weren't just ordinary legs, they were sexy legs. Part of a sexy body. None of his farmer friends had ever had to put up with a sexy wife, and he was at a loss. It sapped morale, it sapped the will to farm, and it had certainly sapped his baby-making facilities.

'I mean, that Trystan wasn't even a *second* cousin, for God's sake! Fifth, more like it! Go that far back and we're all related to Adam and Eve – you could put a claim in for half the Earth. And now he's flogged my birthright to some townie wanker in flannels. As a weekend pad!'

Eryl reached over the bar for another bottle. Since the early death of his adoptive parents, the prospect of being heir to Crug Caradoc had been integral to his career plan, key to his pulling-power. The sudden emergence of a smooth-tongued fortune-hunter from the family woodwork, oozing chat and charm into gullible old ears, and guiding shaky hands over bills of sale, had been as life-changing as a boot to the genitals.

Gareth had spoken to the vicar about his own problem with genitalia, though in a very oblique, roundabout way, when they had been following the hunt one Sunday. He had couched the matter in an allusive marital harmony format, and for several hedges the vicar had been unaware what they were discussing. His parishioners usually fretted about low milk yield. Regrettably, Reverend Oliver, a lifelong bachelor and victim of an even more unfortunate body-shape than Gareth's, had been unable to find a biblical text to cover the sexual crisis in question and the conversation had petered out.

'Did you know that even *before* she signed, he tried to remove the Dresden in a horsebox at midnight?'

A pew scraped back across the flagstones. The clatter of violently discarded dominoes reverberated off the cold stone walls, the noise forestalling a catalogue of Trystan's perfidy.

'I'm sick of playing!' said an angry Teg, and he stood up, reaching for his sack of moles.

He was a shambling mass of a man, his bulk at odds with the delicacy of his work. By nature blessed with endless country courtesy, his temper had been sorely tested that day. For over fifty years he and Ben had tracked and trapped the little gentlemen in velvet. They had eschewed the crudity of poison and the brutality of gunshot. Instead, they had mined for moles, employing a mix of acoustical subtlety and kindergarten mechanics. Armed only with a spade, a length of pipe and a bucket, they were the true, traditional countrymen, the provisional wing of Morris Dancing. Their work was an art form, and they could void a field in a day.

And now their life's work was to be municipalised. Their skills were to be rendered redundant. The mighty minds of the council were to create a Mole Operatives Unit, and kit it out with strychnine. The cost-effective kill would soon sound the death knell of Teg and Ben.

'Forget your bloody million,' said Teg, looking pointedly at Eryl. 'A thousand'd be quite nice for most of us.' He had little time for ponytails, except on ponies.

'Be up to do your new field in the New Year,' said Ben to Gareth.

'Hurry up and fuck off,' said Gwillim.

The motley four ignored him. Teg and Ben were born contrary, and Eryl and Gareth were intent on dragging out their drinks (well aware that, by the rules of the house, a glass put down was a glass confiscated, unlikely ever to be replenished). These rural diehards had come to lean on a five-barred gate indoors, the only place for a long moan in the dry. They also knew that the lunchtime session deprived Gwillim of his ultimate sanction, that moment when he appeared behind the bar in his pyjamas, emptying a kettle into his hot-water bottle, and turning out the lights.

'D'you do food?'

All heads turned.

A pretty dark-haired woman in a short skirt and a slender man

47

with T-shirt and stubble were standing in the doorway. There was a shocked silence.

'Food . . . ?' Gwillim's body tensed. 'You want food?'

'Yes, some pasta perhaps, or a small salad?' said Jane.

'This is not a restaurant, madam. This,' replied Gwillim, 'is a public house.'

'Is it, bollocks!' snorted Ben.

The regulars erupted into laughter, delighted at such a public put-down of mein host. It was the first recorded laughter in the Dragon's Head for several weeks and the hilarity threatened to develop into full-blown hysteria, much to the bafflement of Rob and Jane who were already nonplussed by the sack of moles.

When the guffaws died down, it was Eryl, the thwarted playboy, who spoke. 'Best try town. Abernant. About twenty minutes down the valley.' Then commented with what may or may not have been irony, 'That's where it all happens.'

Chapter 6

The Mayoress of Abernant was running late. Half a dozen dresses lay in a heap of civic indecision upon the bed. Myfanwy Edwards was not by nature indecisive (her capacity to give orders – on any subject, to anybody – would have fast-tracked her through the Paras had not God called her to the voluntary sector) but her mind kept drifting back to the Queen. Many citizens have fantasies about the royal family; they fantasise that the Queen requests the pleasure of their company at a royal wedding, or that she invites them to share a picnic at Balmoral, or suggests an early morning canter *à deux* at Sandringham. Myfanwy, however, always fantasised about Her Majesty opening the mail. And it was always a letter about her.

For over thirty years, Myfanwy had been busy raising the artistic consciousness of Abernant's 5,000 inhabitants. Be it the sponsored harpist in the Indian restaurant, the campaign for a love-spoon exhibition in the defunct abattoir, or the production of a Young Farmers' AmDram Night every Christmas, Mrs M. Edwards was always the name in big type on the publicity leaflet. Such were her powers of persuasion that fully grown dignitaries had been known to hide in alleyways at the sight of her fifteen stone in pursuit of a pledge.

Eventually, with a fourth decade of her initiatives looming, the council had bowed to the inevitable and announced that Mrs M. Edwards was to be Mayoress of Abernant. The official statement said this was 'in recognition of her long-standing services to the arts' and offered a polysyllabic tribute to her energy levels. In private, the councillors' preferred choice was Mr Capstick the butcher, for he was not only male but also brought credit to the town with his specialist sausages. Myfanwy's popularity was not aided by her acceptance speech – reminiscent of a diva accepting the freedom of the city – and her advocacy of an arts festival caused a mocking rumour that she had plans to twin the town with Salzburg (wherever that was).

The mayoralty attained, however, her thirty-year-old royal fantasy had grown ever stronger.

Although common sense told her the Queen would have flunkeys by the dozen to open her mail, Myfanwy had always envisioned Her Majesty delicately holding her own letter-opener, discreetly monogrammed, with a select pile of envelopes laid upon her lap. She would be seated on a chaise longue, open French windows leading on to terraced gardens, a cold drink of crushed lemons by her side, her handbag on a small Edwardian marquetry table. A faint breeze would have tried in vain to ruffle her hair. After taking several sips of drink – there was never a rush: the slow, ordered ritual of events merely heightened the thrill of expectation – Her Majesty would then slice open the pale azure-blue envelope . . . and withdraw a handwritten note.

The mayoress was never able to discern who had recommended her for the OBE. Always at this moment the fantasy would dissolve into an orgasmic haze of satisfaction.

Myfanwy gazed again at the choice of frocks. Today it was the Chamber of Commerce, and she was searching for an ensemble appropriate to the ways of small business. Her elevation to mayoress had exposed her tenuous grasp of fashion and made her cautious. Being in the public eye, her body was now suffering the oxygen of publicity. The lifeblood of the local paper was public events – or 'captive news', as the editor gratefully put it – and hers was the face that had to launch a thousand fêtes.

Her public image was, unfortunately, little helped by Auberon, the paper's freelance photographer. Dividing his time among set-piece weddings, events of municipal record, and his evening job as a petrol-pump attendant, young Auberon had darkroom skills that were not yet cutting edge. In every edition of the *Mid-Walian*, his portraiture transformed the world into a uniform fuzzy grey, depicting a population that was either living underwater or in an earlier century.

Myfanwy had twice complained, arguing that her weekly appearance as a corpse-coloured apparition was a threat to the dignity of her office – a complaint without success, for the neophyte was also nephew to the proprietor, Miss Nightingale. But the mayoress's concern for the public weal was also partly a fear that one of her over-eager fans might include her press clippings in that azure-blue envelope. And for ever stymie the gong.

Pink and orange, she decided. She had a ceremony to perform, an important initiative to stimulate the economy of the town, and she wished her colour co-ordination to convey a mood of dynamism. Insinuating herself into the size eighteen, she rehearsed the orotund sentences of welcome she had prepared earlier. Speeches were her strong point for she had been gifted with lungs undaunted by sub-clauses. Then, having urged her zipper the final yard, she glanced over the guest list, a Who's Who of banking and business in Abernant.

At the door she paused for a moment in front of her full-length mirror to wonder if the gold chain of office might clash, but dismissed the thought. A gold chain of office went with everything. Her appearance did, however, suffer from another problem, a problem which, though known throughout the town, and much commented on in the bars, had never been raised in her presence. Now past fifty, her age at last exceeded her bust size. But it was a bust of such prominence and disproportion that it relocated her centre of gravity – with the consequence that her profile varied from the vertical by several degrees. When on the move – and especially when on the move with a grand *décolletage*

– Mrs M. Edwards bore a quite startling resemblance to a figurehead on the prow of a great galleon.

And so, resplendent in her multi-coloured glad rags, the mayoress left for her official car at full tilt, like a ship of state heading into a severe south-westerly.

'Yeeugh!'

Bryony poked at a second nut. And a third. And then gingerly juggled their container. She was right, the nuts *were* moving. Independently. Although still only in her first month at the health food shop, she knew that nuts were meant to be stationary objects. And, *ergo*, that small wiggly creatures were not part of the deal. She looked around for a binbag.

'What are you after?' A wreath of pipe smoke emerged from a darkened recess nearby.

'Something to put these nuts in. They've got maggots.'

'Maggots?' She heard footsteps on the flagstones, and then Hubert appeared behind her in the storeroom. He looked over her shoulder. 'Don't waste good nuts. Put them in the oven for five minutes. Two hundred degrees.'

'You can't do that!'

Hubert raised an eyebrow, a boss's eyebrow.

'You could poison someone,' she insisted.

'I doubt it. Good nutritional value – don't you read survivalist magazines? Juicy maggots, we could put them on special offer for the SAS.'

Despite herself, and despite her wishy-washy 'alternative' views on life – a mindset he delighted in mocking – Bryony could not resist a grudging fondness for anyone still an *enfant terrible* at the age of sixty-two. Less admirable was the fact that he was serious about selling his superheated nuts. With a large profit margin.

'Well, I'm not doing it,' she said flatly.

Again he raised an eyebrow. He was a tall, well-preserved man – such were his margins that he had a six-seater sauna and solarium in his substantial townhouse – and he exuded the residue of a once-potent charm.

'I'm not.' She had faced him down once before, and achieved a victory . . . of sorts.

One of her ill-paid functions was that of cook, and her daily creation of *amuse-gueules* was much prized by the local bourgeoisie. Their enthusiasm for such delicacies would, however, have ceased mid-gorge had they known the use-by dates of the ingredients. And this information Bryony had threatened to let slip. As a concession to good housekeeping, he eventually agreed that items such as flour would only be kept for one year after the date they should have been thrown away.

In the battle of the nuts, Hubert blinked first and took them from her. Then, shuffling the nuts so the maggots were uppermost, he laid them out on a baking tray in the oven. Bryony returned to the till, attributing her calm resolve to her skilful use of essential oils, of which she now knew twenty-three.

The health food shop had been a runaway success, a place where the word aubergine had been heard in town for the first time in three hundred years, where chocolate was to be seen in individual pieces instead of bars, and where occasionally it was possible to buy pitta bread and hummus on the same day. Key to the shop's triumph was Hubert's exquisite calligraphy, which provided labels that enabled him to double the asking price.

Less masterly was the retention of staff, who sometimes lasted a shorter time than the fresh veg, and on average possessed a sack-by date of six weeks. In part, this was down to Hubert's delight in the role of curmudgeon, but credit must also be given to his temperamental wife Gloria, a former leisurewear model who no longer looked good in colour. Not merely did the pair issue contradictory orders at the speed of ping-pong finalists, but the faded Gloria brought the rules of absolute monarchy to management, apparently driven by the delusion that every female employee had the hots for Hubert. As Bryony's current partner was Eryl the ex-heir, now a man with the ability to provide for little more than a ferret, she was keen to avoid dismissal; accordingly, she took meticulous care never to be late or idle or give generous portions or go down on Hubert.

Hubert reappeared and slipped into his newly adopted vantage-point, half-hidden in the corner of the shop yet still within sight and sound of money changing hands. There was something indefinably, universally mercantile about his posture as he stood brooding in the shadows by the baguette basket. He stayed almost motionless, like a Dickensian overseer, puffing constantly on his pipe and never losing sight of the High Street.

His old vantage-point by the front door, where he used to play the old-fashioned proprietor and exchange banter with each of his customers as they came in and went out, was now a no-go area. It had been a no-go area for over three months and the pettifogging lunacy of the ban still enraged him. It was *his* shop, *his* health food, and so whether or not he smoked a pipe in it was nobody's business but *his* – as he had told the Public Health and Hygiene official in simple four-letter words. He had wanted to go to court, to be a martyr if needs must, but the tyranny of political correctness was now the tide of the times and had captured hygiene as its latest fad, and so the certainty of legal failure – with costs – had forced him to retreat. And now he skulked in a bolthole, puffing with phoney defiance, and praying the gloriously pungent fumes that drifted across the *petits fours* would not be seen by any passing agents of the environmental Stasi.

He had even had a speech ready for his arrest. Or at least, a loose compilation of the aphorisms he daily let rip on his customers. For this was not the first time he had fallen foul of the men with clipboards and a nose for killer cockroaches. 'Dirt is good for you,' he would have declaimed to the bench. 'Bacteria are an invention of bored bureaucrats.' 'The biggest cause of death in catering is falling over the Hoover.' He enjoyed the notoriety of iconoclasm, though uncannily his iconoclasm always served the cause of saving him money. Nonetheless, his attacks on red tape, sell-by dates, smoking bans, hygiene regulations, rang a chord among the small businessmen of the town and for three years in succession they had elected him President of the Chamber of Commerce.

'I think you're on soon,' said Bryony, who was nearer the shop window. 'The paparazzi are here.'

He diverted his attention from the High Street and the small crowd gathering outside the bank, and watched a florid Clydog struggle towards the shop, accompanied by young Auberon, the photographer.

Hubert cut and wrapped a portion of Mississippi Mud Pie, in anticipation. Clydog came in, ignored the new Virgin Olive Oil display, and wheezed his way to the counter.

'Not a bad turnout,' he said, with the authority of an expert in local crowd size. 'Rain coming though.' He laid down some change and reached to pick up his treat.

'No eating in the shop!' Hubert warned him fiercely. Clydog reacted with surprise. '190 over 110. We had dinner with Dr Frost and his wife last night, heard all about your condition. You could go blue at any minute.'

'I've just been chased by a heifer.'

'I hope it wasn't after sex,' Hubert said. 'And no photos of him!' he added sternly to Auberon. 'Pictures of dead people face down in my patisserie put customers off. Got to protect my interests.' Then Hubert twinkled, his face lit up by the joys of mischief, and handed over the cake. 'You are looking a bit iffy though, Clydog.'

'I've just been chased by a heifer,' he said again, irritably. 'What else did he tell you about my medical history?'

'Oh I couldn't repeat that, it's confidential. I'm sure you understand, having once been a journalist.'

'It's my mother's fault,' sighed Clydog, who, though fifty-three, had yet to leave home. 'The food she cooks is too rich. Makes me go this colour.'

'What happened with the heifer?' Bryony asked the non-speaking Auberon, whose private education had omitted social skills.

'The usual. Es-esc-escaped from the pen, just as it was going into auction. Then ran halfway round the town,' he said.

'Get a good picture?'

'C-c-camera got c-caught in the c-case.'

'Oh.'

'Thought we might not make the grand opening,' said Clydog. 'Until we saw the mayoral car stuck in the chaos. You down for a speech today?'

Hubert shook his head. 'I'm just there as decoration. Icon of Welsh capitalism.'

'Again?' Clydog fondled the profile of his mud pie through the paper bag. A pretty, dark-haired woman in a short skirt and a slender man with T-shirt and stubble had just entered, and Clydog was reluctant to gorge himself in front of strangers. He moved aside to let Bryony show them the allegedly home-made pasta.

'Well, guess Auberon and I'd better get over there, get into position. You coming now, Hubert?'

'Might as well. Abernant calls.'

The other two turned to leave.

As Hubert removed his gastronome's apron, the timer on the oven rang. 'D'you like nuts, Auberon?'

'Of course, I should have realised the bastard wasn't interested in art,' she said bitterly. 'I mean, he even used to choose crap Christmas cards! But I just thought he wanted to widen his horizons. When all he was after was to widen her legs.'

Mr Blake nodded sympathetically.

'Fruit, he told me. In bowls. He lied from the bloody start! Seems the shit was in the library, getting out of the rain, and he saw a poster for a life class. So he goes off painting some tart in Llanbedr Village Hall. Llanbedr Village Hall! Hardly the last word in passionate romance, is it? 'S even got a corrugated iron

56

roof! *I* certainly wouldn't want to go lying around naked in there. Not for anybody's art.'

Mr Blake's encouraging silence continued.

'So off my husband trots with his charcoal, week after week. Capturing essences, he says. And apparently one pose leads to another . . .' She paused briefly, her feistiness suddenly fragile. 'And they've been in Cardiff for a year now.'

Mr Blake sensed the possibility of a tear, and moved a pre-emptive hand gently forward across his desk.

'I went and met the class tutor, you know,' she said. 'Wolfgang. Another incomer. Said it's a first. Never happened when he ran the classes in Berlin. According to him, the cultural history of the nude has bypassed mid-Wales. Can't say I'm surprised.'

Mr Blake felt the conversation was in danger of drifting. 'So you found out about them, what, eighteen months ago . . . ?'

'Approximately, yes. It was the caretaker. Saw a light still on and came over to investigate. Found them re-enacting Rodin by the boiler. Now it so happens that the caretaker's sister is married to the brother of our postman, Dafydd . . . Just twelve hours, the news took to reach me.'

In the throes of truth-telling, a sob can burst through the surface at unforeseen moments. It burst through now. Lionel Blake reached across his desk and compassionately squeezed her hand in his – for perhaps a touch longer than was strictly professional. Yet his was a tall, reassuring presence, the well-cut suit, the authoritatively greying hair, the oak-panelling backdrop.

'She's twenty years younger than him, you know. A student. Psychology student. Hope she's got *his* personality disorder sussed!' Not once had any names crossed her lips. 'Seems she modelled because she was struggling to make ends meet . . . ! So we have something in common now I've had to sell the house.' She tossed back her shock of frizzed auburn hair, a bitter smile tweaking a physiognomy that would itself make a fine portrait.

'So the divorce settlement didn't bring a pot of gold, then?'

'Correct. Which is why I currently live in a caravan. A very undes res. And a bastard for dinner parties.'

Lionel Blake smiled. 'But you're still working?'

'Yes. Yes, still supply teaching. History. So there's a sort of income. Oh, and there's the eggs from a dozen Buff Orpingtons,' added Mrs Whitelaw. 'Which I don't declare.'

'I think that's a secret we can share,' replied Lionel. 'So . . .' He made a pretence of consulting the file before him, leafing through the notes of his predecessor. 'Shall we say an overdraft of £2,000 and see how we go?'

'Oh, that would be wonderful! Oh, thank you *so* much.' It put Marjorie's teeth on edge to overdo the ingratiating, but she felt it was probably in keeping with the role of vulnerable, tearful divorcee.

Lionel Blake smiled comfortingly in response and before putting the top back on his fountain pen he discreetly scribbled a note for his records. 'Breasts 8/10, legs 7/10.'

He was about to express interest in the period of history that she taught when there was a knock on the door. The senior cashier, a plump, resentful woman in her fifties, intruded her head.

'You've not forgotten the mayoress is due at three, Mr Blake?'

'No, I haven't. Thank you. I'll be there.'

He and Mrs Whitelaw rose together and made their way across his office suite. As they passed the second palm, he said, 'So what sort of eggs do you supply, Mrs Whitelaw?'

'Oh, big and brown,' she replied, rightly sensing this was a moment meant for direct eye contact.

He was on the verge of jokily suggesting he place a standing order for omelettes when the thought of a cashier within earshot inhibited him, and he merely bid her farewell, offering a banker's handshake. Mr Blake then briefly delayed his own departure as he had hair to attend to.

It was the trajectory of the manager's career path that made his head cashier a watchful colleague. Depicted as a line on a graph, it rose steadily . . . and then fell with unhealthy detumescence. A high-flier in the Welsh capital until just a few months ago, with prospects of executive nirvana, he had chosen to decamp to a small rural outpost. To locals, he sold the change as a rejection of the rat race, a return to life's truer values. He even joked about it as managerial menopause. But beneath his carapace of polished charm the cashier sensed some blotting of a copybook, some faint whiff of scandal, and she rarely missed a chance to count the spoons.

Over two dozen had gathered in the narrow High Street outside the bank in the rain, awaiting the arrival of the mayoress. This lacked the drama of an escaped heifer, but still qualified as excitement in Abernant. Various councillors and several dignitaries were in attendance, including the Traffic Warden, who was wearing a special sash for the occasion. Unfortunately, because of limited space, there was no opportunity for the town band, and, it being a civil rather than military event, there was no call for the goat.

Even though a red-letter day for the town, the council factions had still assembled on separate pavements. Schism had recently rent the body politic and so great was the enmity that the opposing councillors insisted on breathing separate air. Like the Corn Laws and Home Rule, the burning issue was one of human rights: car-parking charges. The morality of the meter. The *Mid-Walian* called it the Debate of the Day – an entire page of letters was dedicated to the issue of Free vs 10p – and their coverage of meter-related matters was so extensive that Hefin's tragic suicide had been held over for two weeks. Today's occasion, though, was without controversy and had widespread support.

All that was lacking was the mayoress. With hindsight, it was unwise to have chosen Friday for it was market day, the day of dawn-to-dusk gridlock along the town's few key streets. Relocation of the market had been under urgent consideration for thirty-five years, but had so far proved too complex a problem for the council's special sub-committee. As a result, the mayoral limo was now victim of a ritual dispute for territory between the town dustcart, a hay lorry and a cattle truck. And, in the absence of the Traffic Warden, no help was expected before nightfall.

There was little option. Although conscious that her action lacked civic grandeur, the OBE-in-waiting decided to abandon her limousine – and walk. Which is why, watched by smirking farmers and pointing children, the Mayoress of Abernant was to be found in full regalia – and chain – powering her way through the puddles of the crowded town centre.

A hundred yards away, the official welcoming committee stood waiting. In pole position was the President of the Chamber of Commerce, giving his views on town planners and the use of cattle prods. Downwind of his pipe stood the specialist butcher, Mr Capstick, quietly regretting that his unsuccessful campaign for mayor had cost him 117 kilos of hand-rolled sausages. Upwind was the town's leading hotelier, a Mr Porth, trying to brazen out the embarrassment of the AA's recent visit, which had obliged him to place black adhesive tape over the two stars on his illuminated hotel sign.

Behind them, the lesser mortals of the business world, men who had yet to contribute as fully to the life of the community, shuffled their feet and talked of slices and swings. The more political among them spoke of strengthening the local ordinance against urinating in shop doorways. At the back were some out-of-season tourists and a puzzled Rob and Jane, who were struggling with some very chewy pasta and trying to get the measure of their new home town. Then all were interrupted by a stir in the vicinity of the launderette.

'Here comes Cutty,' murmured Hubert, in a naval *jeu d'esprit* lost on his neighbours.

Suddenly, the wet mayoress hove into view, breathless from her voyage, and docked by the microphone stand in front of the bank.

At the same moment the bank manager emerged suavely from his branch bearing a de luxe pair of kitchen scissors on a small velvet pouffe, protected from sogginess by the head cashier's umbrella. These he offered to the mayoress before guiding her, with ceremonial aplomb, to the waiting red ribbon.

The photographer chose a viewpoint that would minimise the mayoral mammaries, the councillors emitted a ripple of sycophantic applause, and the mayoress made the much-awaited deft cut.

Then, turning to the crowd, the Mayoress of Abernant announced to the world, 'I declare this cash machine open.'

Part Two

Part Two

Chapter 7

Stéfan pressed his stubby finger over half an inch into the rotten wood of the window frame. Had there been an audience he would have pressed his finger all the way through the frame. And then smashed the window for good measure. Amid immoderate effing and blinding.

Christmas had come and gone. The window maker had done neither. Being a master craftsman, he had not even acknowledged letters marked 'Urgent'. The occasional painter had wandered by, trailing Dulux drips, and the visit of a plumber was evident from a note outlining his failure to find a stopcock. But, in its essentials, the three-month schedule of works was three months behind schedule. And the hand-made window frames had yet to become a gleam in their artisan's eye.

Stéfan had been masterminding operations from his London base, or so he thought. Only on his weekend visits did he learn the limits to the power of an absentee squire in a Pimlico penthouse. Where he came from, and he was never too specific about where that was, people jumped when given orders. And if they didn't jump high enough, or quick enough, they regretted it. They certainly didn't yawn and scratch their buttocks.

'I'm sorry, Mr Griffith Barton is ex-directory.'

'Ex-directory? He can't be!' Stéfan took hold of the phone, cradled in businessman style between his shoulder and cheek, and placed its mouthpiece where he could better bellow at the operator. 'You've got that wrong! Check it again!' His annoyance was heightened as his latest status symbol from London, a mobile phone, had ceased to work the moment it caught sight of a Welsh mountain.

Stéfan continued to stand and glare at his offending windows while he waited, his urge to sit curbed by the dust-sheets. The dust-sheets lay over every item of furniture in the study, over almost every item of furniture in the house. They constituted the decorators' formal declaration of intent, a time-honoured pretence that work was imminent. But the effect was a house closed down for the duration of a war, its inhabitants gone to die far away. So yet again Stéfan had cancelled his plans for a grand house-warming. Flamboyant host though he was, he could see no way to create a *succès de scandale* out of a dust-sheet party.

'I'm sorry, sir. Definitely ex-directory.'

'It's his business address, for fuck's sake. Why would his business address be ex-directory?'

'Perhaps he's shy, sir.'

The dialling tone returned to the phone.

Stéfan disliked driving on country lanes. He belonged to the Mr Toad school of roadcraft, and found anything narrow and winding an affront to his freedom. Even the briefest relationship with the backside of a tractor was a test too far of his patience. But anyone's patience would have been tested by the lattice of lanes that led off the Nant Valley into the hills. And of the six miles Stéfan had to negotiate, he had so far driven ten.

The directions to Mr Griffith Barton and his window workshop were scribbled on a strip of wallpaper, courtesy of the decorators, and verged on hieroglyphic. Best advice was that, if lost in them there hills, he should find a local, any local, and simply ask for The Windowman.

But as the Jaguar rattled over a cattle-grid and up on to common land it was not merely the replacement of windows that was preoccupying Stéfan.

Although his mansion had twenty-eight rooms and three storeys and stood on a tump, Stéfan frequently worried that it didn't make a big enough statement about him. While he had it on good authority that Jacobean was an historically kosher architectural style, and widely seen as a sign of serious money, it caused him regret that its key design features were short on triumphalism. Culturally, he had a penchant for pillars and plinths, though drawn to a generosity of dimension that seemed to imply a march past might be imminent. If Stéfan could be said to have a personal architectural style, it would best be described as Imperial Domestic. Indeed, on a business trip to Athens he had been much taken by the vision of the Parthenon at night, and was currently considering a plan for the permanent floodlighting of Crug Caradoc.

Of course, what he really wanted, as always, was for a spotlight to fall on him. Ever since the tantrums of childhood, he had nurtured the need to be treated as a big player in his adopted land. In some countries, as he well knew, being a big shot came, literally as well as metaphorically, from a casually slung AK47. But in Britain the key to social standing often proved more complicated. And so his mind had turned to statuary.

There existed a circuit of local grandees who opened house and gardens once or twice a year, donating their takings to worthy causes such as bowel cancer or the hunt. Though botany did not appeal to Stéfan, magnanimity did. (Provided it was well publicised.) He had the requisite rhododendrons and the Wellingtonia pine, a lakeside walk, a couple of arbours, and a gardener with a shedful of shears. All he lacked was a set of goddesses.

As yet, exact details of the sculptures eluded him, but he favoured busty goddesses. The classical look, he reckoned, in white stone. About fifteen deities in varying poses, with labels in Latin, along a woodland way. Full lifesize, maybe a 38DD. Leading steadily up to, and around, the swimming-pool-to-be. Thereby recreating the authentic ambience of a Roman bath.

His other current obsession was Rhodesian ridgebacks. Every

proper countryman had dogs, but they were all collies, or spaniels, or labradors. Stéfan wanted his dogs to be different. And bigger. Given that ridgebacks were the only dogs in the world who could take out a lion, he felt this would be hard for anyone to trump. He was at present trying to obtain advice as to whether or not they made good pets. (And, failing a lion, what exactly one fed them.) But he loved the image. Perhaps this Windowman could knock him up a zoo-size cage.

The thought brought him back to the business in hand. He had just crossed a plateau of upland meadows, almost more Swiss than Welsh, and was nearing the end of his scribbled directions. The empty reaches of the moorland, a moorland much used by the military, were almost upon him. He had only seen two people in twenty minutes, but had been reluctant to ask them directions since the Stéfan method of cornering had forced their old Morris Traveller to leave the road. The last miles began to wind past, and the land became an arbitrary mix of windswept bogland and rectilinear pine plantations, of bright open spaces alternating with abrupt stygian gloom. It was a terrain of bleak beauty. And a setting tailor-made for Mr Griffith Barton, a man variously described by the decorators as a recluse, a misanthrope, a mad widower . . . and a genius with wood.

It was wood smoke, a slow, upward trickle of wood smoke, that gave Stéfan the clue to the cottage. Down a forest track and bounded on three sides by the grim symmetry of pine, the plain Victorian building was set back in a half-acre clearing. A large prefabricated shed with a corrugated asbestos roof stood to one side, half-hidden by the overgrown debris of offcuts, and giving little hint that it might be home to artisanship worthy of a Renaissance kite-mark.

The dull fusillade of mud on mud-flaps ceased as the Jaguar pulled off the track on to wet grass. Stéfan turned off the engine, and sat and looked in some bemusement at the ex-directory business premises. He watched the smoke rise for several minutes, resisting his impulsive restlessness.

Drumming his fingers on the steering wheel, he pondered the matter of Mr Griffith Barton. A matter on which every one of his fitful workmen and even the postman had offered much advice. He was, on all sides, judged to be a temperamental man – so temperamental a man that he had actually been known to *refuse* business, *to turn away* customers if the mood so took him. The consensus held that Mr Griffith Barton should be thought of as a fish, a fish to be slowly, patiently, reeled in over an indefinite period of time, and then given much tickling of the gills.

But Stéfan was not keen on patience – indeed he thought fishing was best done by dynamite – for he knew the persuasiveness of cash. The faint-hearts had counselled caution and cunning but Stéfan decided it was down to price. And so he got out of the car ready to deal – thus ignoring the advice that, upon meeting The Windowman, the recommended cry of greeting should be: 'Hallo! I don't want any work done.'

The first hurdle came immediately inside the gate, and it was a goat. Typical no doubt of its owner, it was not a normal goat. It had just the one horn, and was eating a piece of two by four. Any hope that it was a receptionist goat rather than a guard goat vanished when it charged. Stéfan's resolve to remain in control of his visit was much diminished by having to run to and fro through the triffid stumps of the previous year's nettles.

After some fancy footwork and double shin damage, he managed to grab the goat by the horn. He then had to drag it up the path so that he could ring the doorbell. No one answered.

He rang again. There was still no answer. Unable to let the goat go, Stéfan wrestled it across the clearing towards the workshop, where he could see a light. As he tried to force open the ramshackle garage-sized door, the goat got its teeth round his shoelace. Kicking at the goat and shoulder-charging the door, he stumbled into the workshop.

When he had regained his balance and the goat, he looked about him. The place was stacked with wood of every length and width, the floor awash with shavings, the air redolent with the sweetness of resin. Sheets of papers filled with screeds of figures lay beside lethal cutting machines. And a white dust lay over every surface. But it was empty of human life.

'Pegasus!'

The goat pulled from his grasp and ran towards the cottage. Stéfan turned. A tall figure in military camouflage was standing beside the glass lean-to at the rear of the cottage. Stéfan found it one of the more baffling features of country life that people never emerged from the logical exit to their house, but simply appeared round hedges and walls.

'Hallo there!' called Stéfan, dusting down his brass-buttoned blazer. To his great annoyance, he felt the initiative was slipping from him. And loss of power was what he hated above all else. He dragged the door shut and moved across the scrubland to where Pegasus was playfully butting his owner in the balls.

Stéfan held out his hand.

'I hope you don't want any bloody work done!' said the man in mottled khaki.

Stéfan paused, putting his plans on hold.

Mr Griffith Barton was not the effete artisan of his imaginings. Clint Eastwood was the doppelgänger that came to mind. Gaunt, austere, and in his late, great period as lone avenger in the West. As refinements, The Windowman had the charmless lavatory-brush hair of a lapsed Marine and was wearing army boots without laces, though whether due to eccentricity or to the goat was hard to say. Nonetheless, while such asceticism was a far cry from the smooth, soft fleshiness of Stéfan, it was their two faces that offered the truest contrast. Where the older man presented a lined and weathered look to the world, young Stéfan's visage bore all the angst and torment of a puffball.

'Work . . . ?' Stéfan tried his braying laugh, searching in vain for some conversational high ground. 'No, not at the moment, no. Perhaps later.' But now it had become personal. Even if Crug

Caradoc burnt to the ground, he would have his fucking windows made.

There was a brief stand-off, for the chitchat was in The Windowman's court and Mr Griffith Barton was not big on social graces. But then the whistle of a kettle began, and soon its high-pitched insistence could not be ignored.

'I'm making tea,' he said. 'Without sugar.' And he turned on his heel and went in.

On the assumption that, technically, this was an invitation, also without sugar, Stéfan followed him.

If Mr Griffith Barton had not been as expected, neither was his cottage. Probably a gamekeeper's cottage when first built, it had had the usual extensions for twentieth-century mod cons, and the lean-to was but the latest. Yet inside, the guiding aesthetic was breeze block – for the work had ceased, circa 1975. None of the new internal walls had ever been completed, and they stood like a crude and uncertain art statement. Over the years, a chaos of personal effects had cloaked the stark concrete, like flotsam on a rising tide, and had humanised the dereliction. In the primitive kitchen and glass lean-to the only virgin space was a small white Formica table, on which lay that morning's *Financial Times*, folded open to the shares page, and a pair of donnish half-moon spectacles on a silver chain.

Stéfan stepped around a two-foot pile of *National Geographics* and unfolded the spare deckchair leaning against the Belling cooker. He reflected that no matter how long he had considered the question, he would never have been able to arrive at the correct dress code for this cup of tea.

Among the many skills of his in which he had great confidence, none did he set more store by, and rightly so, than his powers of negotiation. The flattery, the bullying, the chivvying, the brinkmanship, the brazen lies, the bear hug, all had been passed down in perfect working condition from father to son, and then fine-tuned some more. Now, for the first time, he felt in need of a manual.

He placed his deckchair to give himself the widest arc of vision, and watched the boiling water make it safely into the two chipped white mugs. As he looked around the lean-to, he felt he was staring at the student digs of a man in his fifties. The geological strata of unwashed dishes, the objects left to lie and die where they dropped, the random profusion of hardbacked books, this was testimony to a time warp.

And then he looked to where there should have been a door into the rest of the house.

The design concept of the door had not advanced beyond a very large lumpy hole, but such size helped give a view of the room beyond. The only daylight came via the glass of the lean-to, for the windows at the far end of the room seemed to be either shuttered or thickly curtained. And this light was glinting on gold.

It was not gold as in gold bullion or gold robbers, but was the almost more surprising gold of gold-leaf. And in abundance. Along both the walls that he could see was hung a series of portraits in oils, with huge and elaborate gold-leaf frames. The portraits were of a type and size that he had not seen since rain once drove him into the National Gallery. And, like them, the imperious subjects in the lounge were posed and grand and formal. But, try as Stéfan might, the goo of the oils and the gloom of the light and the black of the backdrop made details difficult to discern, except that most were women.

'She's thirty-six. Oldest ever known.' The Windowman put a carton of milk on the small table and handed Stéfan his tea. 'But we never had a birth certificate for her.' He cleared a pile of papers to reveal a foam-topped bench and sat opposite, warming both hands on his mug. 'Otherwise we could put her in *The Guinness Book of Records*.'

Not a word had made sense. Wondering if he were witness to signs of psychosis, Stéfan focused his attention on the milk, which he poured in with due deliberation. And sought in vain for a suitable response.

Very discreetly though, as he raised the mug to his lips he ventured a glance again into the lounge, to sneak a second look at the nearest of the portraits. He thought he could just detect the outline of a regal *décolletage*, the breasts graced with a purple sash. No light fell on the face, but the flesh-coloured paint suggested the features of a young woman, and possibly a very beautiful one.

'Bloody miracle, given the rubbish that goat eats,' added The Windowman.

'The goat?'

'Yes. Pegasus.'

'Oh, Pegasus!' Stéfan fell untypically silent for the second time.

'Snuff?'

'I'm sorry?'

'Snuff?'

'Er . . . no. No thanks.' What he really wanted was a line of cocaine. He was in a social world entirely new to him.

The Windowman took a tiny enamelled box from his trouser pocket, clicked it open, and put a pinch of snuff to each nostril. He sneezed twice, then placed the box on the table. A thick browny-yellow film, disconcertingly the colour of wood shavings, remained on his upper lip.

'Buggers your tubes, carpentry.'

Stéfan took another mouth of tea. And wondered at the cost of the spectacles lying on the table. The Windowman offered no more thoughts, but sat sniffing deeply. He had a stillness to him, and the inscrutability of a scraggy Buddha.

'So you play the market, then?' said Stéfan, tapping the *FT*. 'What have you got shares in?'

'Nothing. Wouldn't give the bastards the pleasure.'

'Oh. So why—'

'Because it tells you what the smart money's doing – before you see the ripples. Tells you where the power is, what's *really* going on. That and the court pages. Court pages give you more than all

73

the news stories put together. Who's in town, who's meeting who, at what fancy dinner; it all tells you which fucker's up to what. Then a few weeks later you see some dodgy deal's been stitched together, and it all falls into place. All falls into place.'

'Wouldn't have thought it mattered up here.'

'If I'm going to be blown up, I like to know why.'

'If you're going to be blown up, best get shares in the bombs, I say!' And Stéfan tried his first matey laugh of the day.

There was no returning laugh.

'They train up here for World War Three, you know. Paratroopers, SAS, Gurkhas. And they all make the same mistake. They think the next war's going to be between countries. Between governments. It won't be. It'll be between multinationals. They'll be fighting the next wars. Nissan bombing Ford, Nike bombing Reebok. All dying for market share. That's what the new vested interests are about.'

Political philosophy, indeed abstract thought itself, had no designated space within Stéfan's brain. But his normal mockery of such ideas would clearly serve none of his own vested interests. So he just kept on with the nodding.

'System's so rotten the governments act like bloody agents for these companies. Probably be paid commission for running their bloody wars!' This forced a smile from him, his first. And for the first time Stéfan noticed the intense gaze of his deep-set eyes. 'We always used to have private armies in this country. So it wouldn't be such a change. Except this time the armies'd be run by the likes of BT and British Steel. After all, they already have security forces of their own.'

He smiled again, an unexpectedly warm, apologetic smile. 'Sorry. Hobbyhorse of mine. Been reading too much Chomsky.'

'Understood,' said Stéfan.

Mr Griffith Barton might also have said that even recluses occasionally like conversation and company. But he did not say it because his emotions had been kept in cold storage for too many years.

'Were you army?' asked Stéfan.

'Good God, no! Army surplus. I just don't like wasting money on clothes.'

At last! A word familiar to Stéfan had entered the conversation and he lost no time.

'Must be a lot of money in your line of work though. Some classy designs on your workbench. You could build half a palace with what's in your shed.' Although Stéfan would never admit it, the words 'fish' and 'reel' were silently taking up residence in his head. 'Looked like good wood out there. Not just rubbishy pine. Those architraves were oak, weren't they?'

'Probably. More money than sense, most people. Even had them come by helicopter just to check the grain.'

'Helicopter?' Stéfan felt a surge of pique at being upstaged, even though he had no idea by whom.

'Oh, the aristocracy like their wood. Though lately I've had sheikhs, pop stars, all sorts come here,' he said contemptuously. He glared at Stéfan. 'And I take it you're not just out for a picnic.'

'I have tried writing to you. Don't you reply to your letters?'

'Don't read them. Expect they'll be in that pile over there.' He gestured under the table at the heap of papers he had swept off the bench-seat earlier. 'Anyway, forget it, I've got a nine-month waiting list.'

'Nine months . . . ? Money's not a problem.'

'I'm very pleased for you.'

'It's just some windows, windows for Crug Caradoc.'

'Waste of time, windows.' He reached for his snuffbox a second time.

The comment went unnoticed by Stéfan. 'They're Jacobean windows. Very ornamental. Absolutely beautiful, but rotting.'

'They would be. As I said, waste of time, windows.'

'Waste of time? What do you mean, "waste of time"?'

'Why do people have windows? To close them. What do you get if you close them? Condensation. And then they rot.'

'Well, eventually, yes, but—'

'So if you're going to have windows, have plastic.' At this point, Stéfan noticed that the few window frames he could see were plastic.

'If? What do you mean "if"? You've got to have windows.'

'Of course you don't have to have windows. That's just propaganda. Modern sales nonsense. What you need is free circulation of air.'

'I've got a Jacobean manor house worth over half a million. You want me to take out the windows?'

'If you don't want them to rot.' He sniffed deeply at his pinch of snuff.

'So what would you have people use instead of windows?'

'Sacking.'

He sneezed. And sneezed again.

'Sacking?'

The Windowman nodded, yellow snuff flakes falling on to his camouflage outfit, where they lay disturbingly visible.

'Come off it! *Sacking*?'

'Ideal material. It was used for centuries. Allows the air through, keeps the cold out, and you pin it up if you want daylight. And it's cheap.' Stéfan started to smile at the joke. 'Had it for the first five years of married life.' Stéfan's smile faded.

Stéfan allowed no one to take the mick out of him. It was the golden rule of all his friendships and relationships. But he could not tell if the mick was being taken or not.

'You had sacking over your windows . . . ?'

'Can't beat it for staying healthy. Gives constant fresh air. None of those colds and sniffles and 'flus. Because there's none of the fug and the condensation you get with windows, and central heating. Sacking keeps you in perfect health all year round.' Then he paused, and said almost to himself, 'Though the wife did die.'

He said it so matter-of-factly, as a virtual throwaway, that Stéfan almost doubted he had heard correctly.

Then The Windowman finished his tea in a single gulp and

stood up. 'Nine months,' he said, and walked across to abandon his mug in the kitchen.

This, however, was not the wait needed before he could start work. This nine months was the length of time that he judged necessary to effectively deter a customer. And he judged Stéfan to be the impatient type. For reasonable, patient people, he sometimes found it necessary to say two, or even three, years.

Stéfan, however, always ignored the deadlines of others. He had absolute faith in the power of his personality and the aphrodisiac of cash. And he regarded 'no' as an answer only ever accepted by the little people. Admittedly, he had yet to get the full measure of Mr Griffith Barton, whose negotiating strategy he found brilliant in its waywardness. But he felt confident that a second visit would crack him. That then he would reel him in to the river bank.

Stéfan got to his feet. 'There were some big oil paintings like yours at the place I bought,' he said casually, trying to build up rapport as he walked towards the kitchen door being held open for his departure. 'Are you a collector?'

'No. No, not at all.'

'Oh. So those . . . ?' His arm waved vaguely behind him.

'They're of the wife, and the wife's family. Well, her ancestors.'

'Oh. Big family?'

'The Hapsburgs. Watch out for the goat.'

Chapter 8

Rob and Jane peered down the hole in Gareth's field. It was a neatly dug hole, precisely placed, and about two foot square by two foot deep. Inside it was a bucket, and the bucket was full of tap water. Beside the hole lay a section of plastic drainpipe. Several times the couple shifted their stance for a better view of these objects.

'Well?' said Teg.

'No,' said Rob, after a long pause. 'I don't get it.'

Jane shook her head.

Teg smiled, quietly pleased by the stupidity of townsfolk. 'It's an art,' he said. 'Catching moles runs in the family.'

As they stood up, his huge outstretched arm drew the eye down a row of molehills in a mazy landscape of the mounds. As linear as the Greenwich Meridian, the little piles of earth were marching past his feet.

'That's a run,' he said. And in the middle of their run he had dug his hole. In the distance, Ben was bearing down on another spade, digging out another hole.

Like a magician with a prop, Teg then held up the pipe for them to see. It was a normal pipe, a pipe of some two foot six, but with a small circular piece cut out. He laid it on the ground, across the hole. And raised an enquiring eyebrow again.

Rob and Jane peered into the earth again.

'No,' said Rob, shaking his head after another long pause. 'I still don't get it.'

'Clickety-clop, clickety-clop, clickety-clop, splosh!' said Teg. With an air of helpfulness.

This time they both shook their heads.

The massive molecatcher eased on to his knees, and pointed out a small aperture that had escaped their notice on two walls of the freshly dug hole.

'The mole,' explained Teg patiently, 'runs along his tunnel . . .' As a visual aid he wiggled two vertical fingers like legs. '. . . and then suddenly the tunnel ends. Because of the hole. But . . .' He flourished the plastic pipe a second time, then inserted first one end, and then the other, into the equal and opposite apertures. '. . . the mole does not realise this. Because of the pipe. Which he now enters . . .' Teg twisted the pipe round, so that the missing piece was on the underside. '. . . and continues running along . . .' The sausage fingers doubled furiously as legs again. '. . . until he reaches the gap and . . .' The legs spiralled downwards. '. . . he falls into the bucket full of water!' Teg impersonated a depth charge. 'And drowns!' He beamed with pleasure. 'Followed by all his friends and family. Clickety-clop, clickety-clop, clickety-clop, splosh!'

There was a silence while Rob and Jane pondered these ancient mysteries of rural life.

'Amazing,' said Jane eventually.

Easing his bulk upright, Teg gave a satisfied smile.

'No denying it, with poison you lose the artistry.'

'I can see that,' said Rob.

They each admired the hole some more.

After leaving the offer of carrot cake and a copper kettle simmering on standby, Rob and Jane returned up the meadow to the long-house and the warm bosom of the Rayburn. Not a townie word had passed their lips, not a hint of any molist critique, for already they knew enough to observe the rural rules of integration. For them, the Country Code meant swearing fealty to all farm subsidies, never mentioning the local lamb without prefacing it by 'world-class', and making no public jokes about sheep-shaggers. Being far from socially acceptable in their own habits – sexually liberal, environmentally radical, artistically original, and now owners of a Vietnamese pot-bellied pig – they were not about to raise the contentious issue of multiple mole deaths.

Indeed, although the pockmarked meadow was not their property, they had a personal reason to welcome the traditional molecatchers.

On several days of late, the morning mists had evaporated to reveal the motionless, wraithlike figure of Gareth standing in the field, armed with a loaded shotgun. It was aimed at the earth, but was held with a neurotic, silent intensity, his body coiled tight in anticipation of the bloody blast. And there he stood an hour at a time, poised and primed, in an act more of therapy than rodent control.

Gareth was an only child, and like the Prince of Wales had waited humiliatingly long to take over the reins of the family firm, a 120-acre farm. His parents had delayed retirement well past three score and ten, and had then erected a bungalow within criticising distance of the farmyard. Farming was all he knew, but like a dullard pupil he knew it only by rote; had there been a litter, he would have been the runt. So Gareth would dutifully tramp the land, and plough the fields, and check the stock, and soak up the rain. And still the older cows deferred first to his father.

It was to make his mark, to stamp his authority, that Gareth had gone out on an upland limb and bought the unimproved patch of pasture that had helped put paid to Hefin. But this rare burst of derring-do, which had so surprised his neighbours, was not entirely at the prompt of agriculture. Dating a year from his marriage, which had equally surprised his neighbours, such an independent action was for him some proof of manhood, a confused sexual response to the length of Moira's Irish legs.

Over the years, Gareth had tried various ways to assert his uninspiring sexuality, even being the local pioneer of the bumper sticker 'Help Stamp Out Aids – Run Over a Queer', but had found that the force of his personality frequently fell short. And in this remote field he found both a virility symbol and a refuge.

Standing in the white mist, in deepest silence, waiting for the earth to move, offered an emotional release. Here it was *his* land, *his* law, and life became simple once more. To be unseen, to act unseen, was primitive and thrilling. It was jungle time. And the power of the gun, the size of the mole, they made him a man again.

Rob and Jane had offered him the occasional cup of tea, but he was not a great conversationalist. His face interested Rob, though only from the technical standpoint of its flatness. Somehow it had a shortage of features, as if his character had given up on the idea of personal growth, leaving a physiognomy shortfall. This offered an unusual challenge to the art of portraiture. But Rob's friendly words, 'Would you mind if I sketched you?', had merely caused his hasty exit, fuelled by a fear that art was intimacy with a pencil.

Tinkerbell, the Vietnamese pig, was snuffling the morning mail by the time Rob and Jane made it back from their hole and mole inspection. A miniaturised pig, shaped like a barrel, built like a battleship, and inky bristly black all over, it seemed to hold no resentment for the war and nuzzled allcomers with great charm. She had been their first country purchase, managing to square that difficult circle of being both lovably cute and an all-terrain Rotavator. And if Tinkerbell harboured any regrets that she was never walked up and down Hampstead High Street on a studded leather leash like her contemporaries, she kept them to herself.

Quite why purchase of a pig had taken priority over the guttering, the slates and the peeling paintwork was one of those mysteries that make life in the country so different from life in the town.

'Oh jeez! She doesn't eat envelopes as well, does she?' yelped Jane, rescuing the mail from the doorstep.

'Probably just collecting the stamps.' He took a brown foolscap envelope from Jane's hand.

Installation of a letterbox was another of the architectural refinements that had yet to make it off their long 'To Do' list. But as time passed, items like a letterbox had begun to feel more and more like a foolish fad of the twentieth century. The physical remoteness gave the most normal of possessions an air of irrelevance, almost pretension. A little longer, and even hot water and unflickering lighting would seem the frippery of a mad consumer world.

'Is it about the ducks?' asked Jane.

Rob glanced at the franking, and looked doubtful. He pulled out the letter, read its brief contents, and sucked his teeth with what Jane knew to be irritation. 'No, not about the ducks.'

The six ducks, like the pig, had been a perverse priority.

Mr Probert had neglected to mention that in the event of heavy winter rain (an event of almost hourly occurrence) the source of the Severn would appear in their garden. The first time had been quite entertaining, as is many a rural drama to incomers, and they had some rather jolly photos of Rob rowing the wheelbarrow across the kitchen. But the joke had soon palled.

The two obvious solutions had been diversion or drainage. Rob and Jane went for the duck-pond option. With ducks. Perhaps less understandable was that they had to be exotic ducks. For Rob fell victim, as so often, to aesthetics. And having seen the brochures, he had elected for their ducks to be Cubist in design (a colour scheme also favoured by the foxes). Now they were waiting for literature on their ducks' special dietary needs and hobbies.

Not all developments had been of such dubious practical value (for the eggs also had an exotic, somewhat specialised taste). Wiring – hence lighting and heating – now reached the studio *né* barn, and a polythene mantle hung over its entrance. The joys of multi-tinted emulsion had created a softer mood music in the living quarters, and the Rayburn had been rejuvenated by a d-and-c of its baking bits. And Nico swore on his chequebook that the Massey Ferguson would be gone any day now, probably to Ohio.

The couple also still loved each other, a statistical oddity among the records of those who forsake urban comfort for rural fastness. Mid-Wales was hardly the last frontier, but both Rob and Jane got a primitive pleasure in going head to head with the elements. A wind that wrenches doors off, a rain that penetrates the bones, a night that is black without break, here was all they needed to play at pioneering. Jane had long suffered the curse of a pretty face, that fanciful proof of an empty head, and was delighted the rigours of roughing it gave the world a two-fingered testimony of her true grit. The physicality of their existence was a far cry from the skills honed by her arts degree, but still she admitted to relishing its John Wayne simplicities.

And then there was newness. Each day had a different script, a different menu for the senses. Sunday's double rainbow that had arced with kaleidoscopic precision on to the distant pine sentinels would not repeat its performance for another thousand years, if ever. The climatic quirk that had encased their bushes in filigree ice had its origins in chaos theory, in a far-off Atlantic low. The lamb that had bleated for help in their hawthorn hedge at midnight had left a unique imprint of its quivering ribcage upon their memory. And spring, the season of a million greens, was still to come.

'It's about the wind-pump,' said Rob rattily, screwing up the letter. 'That 2,000-year-old technology yet to arrive in Wales! No wonder the estate agent didn't want to answer questions about wind-pumps.' He scrunched the paper some more and gave it a badminton-type tap towards Tinkerbell.

'Another blank?'

He nodded. 'The fifth.'

'Someone must make wind-pumps!'

'I think they're covered by the Official Secrets Act.'

Mains electricity had long thought better of the journey up to Pantglas, and so the farmhouse had the fitful services of a generator, fed by oil. Noisy and temperamental, it intruded on their rural idyll with the unseemliness of a burbling fart. It also offended their notions of eco-sensitivity, and every day further whetted their desire to give the gales something useful to do, like power the shower.

'If we wanted to heat Cardiff we could probably get a grant. And put a whole bloody wind-farm up here! But keep one house ticking over? Wacky!'

'Dafydd said we'd be the first. He's never delivered mail to anyone with a wind-pump.' Jane handed him the only other post, a Jiffy bag of paint tubes.

'I reckon he'll have spread the word that we're seriously odd. Special Branch will be mingling with the sheep soon.'

'You want to mention the word money-saving to Dafydd. Have that spread down the valley and we'll pass the normality test. Probably for the first time.'

'It is a bugger though. I thought we'd just need to look in Yellow Pages. Under Wind.'

If asked to locate their position on the political spectrum, the pair would probably have pointed the needle to medium-green, their anti-consumerism scoring highly if only by virtue of their poverty. Previously, their main ecological commitment had been the separation of glass from paper, for Manchester offered few opportunities to save the Earth in other than token ways. It was thus a frustration to find the holy grail of energy-saving used up so much energy, and to little effect apart from ridicule.

They moved into the warmth of the parlour, Rob struggling with a staple as he tried to reach his cerulean blue. 'I mean, they were even in that old James Dean movie, for Chrissake! Whirring away. And that was Texas back in the Fifties!'

Jane looked at him. 'You talking about *Giant*?'

'Yes, that's right.'

84

'With wind-pumps?' she said sceptically.

He nodded.

'You sure they weren't oil derricks?'

Rob hesitated. He tried to visualise the fading Cinemascope footage.

'Well, they were going round all the time,' he said, and then was hit by doubts. 'Or was it up and down . . . ?'

Chapter 9

The reluctance of electricity, as well as phones, and sometimes even mains water, to go that final costly mile up into the hills had done more than breed candidates for Cold Comfort Farm. It had given an opt-out clause for the twentieth century. Indeed, in conversations with some locals it could not even be assumed that the Enlightenment was a shared cultural value. Here, the company of beasts and an ignorance of Hansard had led to an individualism, sodden and sullen rather than rugged, that believed rural life had no need for such pedantries as law. 'Hillbillies!' was the putdown view from the valley proper, but in reality their hillbilliness fell far short of Appalachian, the oddball behaviour showing no sign of banjos or beards or any religious hoo-hah with snakes.

Most pronounced of their quirks was an alternative jurisprudence. Landlord–tenant disputes were resolved by shotgun, boundary fence disagreements by chainsaw, and contested water rights by the strategic abandoning of dead sheep. Occasionally, disaffection was more inventively expressed. Mrs Whitelaw, the impecunious teacher of history, came to regret her impulsive detention of the young Dickinson boys: the second-hand caravan on which she had lavished her loan was not improved when the parents resprayed it with liquid manure.

Yet such behaviour was less about maliciousness than Wild West unworldliness. When the ageing Owen brothers – still bachelors at seventy-nine and eighty-one – finally gave up drinking water from their well and sold their candlelit farmhouse, with its fertiliser-free farm, they were ill-equipped for the six figures it brought them. Retiring to a bungalow, where they continued to eschew carpets and curtains, Jack and Arthur allowed themselves only the one luxury – a 26-inch colour TV. Determined to maintain a lifetime's habit of good husbandry, they kept it in its cardboard box, cutting out just enough to see the screen, in order that it remain dust free.

It was a false economy, as the television overheated and burnt the house down.

The brothers both survived, but for the rest of their lives they loudly lamented the follies of the modern world.

To them the modern world was Abernant: they had rarely been beyond the Nant Valley. And, though Welsh to their taproots, they knew almost nothing of mid-Wales. Nor were they alone in their ignorance, for mid-Wales was a mystery to many, a shadowy blur at the core of the country.

The very name itself, 'mid-Wales', rang loud with the failure of confidence. An undefined confection of some foreign cartographer, it referred to no known shape. It was a non-name given to an identity crisis. There is felt no need for a 'mid-Ireland' or a 'mid-Scotland', and middle England represents not a geographical location but a state of mind. The place 'mid-Wales' is the bit left over after the coast, the valleys, the Marches and Snowdonia have been ticked off and signed up for tourist duty. Mid-Wales is the bit without the castles, without the singing in fancy dress, without the folk memory of pits. Here are the parts where motorways don't reach. Here they burn no cottages.

Finding it empty, the English used it to store the rain, to build the reservoirs that gave them baths in Birmingham. Then, when these were awash with water, and the desecration done, faraway financiers planted battalions of pines that stretched to infinity across the hazy hills, creating a view that offered only tax breaks and fire breaks. And all because this no-name place was that joy of central government, its very own Empty Quarter . . . a giant in-fill site that had no votes and needed no governor-general.

The only hint of a heyday had been in Victorian times, when its municipal springs discovered the secret of eternal youth. All it took was a mineral with polysyllables and you had a spa. Baden-Baden, boyo, boyo, cried the hucksters! So little town after little town tacked 'Wells' to its name, a proof of miraculous properties not dissimilar to the dotcom of today. And the charabancs and the parasols poured in. Unfortunately, the Nant Valley had the wrong geology for bubbles, its Old Red Sandstone producing a dishwater that suggested the sludge of death rather than the elixir of life. Elsewhere, however, the bathing in early Perrier paid off, and the inland esplanades linger on to this day.

But this abused and empty landscape is now a challenge to the image consultants. If mid-Wales has an etymological soulmate it is perhaps *Mitteleuropa*; for both the names have Tolkienian overtones, hinting at a dark land full of trolls, where writs do not run. Yet while Hungary boasts its gypsy violins and Transylvania has Vlad the Impaler, mid-Wales is a land where the national characteristics have gone to ground. This hole in the heart of the country runs true to few stereotypes.

Here, the accent is liltless. Not for mid-Wales the adenoidal whine of the north, or the nasal squawk of the south, or the bouncy castle rhythm of the films. The speech is slow, the pauses demoralising, the thought processes opaque. This is country speed, but the speaker leaning on the post could have harvested his values in Devon, or Cumbria or Dumfriesshire. His mores are shaped by remoteness, not by National Awareness Week. He is no candidate for the national character.

Stolidity is his character of choice, and, like his tweed, has long been out of vogue. Subfusc and orotund, these are the traits of the Nant Valley role model. The maintenance of respect and dignity when in public, as if on the *qui vive* for a corpse, are the ground rules for parish behaviour. Queen Victoria lives on in the blood and formalised courtesies usefully dull the emotions. It is as though gravitas began with the first rusks.

Few here are ready for the cultural melting pot, for the coming together of minds from different postcodes.

Chapter 10

'Second track after the bridge, she said?'

'Yeah.'

The Volvo slowed, both occupants looking for a break in the overgrown hedge.

'Didn't get a house name, I s'pose?'

'No.'

Nico flicked the screenwash and sighed. The young lad never got a house name. Rarely got the message right either. Nico sometimes wondered whether he found the phone a technology too far.

'Hope the old dear wants to flog more than a pair of candlesticks. Head of the valley and back, it eats up the diesel.'

Sion said nothing. He was at that post-acne age when only direct questions stood any chance of response.

'But then it's usually a waste of time up here. All fucking Formica! *And* they think they're doing you a favour!' They were now several miles beyond Crug Caradoc, and Nico was miffed. He had fancied he might catch sight of Stéfan, and had entertained hopes of giving him a cheery wave that subtly encompassed derision and triumph in equal measure. But all he had seen was scaffolding.

'Ah, this must be it! "Ty Mawr".' A hoary plank lay wedged in the hawthorn, the six letters daubed in red. Nico swung his Volvo on to the track, and soon they were bouncing along beside a bubbling stream. Half a dozen fields away they could just make out a farmhouse sheltered by a windbreak of pines.

'Be full of shagged-out salmon here, come the summer. Last lap before they burst, this is. Get more baby salmon on the moors than lambs most years.'

Nico was always full of facts. Like many of the antiques he sold, they were of doubtful provenance. As indeed was he.

Despite his name, despite his accent, Nico's roots were local. Nico's name was Nicholas. Guided by greed from an early age, he had done a runner to London. But to be Welsh from Abernant gave little street cred as a fixer, little edge as a wheeler-dealer, and he had gone for Greek. Initially, this had meant just the loss of a syllable, but then the need to get girls grew and he had come to act as if kebabs were in his blood. Yet for all his graft he remained a small-town boy looking for the big time, a fate made worse by ending up in Hackney before it was hip. And after ten years of talking the talk but tripping on the walk, he had come home where he could act the big shot, and run rings around the locals.

'Glaciation. That's why it flattens out up here. Glaciation. 500 million years ago all this used to be under water.'

There was still a fair bit of water left in the potholes and the Volvo bumped along the mud track leaving caramel-coloured streaks over the meadow's edge. As Nico looked out across the recently sown crop, several months away from being hay, he had a sudden insight into the farmer's needs. A 1957 Massey Ferguson combine harvester. Red. He made a mental note.

The estate car continued to rise and fall, not unlike a sluggish yo-yo, as they made their way past the fields. Its ancient suspension had been adjusted to accommodate the farming community's Brobdignagian taste in wardrobes, and now it preferred to handle freight.

'Remember, simpatico body language. Old ladies need TLC. So smile and pat any cats you see. And leave me to do the chat.'

This was the lad's first time out of the shop. Taken on a few weeks earlier, Sion was strictly for dusting and lifting purposes.

Supposedly he was also there to learn, one day perhaps to be a fully fledged dealer, but his provincial gawkiness gave little hint of a silver tongue. He did not seem to have answered the job advert as part of any long-term career strategy.

The approach to Ty Mawr revealed a trim if unglamorous farmhouse, its grey-walled farmyard freshly hosed clean of the day's dung. Its double-fronted exterior lacked the homely touch of a climber, in deference perhaps to the altitude, but the primrose paintwork was recent and the windows retained the charm of small panes. It was the typical abode of a typical farmer making a typically limited living out of marginal land.

As Nico drove up, two unkempt border collies went through the motions of ambushing the car, growling and baring their teeth at the tyres in a familiar charade of aggression. (See Terms and Conditions of Employment for farm dogs: 5 [iii], pointless defence of farm against all vehicles.) Nico wiggled the wheel, taking malicious pleasure in adding some real danger to their game, and then swung the Volvo full circle to halt beside the front door, making a mental note of a wrought-iron foot-scraper as he braked.

Out of the car, Nico and Sion were as ill-matched a pair as in. The middle-aged Nico acted as a spur to the memory by being stubby, scruffy and pasty. At nineteen, Sion was a head taller, clean-shaven and accidentally clean-cut in his jeans and T-shirt; had he not a deferential droop, almost in apology for his presence, he could have passed for a village prop forward. But his most remarkable feature was his tan, a deep, serious and apparently overall tan. Nico, never abashed by nosiness, had enquired several times about this feature, but had only ever got a mumble out of him, in which the words 'been away' seemed to figure.

They stood for a moment to register the view. The true pleasure of each unknown house in the hills is that it comes with an unknown view and is a fresh piece in the jigsaw of the landscape. Far below them the Nant wound south, as yet almost too trivial to glint in the spasmodic sun, and the valley contours had the clarity of a painted clay model.

'Thank you for coming.'

A buxom farmer's wife, silver-haired and sixty-something, was standing in the porch. The barking dogs had served their purpose. Or perhaps she had been watching the slow, unstately progress of the car.

'Not at all, madam. My favourite part of the valley.'

Fiddling with the ties on her apron, she looked from him to young Sion, who had just stepped from the shade into the sunlight. 'That's a very nice tan.'

'He's been away.'

Nico smiled, introduced himself and his 'colleague', said nice things about the farmyard, and was soon, as expected, face-to-face with faded floral wallpaper. And a mahogany-veneer coat-stand, slight woodworm. It was a world of archetypes. Mrs Matthews herself looked as if she had stepped out of a pop-up picture-book on farming: sturdy, motherly, rosy-cheeked and clearly fond of a roast dinner. Yet, as the three stood huddled in the hall, she seemed uneasy.

Nico was a veteran of these early moments. 'Nico the Knock-er' was how he had begun, all of twenty years before, when he returned to this land of rich pickings. Cold-calling in the hope of antique linen presses, or glass-top corner cupboards, or birdcage tripod tables. And being spurned at the door, and being abused as a gippo. Or smooth-talking his way to the heirlooms.

But nowadays it was they who called him.

'D'you arrange these dried flowers yourself?' he said admiringly, adding as she nodded, 'I imagine you exhibit. These'd be worth a rosette or two at the valley show.' And to Sion he said, 'It's a real art. Colours, shapes, sizes, all subtly blended. Takes years of practice.'

Mrs Matthews murmured her appreciation, yet her manner seemed slightly distracted, and Nico noticed that her gaze wandered.

'So! After an expert eye then, Mrs Matthews. What were you hoping to sell?'

'Er, I don't know exactly . . . I haven't decided.'

Sion's fixed smile started to show the first signs of fatigue.

'A few bibs and bobs,' she ventured. 'Perhaps you could advise . . . ?'

'I'll certainly try.' Nico judged it appropriate for the hand-on-forearm moment, which was so often confidence-building for the older lady.

'I thought maybe we'd start with the parlour . . . ?' she said. He inclined his head in acquiescence, and Mrs Matthews opened the door next to her, ushering them in ahead. As Nico squeezed past her he noticed her eyes – and some instinct told him that she had been crying.

The parlour was as he had expected. Kept for best, and cold, it contained a dated suite, some sub-Spode in a spindly cabinet, a few ornaments from day trips, and on the walls was art from the school of cheap sentiment (with animals). While a useful time capsule for a Martian studying twentieth-century cultural anomie, it held nothing to grace the *objets d'art* corner of even an Abernant emporium.

He rubbed his stubble. 'Maybe the fire-irons?' They looked the quirky, one-off work of an obliging blacksmith. 'Twenty-five quid?' He felt no need for the negotiating gambit of world-weary pessimism, and made the offer – which was accepted – almost out of embarrassment. And then he went through the motions, showing a feigned interest in the biographical details of various bric-à-brac. (Emphasising his generosity, he also agreed to give shoproom to a wind-up gramophone behind the sofa, and a sampler that paid tribute to Adam and Eve.)

After the parlour they went upstairs, pausing briefly on the half-landing to remove a vase which might just have known Victoria in her declining years.

Upstairs were four bedrooms and a generous bathroom, and these yielded the obligatory jug and bowl set and an austere commode seat, which he suspected had seen recent service. Set above it was a picture of Jesus, with a friend whom Nico did not recognise, and so on a flaky long shot he offered a tenner, upped to twenty because of the frame. And then there was the old standby of an oil-lamp, to which tourists are drawn like moths, apparently in some belief that their future home life will be taking a Dickensian turn.

Bibs and bobs it was. Like a gold miner, an antique dealer always lives in hope. But in recent years, the Wales of home-grown treasures had been looted. Not by the English, but by the dollar. When Nico had returned to his roots, an over-inflated frog in search of a small pond, the cottages and farmhouses were stuffed with the works of the natives, the arts and crafts of centuries cluttering up the parlours. Original Welsh dressers, hung high with copper lustre jugs, were two a penny. But then the penny dropped, and a pernicious exchange rate opened the door to a new breed of dealer: the American. Like a factory ship scouring the ocean floor, these megabuck-buyers dealt in bulk and Hoovered up the heritage, swearing in aid not the roof of a Volvo but the tonnage of a container lorry. They picked the parlours clean. And then they moved on.

'A potty? Is it cracked?' With the face of Lloyd George on it, Nico would have gone to twenty. But plain white with a Welsh motto? 'A fiver's the best I can do. I'm sorry.'

When, after half an hour, they came back down the narrow stairs, some thirteen items had changed hands, including the coffer in which they carried them. Mrs Matthews led the way, her mood visibly lightened. She would never know that all her objects were going straight to auction – in the junk category. She had had the chat, the charm, the praise of her taste, and she was grateful. The talk had moved to cast-iron kettles when unexpectedly she halted by the coatstand.

'Oh, and your foot-scraper might do well. Say £35?' suggested Nico.

'That's very kind. You've been very kind. But no. No, I've sold enough now.'

'It's a good price. Are you sure?'

'Yes, quite sure. I've got enough now, thank you,' said Mrs Matthews. 'I've reached £450.' Nico nodded agreement at the sum. 'And that's all I need.'

He started peeling twenties off his stash of cash.

'I can bury him now.'

Nico briefly lost count. 'Bury him? Bury who?'

'My husband.'

'You've sold these to bury your husband?'

'It's marginal land. We make so little.'

Nico was a picture of gravitas and sympathy. 'I'm very sorry to hear about your loss.'

Sion tried to look sorry too.

There was a brief but tricky hiatus. Then Nico resumed the count – though more slowly, out of respect for the destination of the money.

As he handed her the £450, Mrs Matthews looked embarrassed, almost flustered.

'I'm sorry if I've seemed rude,' she said.

'Rude? Why rude?'

'Not offering you tea. You've been so kind.'

'Oh, not at all! Don't worry about tea. We understand. You've suffered a loss.'

'No, no, it's bad manners. You're guests. It's just that, well . . . it's a bit difficult.'

'Think nothing of it. Honestly.'

'But would you like some tea?'

'Yes, please,' said Sion.

Mrs Matthews managed to look both pleased and worried. She glanced nervously down the hall towards the kitchen, the one room that had escaped the depredations of their visit. Throughout their time its door had remained shut.

'I just need to warn you that . . . well . . . not warn . . . but just

96

tell you that, well . . .' She paused to let her words regroup. 'I mean, will it bother you that my husband is in there?'

'Dead?' said Nico, somewhat superfluously.

'Laid out.'

Nico did not immediately respond. As the man who had recently put a corpse on his roof-rack, Nico considered himself broad-minded. But the proprieties of taking tea with a corpse stretched sang-froid to new limits. However, the matter was compounded by the issue of manners and the old lady's feelings and even an uncertainty about convention. Yet in the end it was a very simple thing that decided him. He was thirsty.

'Well . . .' he said, 'if . . . if his body doesn't bother *you* . . .' and then, gaining some vigour, 'we'd be very pleased to have a pot of tea.'

He might have been less free with his enthusiasm had he known the specifics.

They entered the kitchen to find another familiar farmhouse setting. There was a flagstoned floor, a ramshackle Welsh dresser, stacked with willow-pattern dinner plates, a corner cupboard, an old hob, a collection of corn-dollies, a sprinkling of brass, even a framed picture of the farmhouse from the air. What was unusual was to have a corpse lain the length of the dining table.

'Milk and sugar?'

'Er, yes. Yes, two for both of us, please.'

Her late husband was a robust man, his stomach rising from his tweed jacket like Glastonbury Tor. Only his formal posture suggested he wasn't simply the worse for scrumpy – although a mortal blue was fast eroding the ruddiness of his cheeks, had the visitors cared to look more closely. There was about him the air of a slain John Bull, brought in from battle. And laid on an *ad hoc* slab.

On seeing the corpse, Nico's initial shock was mixed with regret. It was clear Mr Matthews was not in the market for the '57 Massey Ferguson.

His widow, keen to be the good hostess, fussed solicitously

97

over the pair, gesturing for them to be seated. 'Please, make yourselves comfortable,' she said, more than once.

Their hesitancy was understandable. The only seats available were a set of six hard-backed dining chairs, which stood on each side of the long table. The body lay down the middle as if awaiting a giant Christmas carving.

Nico and Sion pulled out two chairs and sat down beside each other, instinctively choosing the narrow, leg end of the body. Mrs Matthews set out her willow-pattern china teapot and matching teacups on the other side of his legs, then paused as she was about to pull out the chair opposite.

'Biscuits?'

Sion, whose appetite seemed stronger than Nico's, again came out in favour. Mrs Matthews fetched an attractive Victorian china biscuit barrel, full of chocolate digestives, and sat down to join them.

'You must find it interesting to visit all these houses,' she said, giving the tealeaves a brief stir before pouring.

'That's true.' Nico nodded, staring straight ahead in a rather artificial way. Mrs Matthews leaned towards him and handed a disappointingly weak tea across her late husband's thighs. 'Help yourself to sugar.'

The sugar, milk and chocolate digestives moved backwards and forwards across his upper and lower legs for several minutes. The presence of a dead body proved a strong corrective to sloppy table manners. The offer of crumbly cake was refused.

'Only lived in the one house myself,' sighed Mrs Matthews, 'baby and bride, wife and widow. In all weathers, even sun!'

Nico was wishing he had shaved, the one solid contribution to compassion in his armoury. He searched for words.

'How did he die?'

'Milking.'

Nico nodded, and focused on his tea again, clinically stirring and re-stirring.

And it was while he was doing this, focusing without seeing, looking without concentrating, that he idly glanced down for the first time . . . and realised that Mrs Matthews's late husband was laid out on the finest seventeenth-century oak refectory table that it had ever been his privilege to witness.

For several seconds he found it hard to think clearly. Here were problems of sensitivity and logistics that were entirely new to his experience. As a holding operation, he resolved on more tea. He glanced sideways at Sion, hoping somehow to apprise him they had hit gold.

Sion, though, was preoccupied, aware his simpatico body language needed more work. He had just finished his third biscuit and was smiling emptily at Mrs Matthews. Without warning, he spoke. 'Do you have a cat?'

'In the barns. For ratting.'

She smiled back at the young man. In one of the bedrooms there had been a picture of a son, also heifer-like in his gangly bulk, that local hallmark of agricultural youth. 'Had a few in our lifetime. And a dozen or so dogs. He used to do the trials, my husband. Now that's a good test for a young man, controlling sheep. Helps to have your own teeth, of course. For the whistling.

'My husband lost his teeth early – kicked out by a bullock. Metal they were, his first set of dentures. All cold to the tongue. Well, *my* tongue. I used to say to him, "Sit by the fire if I'm going to kiss you!" And he'd threaten to take them out!'

£5,000 at least, thought Nico, who had discreetly checked the legs and found they were chamfered, an added-value feature.

'Now they've got those quad-bikes. Hardly need dogs any more. Except for company. Still, I guess I'm going to need company now.' The old lady smiled at them across her husband's kneecaps. 'A hundred and seventeen in this parish, though. And eighty-seven of them related – one way and another!'

'It doesn't seem right—' began Nico, touched by the germ of an idea.

'And at least fifty of them still speak to each other!' She almost laughed. 'You wouldn't believe the family feuds up here. All over land. And wills. Did you see that derelict house by the bridge? It's been falling down for over twenty years. All because none of the family can agree what to do with it!'

'As I say, it doesn't seem right—' repeated Nico.

'One side want to sell it, another side want to rent it, the daughter wants to live in it, and all the time it's rotting! Soon only be fit for pigs! Not that there's anything wrong with pigs. Sweet, intelligent animals. We used to keep pigs when we were first married. And hang the sides of bacon in this very room!' She paused, and all three looked up at the huge hooks still in the beams.

'What worries me is, it just doesn't seem right,' said Nico in his most caring tones, 'for us to take away all those little mementoes from your life together, all those items so full of memories for you, those keepsakes with . . .' He let emotion slow his speech to a judder.

'Yes, it is sad,' sighed the old lady. 'But what else can I do?'

'I don't know,' said Nico, as if defeated by the enormity of the question he'd been posed. 'Of course, it would be easier for you if there was just the one object to go . . .'

'That's true, I suppose,' mused the old lady, struck by the ingenuity of his idea. 'But like what?'

'Yes. It's tricky . . .' Nico rubbed his stubble.

The three of them pondered on this problem for several minutes. Nico cast his eyes up to the bacon hooks for inspiration, and let his gaze wander the kitchen in search of a solution, until suddenly, by chance, his eyes lighted upon the table.

'Like, say, this table here?' And he grasped the polished wood with both hands, being careful to avoid her husband's buttocks.

'This table?'

'We could stretch a point and give you 450 for it.'

She was clearly tempted . . . until a thought drew her back. 'But what about my husband?'

Nico was ahead of her. But he paused, to give this the gravity of thought due to a recently deceased spouse.

'It's not really the right place for him, is it? On a table? In the kitchen? A man of his years, his standing, he should be laid out properly, with dignity. In a bedroom. On a bed.'

'But how . . . ?'

'Sion and I. We'll do it.'

'Oh, that'd be putting you to far too much trouble.'

'It's the least we could do. After all the trouble you've gone to with the lovely tea and the biscuits?'

'Really?'

'Yes, no trouble.'

'Oh that is so kind of you. So kind. Are you sure?'

They were sure. In less than a minute the tea had been cleared and Nico had hold of Mr Matthews's legs and Sion had secured a grip under his armpits. Years of beef and beer had made him a heavy man and death had not helped. But Sion was surprisingly strong and they made a spirited run with him to the kitchen door. Advising Mrs Matthews to stay behind – so that the lying in state would be all the more of a pleasurable surprise – they then struggled down the hall with his sixteen stone.

It was the stairs that offered the serious challenge. They were narrow and steep, and they had a right-hand turn. First the pair attempted to carry him, as one would a drunk, but his weight distribution had damaged his centre of gravity and twice he toppled, pinning Nico to the floor. Then the two men laid him on the treads, head uppermost and on his back, and dragged him up for a while, a stair at a time, causing his trousers to slide down his thighs and reveal an unexpected taste in boxer shorts. But the real problem came at the turn, where he jammed. For Mr Matthews had rigor mortis and would not bend. Nico's expertise was with wardrobes, but Mr Matthews would not dismantle either. They took a breather. Of his two corpses in recent months, this was by far the more problematic. Then Sion stood up, and with professional deftness snapped first one leg and then the other. Mr Matthews would now go round corners.

Nico could not hide his astonishment. 'How on Earth did you do that?'

Sion merely shrugged. His face remained as expressionless as ever.

Nico wanted to press him further, but there was no time. Together they hurriedly wrestled the dead, and now floppy, farmer up the remaining stairs and into the master bedroom. Here they made him good, straightened out his clothes and his legs, plumped his pillows, and left him ready for Jesus.

Closing the door behind them, they went down the stairs two at a time.

Back in the kitchen, they found that Mrs Matthews had helpfully polished the eight-foot oak table and its frieze rail, and was keen to give them the coasters that had for so long decorated its surface. But Nico insisted on paying her an extra tenner for these, because, as he said, the reputation of an antique dealer is his most prized asset.

'I would offer to put all your lovely bibs and bobs back in place,' he added, 'but I suspect that's a treat you'd like to keep for yourself.'

'Indeed I would,' she replied. 'I'm in the mood for a trip down Memory Lane.'

And on that touching note, Nico and Sion shouldered the table, eased it out of the back door, along the path, round the farmyard, and into the rear of the Volvo Estate. Speed, they both felt, was probably of the essence, and they paused only to lash the legs to the half-closed tailgate door.

As they jolted back down the mud track, Nico let out a whoop and punched the air. 'So much for fucking Formica!' he cried.

Chapter 11

Eddie had been driving his taxi long enough to know when a bird was gagging for it and these two lesboes were. The dikey one was sprawled out on the back seat prettending she didn't know her knickers were showing, while the blonde nympho one sat in the pasenger seat with her huge nipples hard with lust and protruding through her skimpy T-shirt. Eddie stopped the metre and pulled over into a lay-by and showed them his eight inch dick knowing this fare would be one to remember. At first they acted suprised but as he pushed his fingers towards the blonde bitches' clit he could feel the thick cappuccino froth that he lov

'Oh dear God!' Bryony leaned back from the keyboard in weary revulsion. It was not a good way to spend a Sunday.

She pushed away the author's pages of scrawl and gazed out of the old school window at the pouring rain. Across the river, in the churchyard, the fat vicar was showing a few old ladies round the surveyor's latest holes. Or the 'exploratory holes', as parishioners now put it, suggesting a surgeon with a shovel. From where Bryony sat, looking out over her winter vegetables, the threat to St Brynnach's seemed increasingly to come from a siege by giant moles. It was around their thigh-high spoils that the last surviving Christians now pottered, prodding at the loose earth as if in search of relics whose magic would save their church.

As she watched them, the church clock struck twelve. That it was midday surprised her. She had not heard that the vicar was now bringing the word of God to a total of three unfortunate parishes, and so did not know he had just emerged from his third dull sermon of the morning. Learning the time also angered her, because it most likely meant that Eryl, her absent lover, was on his way to the Dragon's Head, bypassing her and their home as he staggered back from another late-night party. For a brief moment, the hours of overwork and the weeks of worry made her want to cry.

A happy-clappy hippy, her boss Hubert called her. It was a dated expression, but hippydom – like most social trends, from Doc Martens to Victorian Gothic – had arrived late in mid-Wales. Her attachment to the cause, diluted and anaemic by the time it reached the Nant Valley, had meant waist-length hair, a rejection of the vicious careerist materialism rampant in Aberystwyth, and the occasional night of whirling naked at a bonfire party in the woods. It had also meant rejection of her rather well-to-do family, though she retained some innate sense of social standing that gave her influence over the likes of Hubert.

For several months she had tried to be a potter, that interface of artistry and playtime, but found that clay did not respond to her kneads. Her current enthusiasm was aromatherapy and almost every day she smelt different. Essential oils were her one treat; she felt her emotional problems were much aided by intimate contact with the likes of ylangylang oil. She had even begun to think of aromatherapy as a career pathway. Her magazines said it was a niche growth area where your only start-up costs were some oils, a comfortable front room and a certificate. Not a natural student, Bryony was drawn to the idea of a course where taking a long bath could be considered as studying.

Otherwise her résumé was short. Now twenty-six, with easily accessible breasts, she was keen on vegetables and smiled a lot.

But two years of living with Eryl had left her lonely, and with little to smile about. Her man was embittered at ending up a squire *manqué*, and raged at the confiscation of his silver spoon. She, meanwhile, worked six days a week for a pittance and came home to slurred speech and arms that rarely held her. This was hard for a woman who loved to touch and be touched. Effortlessly physical, she was a woman whose soft body filled up the nooks and crannies of a cuddle. But now to the shortage of sex was added shortage of money, and she was growing weary of her unfair burden.

The stress of the day was mounting. She had already had a coconut and jojoba shampoo, but to little effect. Bryony reached for her hand-woven Andean shoulder-bag and started to roll a joint.

It was a week after the auction at Crug Caradoc that she had put the small ad in. One of the few perks of toiling in the deli was free use of its notice board. First reply to the advert was a nice retired railwayman from the council estate on the edge of town. He had spent fifty years operating signals and had changed the points for just about every steam train you could think of . . . and now felt this would make an interesting 500-page book. Then came a cyclist, who had meticulously bicycled along every B-road in Britain, and he too felt his experiences would be appreciated by a wider public. She had typed up both these seminal works.

And then came the Traffic Warden. Who had written a novel in pencil.

No one liked the Traffic Warden. It was not just because he was a Traffic Warden. It was because he was a crooked Traffic Warden. Touched by the entrepreneurial spirit of the age, he would turn a blind eye to infractions if his palm was crossed with gifts, usually of a household nature. Hardly a trader in the town had not stumped up a bottle of whisky, a pair of slacks, a crate of carrots, a transistor radio, even a Moulinex mixer, so that their deliveries might proceed unhindered. It was an arrangement almost enshrined by local statute, a plebeian variant of *droit de seigneur*.

And then one day all the warden's extra income had come to a halt.

A new delivery driver called Rhys had brought the bread to the baker's in Abernant. The hefty young man, a rugby player from another valley, had not been officially advised of the system of traffic tithes. After unloading his order of crates, he came out of the baker's to find the Traffic Warden in the back of his van, helping himself to several square-tinned white loaves. Pretending not to notice him, nor his subsequent cries for help, Rhys slammed the back door and drove off. He then drove, as fast and erratically as he could, twenty miles over the mountains to his next delivery in Llandulais. Where, feigning astonishment, he discovered the now bruised and floury Traffic Warden in the back of his van and released him. Though apoplectic, his captive was quite without comeback – in more senses than one, since he had no money upon his person.

Hitchhiking in rain is never easy, but wearing a Traffic Warden's uniform is a particularly harsh handicap. He took eight hours – and was the subject of much ribald hooting – to cover the twenty miles back to Abernant on foot.

He never again solicited a bribe. But needing another source of income, he had turned his talents elsewhere.

And now the outcome of his efforts lay resting on the old trestle table.

Bryony forced herself to look again at the ruled exercise book, a WH Smith Student Special. The prospect of spending her evenings and weekends buried in the fantasies of a pervy Traffic Warden did not appeal. Especially if it were just for the benefit of Eryl's bar bill.

If she had been a reflective young woman, sensitive to life's many layers of irony, Bryony would perhaps have allowed herself a wry smile – for the formative years of her life had been spent as a pupil in this former classroom, learning right from wrong by rote. Here, where a dozen ink-welled desks used to face across the River Nant, she had once been slapped for offering a provocatively free-ranging view of her black netball knickers to a little boy called Tom, who went on to become a water bailiff. Now, twenty years later, she was lighting a joint from the old school boiler and considering the transcription of hardcore porn.

She and Eryl had bought the tiny village school (none up, two down) a couple of years earlier, when small had ceased to be beautiful in the ledgers of the Educ. Comm. Needing work, it had gone for a song – with a minor mortgage as a chorus.

It was with that unpaid mortgage on her mind that she reluctantly reopened the Traffic Warden's exercise book, and started leafing through its pages in the forlorn hope that redemption and a banjo-playing Jesus might be a late theme. Everywhere the penny-dreadful luridness of the sex lay heavy upon the paper, struggling to make headway against the absence of grammar and punctuation. (Those, the author had informed her, were down to the publisher. 'They know where to put the commas and stuff,' he had told her, the afternoon that he had slipped his brown-paper parcel into Hubert's shop. 'That's their job.') Indeed, the text sometimes had six to a taxi, so the shortage of colons and commas left the complex sexual couplings almost impossible to disentangle, the correct attribution of private parts calling out for the skills of a senior editor. She paused at random.

Their tongues met in the sticky spoils of the girls strawberry-red vulvars after the gear-stick had revved them to a juicy frenzy and the reclining front seat had tipped their already liquid mouths on to the overflowing dicks of –

'Have you got a fiver?'

Eryl stood unshaven and bleary-eyed and wet in the doorway of Class 2.

*   *   *

'Salsa?' said Gareth.

'Salsa?' said Gareth's mother.

Gareth's father would also have said 'Salsa' in a baffled, disapproving tone, but he had a new Dralon sofa and kept Sunday lunchtimes for lying down and snoring.

Moira already regretted her impulsiveness at voicing the idea in front of her in-laws.

Six months as Gareth's wife, and she had learned that impulsiveness, and indeed ideas, were not part of the Richards' family tradition. Nor likely to be so. Death was probably only ten years off, and they did not wish to do, or think, anything untoward in the meantime.

'It's Latin American,' Moira said to Gareth, sliding the Entertainments page of the *Western Mail* across the nest of pine tables.

Gareth picked it up warily. He did not like headlines that contained the words 'The Latest Craze'.

Moira felt this was not the moment to explore the full sensual details of salsa, and merely said, 'It's a new venue. Special offer – course of lessons for beginners. By a real Cuban.'

'Cardiff?' said Gareth. 'That's half a tank of diesel.'

'My hymn book's wet,' said Gareth's mother, laying her gloves to dry in front of the electric fire. 'Thanks to that vicar.' She had never taken to the new vicar, as his size made him sweat, and since putting St Brynnach's last on his list of Sunday services he had ruined her routine for the roast. 'Dragged us round the graveyard in the rain, and talked about nothing but money.' She pursed her lips, a tailor-made expression for her face, and Moira knew the leg of lamb would be consumed to the sound of her sighs.

Moira waited as the old lady fussed her way towards her fitted kitchen, fiddling to no purpose with the table laid by her daughter-in-law, and checking the room temperature was at its optimum sixty-two degrees. As always, there were just the four place settings. It was both a ritual and a duty, this crossing of the farmyard for Sunday lunch in the new bungalow, and only a medical note would have made absence acceptable.

'I must go and chop the mint up now,' sighed the old lady, disappearing into the kitchen as she added, 'Gareth doesn't like dancing.'

Moira did not respond: she tried to have no opinions on a Sunday. It was also her policy to have no personality within a fifty-yard radius of the bungalow. It helped harmony. The arrival of her easy wit and Irish vivacity had not been seen as a boost to the gene pool of the family. There was distrust of her brain and resentment of the dress sense that enhanced her body. And, although no one mentioned a dowry, Moira sometimes felt she should have come bearing a field.

In a valley where every day was a dress-down day, even her yellow wellies were seen as a provocation. Her hair had not brought approval either, as it reached nearly to her waist and lent itself to tossing in an unseemly manner. And her laugh had a decibel beyond what was decent. Moira found it hard to locate the craic in the anal air of Wales. The thought was unspoken, but some in the bungalow felt her to be the type of Celt seen in films with jig music.

'You must like dancing,' said Moira. 'Everybody likes dancing!'

Gareth shifted uneasily in his armchair. He hated dancing.

'Come Saturday night, we'd drive halfway across Donegal for a good dance at a ceilidh. Usually in village halls with no licence. The Gardai would frisk you at the front, so people'd pass drinks in at the back!'

She spoke almost like a woman trying to put a stranger at his ease.

It did not succeed. Gareth remembered his Young Farmers' dances as lonely evenings of anguish, trapped in a body that neither rocked nor rolled. 'Me, I'm not rhythmic,' he muttered.

'Oh everyone's got a bit of rhythm somewhere!' responded Moira. 'And a few salsa lessons would kick-start it!'

It was not just his rhythm she was hoping to kick-start. Her husband was tense to the touch, resistant to intimacy, reluctant to relax. Moira was a tactile woman who found it puzzling, and not a little hurtful, that his body was as cardboard in her hands. Even when she patted his head, he seemed to flinch. By exposing Gareth to the hot-blooded beat of Latin music she hoped to disinhibit him, to let his lusts run free, to soften him up for sex.

'It's like the tango,' she added encouragingly. 'The woman makes the moves, the man just responds with his body.'

Gareth evaded her smile, and glanced uneasily at the photo in the *Western Mail*.

Gareth's father gurgled in his sleep, his head twitching on the antimacassar, his dentures floating free.

Moira wondered again whether she should try low-cut bras.

Her first sight of Gareth had been upon a packed Arms Park terrace, leaping and cheering at a fine, pitch-long three-quarters movement against the Irish. Young and unworldly, her heart had been stirred by this passion. It was a short courtship, lasting several games. Eager to be gone from the poverty of Donegal, the list of qualities she sought in a husband fell rather short of the usual requirements for matrimony; the tenth of twelve children, she was prepared to settle just for *joie de vivre* – as instanced by leaping and cheering. Unfortunately, this was a degree of animation Gareth was rarely to repeat, as the Welsh national team then entered a decade-long decline.

'It's not like the Gay Gordons. You can improvise,' Moira persisted, with a limited grasp of salsa.

Still he said nothing.

'And anyway the lights will be low.'

Gareth looked like a cornered fox. But he gave no vent to his thoughts, leaving it unclear whether the wattage of the bulbs was a plus point.

Over the last few months, Gareth had developed a moodiness that Moira could not explain. He was moody when sober and moody after weaving home drunk. But more often he was simply not to be seen. Although she always knew she would have to share him with hill-sheep, she had not been prepared for the length of his absences. Nor indeed for the force of his silences, and the frequency that he returned home with moles.

Finally, Gareth handed back the newspaper, and leaned forward in his chair.

'I'd better help to shell the peas.'

'Have you got a fiver?' Eryl asked again, rubbing his stubble and yawning bad breath into the air.

In his dealings with the world, Eryl relied on what he liked to think of as a raffish charm. If asked to describe his self-image, he would probably have directed the enquirer to old footage of Spitfire pilots, being rather dashing in the mess. But his power as a charmer had peaked some time ago, eroded by drink and his falling stock, and this left him to operate on a hollow bonhomie and a formula smile. It was not a winning combination.

'Have you got a fiver?' he repeated.

For several moments, Bryony did not speak, relying on silence to best convey contempt. Until, unable to stop herself, she demanded, 'How would I have a fiver?'

Hungover though he was, Eryl recognised a minefield that he had stumbled into before.

'Forget it.' He shambled past her, making towards the newly built staircase in the corner of the room.

'No, I won't forget it. How would I have a fiver?' she persisted, rising from her chair to pursue him.

'OK. Point taken.'

'Don't say point taken. Tell me how I would have a fiver.'

'Oh I'm too tired to play these games.'

'But not too tired for the pub. *Tell me how I would have a fiver!*'

Eryl stopped, turned. By this stage, the correct answer, or at least the one that offered best hope of respite, was: 'Because you do all the work and I'm an idle drunken self-pitying bastard.' Instead of which, he said, 'D'you know how Trystan got the old lady to change her will?'

Bryony let out a groan. 'Left a horse head in her bed? I don't give a fuck what he did! He could have pulled out her fingernails! Just stop whingeing! Let it go!'

'Yes, but you know the woman in the lodge at Crug Caradoc? Her son was at the party. He said that Trystan used to—'

'Oh for Chrissake!' she screamed. 'Does it matter *how* you were stitched up? You were stitched up, period. OK?'

Eryl turned away, and the sight of his back was one provocation too many. 'And,' Bryony added, 'with good bloody reason!'

She had said the unsayable. And Eryl had no answer. He stormed up the stairs in search of loose change. The new pine stairs visibly shook, an unfortunate commentary on his carpentry – his only tangible achievement in their two years together had been a shaky mezzanine, an open-plan floor space where they slept on a mattress below the V-shaped school roof.

Bryony sensed a victory but she wanted more than a retreat. Despite her ideological commitment to niceness, she wanted to see a white flag and spilt blood . . . though somewhere in her heart she also wanted love to be declared. She pursued him up his stairs, belabouring him with abuse.

Eryl's gene pool was unknown. He had never shown signs of gentry and his buttocks would not fit a saddle. His late adoptive mother, Gwendolen's great-niece, had never spoken of his origins, though the Commodore – who hated Llewellyns – had once been heard to say that he came from a remainders sale. By the time Eryl developed into an adult Llewellyn, he had come to resemble a family skin graft that had not taken. But if he knew he was a disappointment, he never said. He just leched and drank and spoke loudly of grand plans. And paid no heed to others, with Bryony just the latest to be ignored.

Half a dozen coins fell from his black leather jacket as he raised it from the floor. As Eryl reached down for them, the Traffic Warden's lurid fantasies were thrust in his face.

'That's what I have to do so's you can go down the pub, you bastard!'

He snatched the WH Smith Student Special from her.

'And while you piss off on your bike to God knows where, and stay out all night getting rat-arsed and boring everyone stupid, I'm here typing that garbage so we can eat! And have a home!'

She dabbed a tear away.

'The Traffic Warden?' laughed Eryl, reading. He started to riffle through the dog-eared text. 'What is it, men in uniforms?'

'No, it's wanking for sickos. And I'm sick of it!'

'I'm broad-minded. You can do what you like while I'm down the pub.' He paused. 'Have the warden round if you want. Dictating.' He laughed again.

'Oh, you shit! You bloody shit!'

'"*Rubbing his exhausted dick*",' read Eryl aloud, '"*in the sticky juices of her—*"' Bryony snatched *Confessions of a Taxi Driver* from him and hurled it to the floor ten feet below.

Eryl grinned and bent to retrieve his scattered coins. Bryony kicked out at him, but immediately thought better of it. Eryl's work on the mezzanine had, rather predictably, failed to include the erection of balustrades. Even on the increasingly rare occasions when they had sex, there was always the risk that any passion might culminate in a death plunge.

'Oh sod off!' said Eryl, and pushed his way past her and back down the stairs. He had found money enough for a pint.

Eryl had always liked Bryony, and had found her easy-going ignorance much to his taste. But since his life had imploded, he had gained an urge for self-pity and self-destruction; his grievance had become a mantra, and repeating it was now his greatest source of comfort. He had no time for the moans and mundanity of her domestic world.

But as Eryl staggered out to join the Sunday drinkers at the Dragon's Head, he was also starting to tire of his own world. Brought up to be squire of all he surveyed, two surplus classrooms offered less and less satisfaction.

Chapter 12

'. . . Lions? It kills lions?'

'Apparently.' The postman was gratified to see his news had scored a direct hit on the world-weary Hubert. In his experience, nothing much short of cannibalism in an outlying village was usually able to surprise Hubert. Dafydd added, 'He calls it Genghis.'

'So it's not a dog you'd kick, then?'

'It's not a dog I'd try to run over.'

'Is there much of a lion problem round Crug Caradoc?'

'Not now. More of a postman problem.'

Hubert slowly tapped his pipe out on the baguette basket as he mulled on the mystery of a country landowner without a black labrador.

'Clydog, you've had audiences with our Mr Big. Is he mad or bad, or both?'

Clydog struggled to free his mouth of mud pie. 'Give us a tissue!' he said, spluttering, and wiggled his sticky brown fingers in the air as Hubert tore a strip from the paper roll behind the counter.

It was the dead part of the afternoon, when Abernant shoppers wait for a second wind. The three often gathered for some men's talk in what Hubert called his high-cholesterol corner. Here, an off-duty Dafydd had the time to be expansive, Hubert had the freedom to be provocative, and Clydog could indulge his greater intestine.

The old sleuth pondered Hubert's question. 'Well, the man's certainly not very British.' After deeper thought, he went on, 'From one of those countries without proper roads, I reckon. Where the electrics only come on once a day and they bug your hotel room. He made a joke to me about part of his bottom being shot off – except I don't think it was a joke. Sort of place you'd need a big dog.'

Although only fragmentary pieces of information, they pretty much fitted with what Abernant knew about foreigners.

'D'you remember Mary Jenkins?' said Dafydd. 'She married a foreigner. A German. Lasted less than two years. He used to block his lane with dustbins, to try and stop the car rallies.'

'Oh, it wasn't just the dustbins,' said Clydog. 'He broke her leg as well.'

'Düsseldorf,' said Dafydd. 'Different mindset over there.'

'I went out with a Scandinavian once,' said Hubert, keen to preserve his cosmopolitan edge. 'I had no complaints. Well, except that she folded her clothes before sex.'

'But you wouldn't have married her,' said Dafydd.

'Oh no. Not with their level of taxation.'

'Which is my point,' said Dafydd. 'Cultural nuances. They're the barrier reef of marriage.'

At fifty-three, and still a bachelor, Clydog would have been prepared to risk some damage from cultural nuance, yet he instinctively shared this view of the worrying world beyond. 'And it's not just abroad,' he added.

'What's not just abroad?' asked Hubert, after a short wait.

'This "mindset" thing. You get valleys where people think differently, even just a few miles from here. No rhyme or reason for it. But somehow their attitudes are not the same, not quite normal. For instance, I could never marry anyone from the Cynrig Valley.' He thought some more. 'Or the Grwyne Valley. . . . Or the Llynfi Valley.'

'Have you had to fight off many offers?' asked Hubert.

Clydog ignored him. 'Then again,' he mused, 'how far would

you have to go to find someone who'd want to pair off with the sort of man who owns ridgebacks?'

'About a mile and a half!' said Dafydd, and grinned. It always pleased the postman when his grapevine was superior to the reporter's.

'You're not serious? Stéfan's got an admirer? Who?' asked Hubert.

'Hunt secretary.'

'What, Felicity?' Hubert laughed scornfully. 'Part-woman, part-horse? Services to the gentry a speciality?'

'I've heard she's after him. Been practising her Lady Di impressions.'

'I'm sure she has, but that doesn't mean she fancies him. If a bloke's rolling in money and paddocks, he could be a Martian, and she'd still be after him.'

'Perhaps that's where he's from, Mars. He's got the dress sense of an alien.'

A sort of communal smirk crossed their faces, and Hubert filled up their glasses again with his cheapest wine. The postman prepared to tell them about the funny-coloured ducks and the black pig that the other incomers had bought.

Chapter 13

Stéfan was dining alone. At home. He did not like to dine alone. Indeed, he did not like to be alone. Alone, there was no gallery to play to. Alone, there was no hierarchy to be head of. Alone, there was no poor sap to pick on.

Stéfan's taste was for groups. Boisterous groups. He took his pleasures in mateyness and horseplay and raucous laughter, with the unspoken rule that he was the funniest. For he was the matey one with money. And for him an appreciative audience was key. Then again, what was the point of a joke if there was no butt?

Stéfan was not only dining alone, he was drinking alone. Forty-eight bottles of champagne, ostentatiously good champagne, lay idling on the shelves of his outsize fridge. He blamed them on his broker. The hottest of Budget tips, he had been told. But then the Chancellor had instead put the tax on petrol, and Stéfan's insider trading at the off-licence netted him nothing. Except enough Bollinger for a wedding, for which there was no bride.

But while to dine alone in your mansion may have a tragic splendour, to do so in your overcoat is more likely seen as pathos. It is not a fun night in for one's hands to be colder than the cutlery.

Even when it functioned, the heating system was deeply moody, distributing its warmth like reluctant sexual favours. Some nights it would reward the attic, on other nights the study.

Only by following its gurgles could one determine where its orgasmic sweats might end. And the panelled dining room had, for reasons that evaded the finest of plumbing minds, become estranged from the boiler.

His one weekend house-party had therefore gone with a somewhat muffled zing. The party mood had been muted, for though dress was casual, gloves were essential. A Jacobean mansion might be a classy venue, but modern high-rollers had yet to embrace the aristocratic tradition that hypothermia was character building.

Nor had all guests been happy to find their view of the hills was framed by scaffolding – useful though it was for the new section of roof. The dust-sheets might be off, and the decorating might be done, but gradually the go-getting Stéfan was starting to gather what he'd gone and got, and it was the domestic version of the Forth Bridge. From jackdaws who nested without planning permission to seventy years of solidified Llewellyn sewage, Crug Caradoc was maintenance man's heaven. Stéfan did not yet regret his impulse buy, but was straining at the bit for the day he would be squire of more than a listed building site.

His family had once before known such a spacious house, long before he was born. He had known it only from the family photo album – and from a large black-and-white portrait that had hung for many years, pregnant with mystery and nostalgia, in the hallway of his late father's flat. It was a portrait of a grand city house, adorned with traditional wooden balconies, and set in the heat and dust of the Caucasus. The money that built it was made from trade – a skill that had stayed in the genes – and through its doors the A-set regularly came to call, usually at the bidding of business.

Unfortunately, his father's judgements on money were somewhat superior to his judgements on politics. His wartime decision to give fulsome backing to the Germans proved, with the benefit of hindsight in '46, to have been a wrong career move. The war over, the Iron Curtain winching down, their palatial family home was judged ideal for the secret police, who were after something nice and central for their headquarters. It was a very sudden house move, which took place without the customary paperwork.

Sitting alone in Wales under his chandelier, Stéfan might well have reflected that the arrival of armed communists would add interest to his own evening. Instead, he had to make do with Mrs Grotichley, bearing meat and one veg.

'The cooker's crap.'

This was her first Saturday night as housekeeper-cum-cook, a post that the *Mid-Walian* classified department had unhelpfully advertised among slaughtermen, water-diviners and purveyors of bull semen. Chosen from an extensive shortlist of one, she represented the first of his planned retinue. (Handymen and gardeners were next on his shopping list, plus a live-in plumber for the heating system.) Eager to establish his reputation as a host, Stéfan had hoped for someone who could whip up a roast ox, advise on fine wines, and tell risqué after-dinner jokes. The unhappily divorced Mrs Grotichley was a squarish woman, little given to speech, who had formerly been a tractor driver. Following the accidental demolition of a wall, she had decided to turn to domestic service.

Mrs Grotichley made her heavy-footed way to the head of the long table, where Stéfan shivered in state.

'I don't do foreign,' she said, offloading the tray. He took this as an allusion to the recipe books he had placed on her kitchen shelf.

The first Delft tureen contained a murky casserole. Uncertain what lay in its depths, Stéfan prodded with his fork and an angry sausage shot Polaris-like to the surface, where it then lay like a truculent turd. The second tureen contained half potato purée, half potato lumps, though of a brazenness that suggested it might be a regional delicacy.

'Almost *français*!' he cried in mock-delight.

It was round about now that Stéfan decided to pay his first visit to the Dragon's Head. Technically it was his local, but for some reason he had never dropped in, partial though he was to drink. And a Saturday night should see a bit of local colour.

'French?' she enquired.

'*Cuisine lourde*, I think it's called,' he replied satirically.

'Whatever,' said the housekeeper-cum-cook.

As he watched Mrs Grotichley recede, the words 'lumpy woman, lumpy potatoes' kept repeating in his head. He flicked a spoonful of her potato pastiche at her back, and was gratified to see it stick to her cardigan.

Gazing after her down the length of his grand oak refectory dining table gave him his only satisfaction of the evening. £6,000 it had said in his *Miller's*, the Bible of the antiques trade. He had bargained Nico down to £5,750, and had had his revenge on the grasping little upstart.

The pub's local colour was almost in double figures – much to Gwillim's chagrin. It had been a difficult month for trade, with an increased number of customers insisting on being served. There had even been attempts to introduce amenities. The new game-keeper on the Commodore's estate had turned up with his own dartboard, possessed by some idea of challenging people to a game. Gwillim had put a stop to that by refusing to allow the fabric of the building to be damaged by a hook. But the following week he had been forced to throw out several Young Farmers who had turned bolshie and repeatedly tried to propose a Quiz Night. There had also been talk of a small executive housing development in the village, and he was gearing up to repulse the sort of outrageous demands that people with porches were likely to make.

Dislike of people is a big handicap in a pub landlord, but perhaps a bigger handicap is an absence of small talk. Or indeed of any size talk. Surly and silent, Gwillim gave away nothing, his mind a permanently closed book even to his regulars. One of the molecatchers, the bolder for drink, had once asked Gwillim what he was thinking about. 'Teat infections,' he had replied.

Tonight the talk at the bar was, as so often, of dynastic disinheritance and sexual dysfunction.

This time Eryl had an audience of two, though to describe Gareth as an audience was perhaps over-ambitious. Synchronised drinking was usually his nearest to a sentient response. Eryl had, however, recently widened the area of emotional pain he wished to share, and the word 'woman' had several times caused a flicker in Gareth's frontal lobes.

'It's obvious now, I've been used by her,' confessed Eryl. 'Used for my money.'

The other listener kept his counsel, but gave a nod, the regulation nod in bars the world over.

'If people think you're gonna be rich, they go all smarmy. Abuse your good nature.' Froth, the inevitable concomitant of Gwillim's pints, was gathering on his quivering Zapata. 'Then they play you for all they can get.'

Another nod.

'Two years I've been used by her. All lovey-dovey, no sexual position too much to ask. But now it's empty your pockets time.' Eryl looked for more sympathy from his fellow drinker, several years his junior. 'It's the "show us the colour of your money" spiel, you know?'

The young guy allowed a non-committal smile to flicker politely across his face. It was a face that was faintly familiar to Eryl, a face that he once used to see around town.

'Typical woman!' he explained. 'Doesn't want to know me now I've got nothing.' Eryl felt almost cheered at finding someone who had not yet heard his full tale of woe. 'Not even my birthright.'

'Go away then.'

'What?'

'Go away. Start over.'

'Go away where?'

'Anywhere. Travel.'

'What, leave the valley?'

'Why not?'

'Dunno.' Why, he wondered, did he feel defensive? Eryl looked at him. 'Is that how you got your tan? Travelling?'

'Sort of,' admitted Sion, with some reluctance.

'Where d'you go?'

Sion looked uneasy, a state that went well with his beanpole posture. He turned to his pint, emptying the glass with a professional, quasi-hydraulic, suction, and muttered, 'Hot places.'

Eryl, who had known little but rain for most of his adult life, felt his self-pity edged out by curiosity. 'Hot places? What, like Africa, you mean?'

Sion seemed tongue-tied. 'Yeah, suppose.'

His limited speech matched Eryl's vague memory of him, a nerdy misfit standing on street corners, plucking up the nerve to watch the girls go by. To be six foot with catatonia was a heavy cross to bear at fifteen.

'You must know where you went,' pressed Eryl. 'It's a big country, Africa.'

Sion poured another bottle into his glass, and looked around. Gareth was resting his face on the bar, Gwillim had retired to the cellar, the farmers were arguing about sheep dip. Sion took another giant mouthful of beer and said quietly, 'I can't say. I'm on the run.'

Eryl burst out laughing. 'On the run? Who from?'

'Can't say.' For a moment he had the air of that frightened fifteen-year-old again.

'You're not serious? You've really got people after you? What, like chasing you?'

'Yes, exactly like that.'

'Woman trouble, is it?' In Eryl's fantasy world, the chances of accidentally sleeping with a Mafia man's moll ranked extremely high.

'No, nothing of that sort! Nothing . . . domestic.'

'Oh . . . So . . . these people, are they dangerous?'

'Very dangerous.'

'And they're in the valley?'

Sion sighed irritably. 'They don't give up. They're famous for not giving up.'

Eryl looked around the bar. 'Will they be in disguise?'

Sion appeared torn between his need to talk and the wisdom of staying silent. Then, perhaps exasperated by not being taken seriously, the need to talk won.

'I joined the Legion,' he said, in a tone both furtive and defiant.

'What legion?'

'What legion? The French Foreign Legion.'

'You can't do that! You're Welsh.'

'That's bollocks! Anyone can join. *I* did. I ran away to join them.'

'You never?' Eryl looked astonished, gratifyingly so. 'Did you leave a note?'

'I don't remember. I think so.'

'But weren't you too young?'

'Yes. So I lied about my age. And they took me. Really. I'm a trained killer now . . . I think.'

'Bloody hell, you can kill people without having to join the French Foreign Legion! I mean, what on Earth made you want to join *them*?'

'I saw this film at the Agora.' This was Latin for fleapit, the local cinema where the town's youth went to give their private parts an evening out. 'It looked kinda fun. Deserts and castles and things. And sleeping under the stars.'

Whether it was the original *Beau Geste* or a later remake was never established. Sion went on to mention Lawrence of Arabia and belly dancers but his exact motive remained murky. The claustrophobia of a small wet community, an ignorance of the outside world, a yearning for adventure, the urge to be macho, a liking for camels, all was muddled up in his adolescent brain and pubescent body. He might well have thought the Sahara was just to the south of Cardiff. And that the guns were make-believe and the knives were rubber. How he had found the Foreign Legion, and what they had made of him, was an unchronicled mystery. Perhaps he was well qualified by virtue of maladjustment, perhaps his height impressed them, perhaps they were just short of bodies. Yet, in the end, his actions had a foolishness that verged on the magnificent.

'So how come they're after you?'

'I left. I did three months and then I went over the wall. You're not allowed to do that. Leaving's against the rules.' He spoke with the simple-mindedness of an *idiot savant*, though so far his air of bewilderment suggested the *idiot* was in the ascendant. 'And now I'm wanted for desertion.' He grimaced.

'Desertion?' said Eryl, incredulous. 'You're a deserter?'

'Yeah.'

'From the French Foreign Legion?'

'Yeah.'

'In Abernant?'

'Yeah.'

'Wow!' Eryl was impressed. He had never met a deserter before.

'So if you only did three months – how long did you sign up for?'

'I'm not sure.'

'Not sure? How can you not be sure? Didn't you ask?'

Sion did not reply. He would have made a good prisoner-of-war, his natural instinct being to say no more than name and number, even in a pub. But this ill-equipped him for foreign travel, or indeed travel beyond the Nant Valley.

Eryl too was now caught up in the excitement and magic of foreign lands. And he was eager to know more. 'So why did you leave?'

Again Sion did not reply.

'Come on, why did you leave?'

After a pause, an embarrassed Sion began, 'They kept hitting me . . .'

'Oh, well, I guess that's good grounds,' said Eryl.

'No, no, I'm sure they had a valid reason,' Sion insisted, with sudden legionnaires' loyalty. 'Probably part of the training, you know, them making a man out of me. But the trouble was that . . . that, well, I didn't know *why* they did it. Or what I was doing wrong.'

'Jesus! And you didn't think to ask them? Like "What's with this hitting?"'

'I couldn't,' Sion muttered, and stared at the flagstones. A long silence, long even by Sion's standards, came over him. Until finally he said, 'I don't speak French.'

And of course, 'they', the hitters, did.

This esoteric aspect of the French Foreign Legion had come as a terrible shock. He had travelled thousands of miles to the Sahara Desert and not realised that the choice of Woodwork for his one GCSE could prove a linguistic handicap. Unable to translate the reasons for being punched in the face and kicked in the stomach, he had become demoralised. Had *Beau Geste* been in subtitles he might have sensed that foreigners sometimes speak a foreign language. But life in the valley offered few such clues to the subtleties of life outside the valley. And now he had returned home, probably for ever.

A serious silence fell. And they went back to their drinks. Sion's load had been shared. And, almost mystically, Eryl's load had been lightened. He too would go and see the world.

It was time, he now felt, for *him* to move on, to get out, to be his own man, to do his own thing. To check out what all those foreigners were up to. Admittedly, he was more Club Med than trainee killer, but suddenly in travel he saw salvation. And if the local retard could make it across a continent (and back), then he could see no reason why not to embark upon his own Grand Tour of somewhere. Except, of course, lack of money – and for that he suddenly had the first inklings of a plan.

He gave his usual pseudo-seigneurial wave to the other drinkers and made his way out of the pub. It was pitch-black outside, and as he, the valley's pretender, stumbled his way out to his battered motorbike he did not notice the advancing figure of Crug Caradoc's new owner. They had each heard tell of the other, but they had never met.

And so it remained. For in the dark their paths crossed – and by several feet their destinies failed to connect.

Stéfan pushed open the door of the Dragon's Head . . . and waited in vain to be hit by a wall of noise. Seven polite nods were his lot. He crossed to the bar, where Gareth and Sion were slumped . . . and waited in vain to be served. He called 'Landlord!' in his best stentorian . . . and waited in vain to be answered.

'Wrong night for the stripper, then?' He spoke so all could hear, and laughed so all could know he was funny.

The silence was broken only by the clicking of dominoes, and the occasional muttering of the molecatchers. The bar and its nooks were dimly lit, and the cracked Barbours merged with the shadows.

'I hear you've got cesspit problems,' said one of the farmers.

In the countryside, neighbourliness can take unconventional forms.

'So that's what that smell is! Thought it was my neighbours' BO!' Stéfan shot back, using his heavy-duty laugh as a backing track. It did not surprise, nor displease, him that he be recognised, but the speed of the grapevine was decidedly not to his liking and he felt the need to assert control. Especially over strangers unduly familiar with his sewage.

'Yes, rodding's no good,' continued the farmer. 'Need a hand grenade to shift that lot! Backs right up, and come the winter rain that whole meadow goes whiffy.'

This was said in a tone of helpfulness, in an offer of local knowledge, but it fell short of the ambience that Stéfan had had in mind. He had recently been to Seville and clapped himself silly on flamenco; he had returned with hopes that in the Welsh hills of a Saturday night he'd find some riotous cross between a male voice choir and indoor Morris dancing.

'Landlord!' he cried again.

'That won't work,' said Gareth, raising his chin.

'What won't work?'

'He won't recognise the voice. He doesn't respond to strangers.'

'What is he, a fucking dog?'

'Gwillim!' shouted Gareth, whose sottishness did not exclude deference to landowners.

Stéfan looked around in vain for a bar stool. There were indeed bar stools near at hand, but they were secretly stacked in the cellar.

'Don't need a password, do I? Or a funny handshake?' Stéfan spoke as if at a public meeting, his ego crowding out all other conversation in the bar. 'Because I do funny handshakes.' He held out his hand to Sion – and as Sion reached to take it, he withdrew it. And then laughed, a manic, machine-gun laugh that made his upper body vibrate. The false handshake was a favourite practical joke of his, and never failed to give him pleasure. That it was childish and churlish and unoriginal seemed not to trouble him; that it gave him the upper hand, both literally and metaphorically, was satisfaction enough.

'So, when's it get busy?'

'It is,' replied Gareth.

'Christ!' said Stéfan, pulling a face. 'Not very fucking folkloric, is it?'

The pain of concentration settled briefly on Gareth's face as he wrestled with this heady mix of irony and rhetoric. He decided to ignore the remark. 'Are you married?' he asked.

'Married? No. Why?'

But Stéfan was never to learn Gareth's views on married life. For Gwillim's head abruptly rose into vision beyond the bar, his emergence from the cellar lacking only a puff of smoke.

'Yes?' he demanded angrily.

'What beers d'you have?' asked Stéfan.

'None,' retorted Gwillim. 'We're closed.' And his body began its return to the underworld.

A lesser man than Stéfan might have slipped away into the night, deterred by the torpor of the bar, trounced by the quality of the service. But Stéfan stood his ground.

'A tenner to reopen!' he retorted in return. And with a showman's flourish he slapped a ten-pound note on to the bar.

The dominoes fell silent.

As *High Noon* it was no great shakes, but the regulars had yet to see anyone get the better of Gwillim. Even on the matter of crisps. However, bribery was a new technique – and a tenner was high stakes.

Gwillim halted on the cellar steps. It was not a good position from which to be imperious, or magnanimous, or even cur-mudgeonly, for his head was at the level of Stéfan's groin. He climbed back out. He moved to where the money lay and looked hard at Stéfan. Keeping his arms rigid, Gwillim placed his palms either side of the note, and leant ever so slightly across the bar. His face remained as impassively dour as always, his body language suggesting a man who had problems with his feminine side.

'Have you ever milked a cow?'

This was the one response that Stéfan had not planned for. He was immediately suspicious, wary of a trap. Was it witty? Was it coded? Was it abusive? . . . Or was it some kind of rustic challenge? He had no ready reply, for it was a cow that had come completely out of left field.

'No,' he said finally.

'Well, I've got fifty to milk, 5.30 tomorrow morning. So I like all the sleep I can get. This place is not a bloody nightclub!' And Gwillim pushed the ten-pound note back across the bar.

Stéfan looked down at his note, now stained by slops.

The Dragon's Head rarely saw human drama, except when Teg and Ben came to blows over a double six, and a palpable sense of interest was taking hold of its phlegmatic drinkers. Even Gareth was readjusting the focus of his hormones.

Stéfan considered pointing out that the time was in fact a quarter past nine, but sensed that reason would not prove a potent weapon. He felt both angry and frustrated. That his local was at one social remove from a morgue, an alehouse across whose threshold wild horses would normally never drag him, was not the salient point. He resented being told 'No' by anybody; he was baffled (yet again) by the failure of money to solve life's problems; and above all he loathed being bested in public. He resolved to bring the experience of years to bear.

'Let's make it twenty,' he said. 'And all drinks on me.' With that, he laid down a second tenner.

A murmur of moistening saliva indicated that he had caught the mood of the bar. He might be an incomer, he might even be a foreign incomer, indeed he might even be a foreign, weekending incomer, but here he had displayed certain universal values that would ensure he did not lack for friends in the valley. The grapevine would add the word 'prodigal' to his file.

For his part, Stéfan found a certain emotional satisfaction was to be had from the farming community. They offered a muted, unsophisticated audience, their silence providing a perfect counterpoint to his noise, their deference providing a stage on which he could perform. His presence in their midst would, be believed, bring some much-needed zip into their lives.

'I serve who I want, when I want,' snorted Gwillim. 'And as far as you're concerned, I'm closed. And you're barred.'

Both the tenners were slid messily back across the slops. And the burly Gwillim stood back with his arms folded.

The small huddle that had started to gather round the bar were now wrong-footed, and empty-glassed. A few embarrassedly swished the odd dreg to and fro and gazed floorward. Sion, the only one who could have vaulted the bar and killed the landlord with a single well-aimed blow, felt it was probably time for bed.

Gareth wondered briefly, and to no effect, about his powers of conciliation.

It was Stéfan who remained apparently unabashed. He simply stared back at Gwillim, smiled disarmingly and, taking the ten-pound notes, screwed them up into a sodden ball . . . which he tossed lightly over Gwillim's head to the far corner of the bar. If money can be said to have an attitude, it lay there contemptuously. Then Stéfan reached slowly inside his velvet jacket.

He brought out first a silver biro, and then a chequebook. He laid the chequebook carefully on a dry section of bar, clicked his silver biro, and looked up at Gwillim.

'So,' he said, 'how much do you want for the pub?'

Chapter 14

Rob was hoeing circumspectly round some early signs of carrots when he saw Glyn's head bob up behind the bushes. Although the painter was surprised to see him, it was Glyn who got the greater shock.

Glyn was up on the hill pretending to look for stray sheep. It was his usual alibi for forays near Pantglas, and it had the ring of truth, for the hedges on his tenant farm had holes the size of rhinos. Even though farming was the only life he knew, and the only life his father and grandfather had known, he had no love of the land. He let his lambs snag on wire, his fields fill with thistles, his cattle bog down in mud, and he ruminated the days away in the half-light of his corrugated cottage. There was a time he had shared his gloom, but Hefin had now gone the way of the beam. Glyn had rarely been beyond the valley, and only a neglected appendix had taken him to the capital. His life had bypassed society and at fifty-two he had yet to attain any social skills of relevance to other human beings. Women from the late twentieth century were not even on his radar screen.

So he had taken to coming up the cleft in the hillside, the common land that ran below the outcrop on which stood Pantglas, with a clandestine zeal. He came without his dog Twm, and walked in the shadow of the trees. In part, perhaps, he hoped to gain solace from the distant company of others, to find bittersweet comfort in the sights and sounds of the normal living he had never known. He sometimes stood for hours. He knew which window marked the bathroom, and the best angle from which to see the bedroom. But he came only by day, to prowl with the timorousness of a distant rabbit, and rarely saw the signs of human life he sought.

The mist had lifted a little after ten, and a warm day was gathering strength. It was through the last dissolving wisps that Glyn suddenly sighted his neighbour, hoe in hand. Hoe in hand and stark naked.

Rob was about five foot eight or nine, with slim limbs and medium hair on his chest. Even when bent, his buttocks were economical and could have modelled provocative underwear. He was wiry in a whippetish sort of way but if push came to shove he had muscles enough. It was too early in the year for a tan and the white of his body stood out against the compost heap. From fifty yards away it was not possible to make a judgement on penis size, but he held the hoe-handle at a good distance, and awkwardly so, suggesting that splinters were a threat to be taken seriously.

Not that Glyn was about to make a judgement on his penis. Glyn was in the ambivalent position of wanting both to avert his eyes from the scene *and* take a closer look for verification. It was this confused reaction that led him to bob about too long for his own good. Seeing him break cover, Rob gave him a cheery wave. Whereupon Glyn fled, fearing the prospect of a chat. (He would, though, be back – drawn time and again by the hope that Jane believed in similar gardening techniques.)

Rob grinned, not without some modest *schadenfreude*, and continued his attempts to put paid to the bindweed.

Had Glyn been equipped to examine his subconscious, he would have realised it was the hoe that most disturbed him. Accidental nudity can happen to anybody – high spirits, drinking, mixing with Swedes – and is a human failing that even the courts can sometimes forgive. Nudism with a hoe, however, has too doctrinaire a feeling, is too arch an exposure. To strip before hoeing, or indeed to engage nude with any garden implement, is too premeditated an act to be just joyous. It was not merely a body that Glyn had seen, it was a sexual statement. And had Mr Probert been called to testify, his moral misgivings about first-time buyers in T-shirts would have rung with vindication.

Sex was what the new owners most missed about Manchester. Nude weeding was a poor substitute, although it had an exhibitionist dimension. In Manchester they had been a liberated couple, their sexual freedom little discussed, almost a given. Here, such open-minded circles had yet to be located. The nearest to rural counter-culture was a life class that Jane had discovered, thanks to Bryony. She had been after mangetout when her new friend pointed out the small ad in the delicatessen window. Jane had done nude modelling before, but never in a village hall, not in the hour between badminton and first aid for farmers. Wolfgang, the tutor, said her body would go down well in Berlin.

Rob finished chivvying the earth along the line of fresh green shoots and then, stepping respectfully around the brambles, lolloped towards the house. A more scheduled visitor was due, a man of some standing, and it seemed politic that he not be met bollock-naked.

The taming of the garden, and the raising of the animals, and the humanising of the house, had not led to any neglect of Rob's other love: painting. Time and again he had been out on the hills, hunched hour-long under an umbrella, struggling to meld the sights into something that might be called his vision. Some dozen watercolours now leant against the walls of the barn. They showed a world where the sky and the land almost merged in angry whorls of wind and grass. The surging clouds had the rhythm of the sea and the trammelled plantlife swam with the eddying air. The colours were near to monochrome, seen as if through struggling eyelids. It was landscape, recognisable wild bleak lonely landscape, but pushed to the limits of abstraction. It was the mountains at their most extreme, it was Turner without the kaleidoscope of colour.

And now he needed to sell. Now he needed to flush out the local art-lovers. Now he needed to spread his name in mid-Wales. Now he needed some cash for a wind turbine.

So he had arranged for the chief reporter of the local paper, a Clydog Turner, to pay a visit, to view – and hopefully review – the work.

They had agreed on 10.30 but, as Rob zipped up his torn jeans, he could see from the bedroom window that the man from the *Mid-Walian* was in trouble making his deadline. Spring rains had washed away the track's latest helping of hardcore, and Clydog, his office car outwitted by the hairpin bends, was not built for a one in seven gradient. Years of Mississippi Mud Pies, courtesy of Hubert, had made his two legs increasingly unviable. For several minutes Rob watched the reporter struggle up the grassy slope in full sunlight, with the purple complexion of a man on life's final journey. Then he went downstairs and made a jug of lemonade, which he waved cheerily at Clydog as he puffed through their gate.

They sat in the shade by the pond for some time, while Clydog got his breath back and was introduced to the pig and the ducks.

'That's my studio,' Rob said, and gestured towards the barn. 'I do landscapes mainly. Not traditional, but more like mood pieces. I'm very influenced by Japanese ideas.'

Clydog stared at the barn and sighed. 'Ten column inches.'

'Ten . . . ?' said Rob uncertainly.

'But then you always get good coverage when you hang yourself.'

'Oh. Mr Phillips.'

'You live a successful life and die from natural causes, you get a couple of lines. But fail, and top yourself, it's news. Sad old world, eh?'

'Yes. Yes, indeed. Very sad.' Rob allowed a few moments for the man's memory. 'I suppose you could say my work is Turner without the kaleidoscope of colour.'

Rob paused, expecting Clydog would want to start taking

notes. Instead, the reporter continued to gaze into the middle distance, and then unwrapped a piece of nougat which he gave to the pig.

'Funerals, that's what people read first round here. Who went, who gave flowers, who sent apologies for absence. Who was the vicar, what were the hymns, how big were the attendance figures. All sent in by the relatives. Miss out a name, and you're in trouble – with apologies to print!

'We sometimes even have a funeral supplement. People appreciate that. Because of course, death here, it's not like the Irish, it's not a drunken wake. The Welsh take death very seriously. They often go to funerals of complete strangers. Just to pay their respects.

'Mind you, vegetable shows come a close second in the summer. Our readers like to see a full list of rosettes every week.' He turned his gaze on the hoe and the garden. 'You planning to grow anything big?'

Rob smiled. 'I think that's down to the vegetables. Ours seem to have a mind of their own,' he added, wondering if the interview had begun.

'Yes, well you're bound to be late, being this high.' Clydog cast a concerned eye over the rows of windswept seedlings. Reaching down, he crumbled a sample of earth between his fingers. 'And the brick dust won't help.' He looked troubled. 'My mother used to have brick dust.'

Although Rob liked to feel he had left urban brusqueness behind, he could no longer contain a townie's urge to organise the conversation, to give some relevance and direction to its sentences. 'So will you be taking photographs?' he asked.

'What of?'

'Of the paintings.'

'The paintings? Oh, no.' Clydog seemed surprised by the question. 'No, old Miss Nightingale – her family own the paper, have done for years – she has a very strict rule about photos. She only likes to see people and livestock. And vegetables, in exceptional cases.'

'Oh. Right.' Rob took a moment to absorb this information, and then with seeming gravity asked, 'What about paintings of vegetables? Would she publish photos of those?'

'You paint vegetables?'

'No. No, that's just a hypothetical.'

'Oh. Well, I suppose I'd have to ask her what she thought best.' Clydog looked as though that were an exchange he'd rather not have. 'People holding golf cups, that's her favourite. Especially the Nightingale Cup, for ladies' pairs. You ever painted golfers?'

'No, can't say I've ever had the urge.' Rob had started to loosen his language, sensing that irony was probably safe from detection. 'I'm not really representational.'

'She was. She represented the county for over thirty years. Played off six, till her hips packed up.'

Rob decided to take the initiative and stood up. 'I still reckon you can't beat nature as a subject. Whatever the weather. You ready for a viewing?'

Clydog was reluctant to move from his lemonade and his seat in the sun, but could not see a good reason to turn down the offer, it being the purpose of his visit. 'Guess so.'

He rose slowly to his feet and followed Rob into the barn. The watercolours had yet to be framed or hung and they rested informally, almost haphazardly, against the stone walls. They ranged in size from a foot square, a blur of horizontal sedge, to a yard wide, a vortex of battleship-grey wind. Jane liked to call them the mood music of the mountains, and the energy of the brushwork certainly showed signs of being applied at Force 8. The man from the *Mid-Walian* pottered round the studio looking at the works in silence while Rob wondered whether to point out the Japanese aspects. Occasionally he would put his head to one side like an owl, and twice he raised a picture to his eye level so as to look more closely at textural details. Eventually Clydog spoke.

'No sheep, then?' he said. 'I thought there'd be sheep.'

Rob decided not to bother with the Japanese aspects. 'Couldn't get them to pose in the wind,' he replied, affecting regret.

'It's a pity, though,' Clydog went on. 'Locals like to see sheep over their mantelpiece.'

Rob was not precious about his work, he never thought of it as a calling, but he did find the need to place farm animals in strategic parts of it to be a touch prescriptive. He felt a twinge of worry about his client base.

'But then,' and Clydog sighed, 'what do I know about art? Art's always been a closed book to me. As have books,' he added with a laugh, the polished delivery suggesting this was a punch line that had seen much service.

'I thought you were supposed to be the Arts Correspondent?' said Rob, more bemused than irritated.

'I am, I am.' Clydog was unabashed and on his way back to the lemonade. 'I'm also the Farming Correspondent, the Crime Correspondent, the Local Authority Correspondent, the Religious Correspondent, the Parking Correspondent, and for many years I used to be Rhiannon on the Women's Page, offering advice on undergarments and the like.' It was a long sentence and he needed to sit. 'Doesn't mean I have personal experience of pantihose.'

Rob could already foresee the article. A painting being more elusive to define than a vegetable, he would receive a bland and inoffensive 'B'. The *Mid-Walian* was not a paper that liked to offend or have opinions. Also, unlike the article's author, there would be nothing florid or breathless about the prose. And there would be no mention of the Japanese.

'Are there any other painters in the valley?' asked Rob.

'There's a woman does dogs. Pet dogs. Usually on a cushion.'

'Do they sell?'

'I think so. But they're a bit pricy because you have to have an oval frame with dogs.'

'Oh. That I didn't know.'

Rob felt ambivalent almost every time he listened to Clydog. To an exile from the city, Clydog's world offered the Promised Land of 'local colour', and contained a people whose thinking was free of fashion. However, with this world came an awkward truth – viz that while the upside of the rural idyll was its absence of urban sophistication, the downside of the rural idyll was, well, its absence of urban sophistication. (This insight had begun with Rob's discovery that Abernant's art exhibitions suffered the visual drawback of being held in the town's launderette.)

'What you need is a patron,' said Clydog.

'True.'

'Someone with a few contacts.'

'I fancy Louis the Fourteenth,' replied Rob. 'So long as I don't have to watch him shit in the mornings.'

Clydog was noticeably fazed by this reference to the *toilette* of the Sun King, but held to his train of thought.

'The mayoress is very keen on culture. Very keen. Think it comes from her father, who was the first man to have a personalised number plate in this area. He used to trim his hedge in the shape of musical instruments. Woodwind mainly. And she's got his energy, she's always trying to get the council to spend money on arts projects. Things like a *son et lumière* of the old market hall. Have you come across her?'

'Big bosoms? Wears an orange tent?'

Clydog nodded.

'I've seen her do street theatre. She was pretending to inaugurate a cash machine. Very entertaining.' Rob grinned. 'Now *that* you photographed!'

Clydog chose not to rise to the bait. 'Yes, that's her. Mrs Myfanwy Edwards. Point is, she knows the Abernant art world. All sorts, woman who writes poems and a wonderful chap who makes matchstick models of Cardiff Castle. A little group of them meet in her conservatory – "to help stir the creative juices", she says. It was her that tried to set up the love-spoon exhibition and put Abernant on the map.'

'I'll bear her in mind,' lied Rob. 'More lemonade?'

Clydog looked at his watch.

'No, I've got a council meeting to cover. There's a vote on this new ombudsman.'

'Ombudsman?'

'You are cut off from the world! The parking meter ombudsman. To rule on whether to put meters in the high street. And risk civil war.'

He eased himself up. All the while Clydog was resting, he had been idly stripping the crispy grey lichen from the bench-seat with his fingers; now he rolled the bits into a small ball and flicked it across the farmyard. The ducks pursued it and prodded away in some puzzlement.

As the two men walked towards the farm gate Clydog looked over at the missing part of the farmhouse. 'That's a splendid old Massey Ferguson!' he said, much impressed. 'Must be what, early postwar?'

'April 1957,' said Rob, failing to reciprocate the enthusiasm. 'No home should be without one.'

Then they shook hands at the gate, and Clydog set off down the steep meadow with the ponderous caution of a man regretting his taste for smooth-soled brogues.

Three days later Rob joined the Friday queue at the newsagents and waited for the wheelbarrow that brought the latest copies of the *Mid-Walian* from the printers. But he found that week's edition did not contain an Arts Page, there having apparently been no art in mid-Wales since the previous Friday.

He did, however, find an article on old agricultural machinery. Describing how a young artist had a vintage combine harvester in his bedroom. It was written by the Farming Correspondent.

Chapter 15

'Please, be a sensible chap. Put the chainsaw back.'

'It's my chainsaw! My home! I can do what I fucking like!'

'What, cause mayhem? I'm sure you don't really want to do that.'

'I want what I'm owed. I know my rights.'

'Yes, I'm sure you do. But is a chainsaw really the best way to get them?'

'Why the hell not? Because *she* won't like it? Fuck that!'

Marriage guidance was not one of the postman's stronger suits. He had had some experience before, when Mrs Whitelaw had trapped her errant husband on their flat roof for two days by taking away his ladder. And he had once briefly sheltered a naked woman in his mail van to protect her backside from buckshot, an old farming remedy for adultery. But counselling the warring parties was a specialist task and it was stretching his postal skills to the limit.

'I'm sure Bryony only wants what's best,' he said.

'Well, go talk to her again then!' said Eryl.

'Again' meant 'yet again'. For Dafydd had been in and out of the old school playground like a UN special envoy, relaying back and forth each twist and turn of the parties' negotiating positions. As yet it was still talks about talks about talks, and he was an hour behind his new schedule. Indoors, Eryl stood nursing his chainsaw in the classroom-cum-lounge-cum-bedroom; outdoors, Bryony sat defiantly tearful on a child-sized swing, scuffing her legs on the tarmac as she rocked.

'Well?' she demanded of the postman, as he emerged once more from the schoolhouse. 'Did you tell him he was a parasite? A useless sleazebag?'

'Er, not in so many words,' said Dafydd, feeling vindicated in his decision to separate them. He walked across the faded white lines in the infants' playground. 'But I think you are probably right about the relationship being over.'

'So why doesn't he just go? Just take what's his and go, you tell him!' She waved him back towards the schoolhouse.

Dafydd resisted. He had, after all, only just come out, and he felt there should be more to negotiating than this.

'That's the problem. I fear,' he said, a hint of the portentous in his tone, 'that may be exactly what Eryl is planning to do – take what's his and go.' There was a spare swing, and Dafydd briefly wondered whether a fuller empathy might be achieved if he rocked with her, in harmony with her pain. But he was a tall postman, and felt he could look foolish with his bottom just a foot above the ground. Instead, he stretched his hand out to the iron upright and leant at a paternal angle. 'You see, there's been a sort of development.'

'What development?'

'He's gone and got a chainsaw.'

'A chainsaw? Good. He can cut his dick off!'

'No, I think he's going to cut his bits of the house off.'

Bryony brought the swing to a jangling halt. 'He's gone mad! . . . What bits?'

'The bedroom and the stairs. He says they're his.'

'His? How can they be his?' Bryony was on her feet, outraged and panicked in about equal measure. 'Seriously – he's planning to wreck the place? He must be bluffing. Surely?'

Dafydd shrugged. 'I don't know. Is there any petrol in the chainsaw?'

'No idea. All I know is he's a bastard.' She bit her nails, and tried to think straight, and then said, 'Go back and ask what his demands are.'

When the postman had delivered the phone bill and found the pair exchanging insults in their kitchen, he had thought the avuncular authority of a Royal Mail uniform would be all the balm required. Now, after an hour of his balm, Dafydd's mind began to fill with loudhailers and police crouching behind cars. He sneaked a look at his watch.

'Go back? Is that wise?'

'Oh, he likes you,' said Bryony.

'He does?'

'You deliver his Giros. That's a meaningful relationship to him.'

With the reluctance he normally reserved for delivering a suspicious parcel, Dafydd went back, once again, into the school-house.

Bryony sat on the stone wall, her kaftanned knees up to her chin, and tried to calm herself by rolling one of her wispy cigarettes. Unfortunately, all her essential oils were inside. She tried to reflect serenely. But her refusal to buy Eryl out of his share of the mortgage – on the grounds that he never paid it – now felt worryingly ill-judged. As were her remarks about preferring a dildo. She was still struggling to light her roll-up when the postman came back out again.

He did not immediately speak.

'Well?'

'He says it was him that built the stairs and the bedroom. *And* it was all his wood. So he reckons he can do what he wants with them. And . . .' The postman hesitated. 'What he wants to do with them is cut them down and take them away.'

'The stairs and the bedroom?'

'Yes. Unless . . .' The postman hesitated again.

'Go on.'

'Unless you buy them off him.'

'What? Buy my own stairs and bedroom off him?'

'Provided you offer a fair price.'

'You are joking! Never! No way! Go and tell him to drop dead!'

Public-spirited though he liked to be, Dafydd felt this was possibly a mission too far. But before he could reply, the chainsaw fired up. Then it subsided, but remained idling away in the background, its menacing whine an aural reminder of Eryl's negotiating position.

Bryony blanched, fury tempered by alarm, alarm heightened by impotence. From outside she could see nothing of any drama within. The narrow, arched windows of the Victorians ended at his modern mezzanine flooring, and provided no view of Eryl the home wrecker.

'But he can't do it, surely? I mean, it can't be legal, can it? Destroying your own home?'

'I suspect it's a grey area,' said the postman.

'What about the police? Would the police help?'

'It's market day. They only do escaped heifers.'

Bryony slid down from the wall and began to pace. 'So what should I do? What should I tell him?'

'I guess it's a judgement call,' said Dafydd, using a phrase whose meaning he had often wondered at.

'But he must know I've got no money. Did you tell him I've got no money?'

'He said your parents have got money.'

'Not for me. Not for him. Oh Jesus! Tell him I need time to think.'

Dafydd looked uncertain. 'Is that a yes or a no?'

'It's a fuck knows! Go and play for time. Please!'

The postman frowned. Next thing, Eryl would be sending out for a pizza. And being interviewed from a gantry by the Welsh TV News. And then the lane would be floodlit and blocked by CNN Winnebagos. In the meantime, a dozen copies of *Farmers' Weekly* were still to be delivered, Mrs Wilkins would be fretting about the date of her eighth driving test, and the Commodore's leaflets for the Sinking Church Fund's Musical Afternoon & Spring Fête were going unread. And his job was on the line.

'How much time?'

'I don't know. Till the pub opens. Whatever.' She looked at him pleadingly.

He hesitated. He wished he had been on more Post Office training courses. He had done 'Relationships with the Public', but that had covered lost motorists, smudged postcards and difficult cats. Nothing about men with chainsaws. But then again, Dafydd reasoned, he had known Eryl since he was about six – and for years used to deliver his birthday cards, until Eryl ran out of friends to send them.

'OK. I'll see what I can do.'

Showered with thanks, the postman trudged off, yet again, into the schoolhouse.

Bryony watched his legs go up Eryl's stairs and out of sight. There was a sordid aptness for their relationship to end with a fight over a bedroom. When they had first met, when he was Eryl the heir, he had promised her a choice of twelve. Enough bedrooms to keep a woman busy for weeks, he said. It was a good chat-up line.

He had a cavalier charm then, of sorts. She had fallen for him because he seemed to be as free as the wind, but in reality he was as free as the windfall, and when faced with poverty he crumpled. She was keen not to crumple. And though it grieved her, she realised she must find some way to buy him off, some porn-free, pain-free way to raise money. And then she recalled a chance conversation with her neighbour, also forced into penury by a man. She was pondering the neighbour's solution when she heard a shout.

'Bryony!' Ten minutes gone, and Dafydd was back out once more. But with a difference, for as he crossed the playground the sound of the chainsaw was no longer searing the air. He smiled at her.

'I think we may have a deal.'

'Really?'

'More or less. He just needs a helicopter for his escape.' Dafydd gave her a big smug grin. 'No, I said you'd agreed, but that you'd need a few days to get that sort of money.' And then added with another grin, 'After all, you'll have to find a gun and where the Securicor vans park!'

Bryony stretched up and kissed him on the cheek, a gesture he modestly pretended to resist.

'Well, at least it's a breathing space,' he said. 'But as for paying him . . . ?' He shrugged. It had not escaped the postman's notice that the phone bill, like all her bills, had been a final demand.

Bryony managed to look upbeat. 'I'm working on it.'

'Good luck.'

'And thank you so much.'

'All part of the service.'

And Dafydd got back in his van and drove off feeling, like Wells Fargo, that the mail always got through.

Bryony went back and sat on her swing. Here she tried to give shape to an action plan. Several times in the past she had considered a bank loan and the response had not been encouraging. It was a colonial tradition that the wages of mid-Wales be the lowest in Britain – no doubt Hubert was the benchmark – and so banking ears were hard to bend. But when paying in her pittance lately she had found signs of a new mood in her branch. A mood that a grateful Mrs Whitelaw, her divorcee neighbour in the caravan up the hill, had described as 'unusually customer-focused'.

Bryony slowly scuffed up the weeds in the crumbling tarmac as she rocked to and fro, allowing this thought to settle. Maybe now was the time to take up the offer of the new bank manager, to go and discuss her needs with him. Somewhere in the kitchen she had a business card that Mr Blake had given her.

Chapter 16

Small cocktail parties for ten, even for twelve, the Commodore could cope with. He had a strategy for coping, as the modern world would say. He would shake hands with the guests – his reptilian handshake had a tenacious grip although his body looked near death – and then would busy himself with coats until Rupert whined. Rupert would whine because, like any twelve-year-old labrador, he needed to do his number ones on a regular basis – and by locking him in for six hours prior to a cocktail party, the Commodore could ensure the whining came on cue. Dog and master would then excuse themselves and exit into the gardens (leaving sister Dilys at the social helm), and quietly spend the evening in the dovecot folly, circa 1782.

More difficult for the Commodore was the 'open house' invitation, the At Home for the neighbours. He still bore the scars of the Silver Jubilee, when five hours of small talk had almost led him to regrets about the monarchy. His only specialist subjects were escutcheons and fly-fishing, each favoured for their solitary nature and neither amenable to a quick joke. Moreover, when holding such events, events required by his status and insisted on by his sister, he was always prey to the worry that his wife would escape from her bedroom and appear in public. (An alcoholic and a royalist, she found irresistible the prospect of constant toasts to the Queen. Her solo attempts to sing the

National Anthem with gestures had twice caused her to trip on the unevenly paved terrace and roll into the rosebed.)

So, as he forced open the glass of St Brynnach's notice board with a twig, and wrote 'T-O-D-A-Y' in black ink across his personally designed Sinking Church Fund's Musical Afternoon & Spring Fête leaflet, the Commodore would rather have been up to his thighs in the River Nant.

The nuns were the first to arrive. Sister Philomena was a little heavy on the brake pedal and left a bald patch in the gravel drive as the Transit van slid to a stop. Their religious order ran some school in the hills, where youngsters were introduced to the world of God and primitive sanitation, and was usually the source of tearful children found loose in the lanes. Public appearances of the sisters were more limited. Sister Philomena's slightly nervy driving stemmed from her last outing, a Christmas mass in Cardiff, when black ice and a bend had re-routed her into a river. That she subsequently became the lead story on page 6 of the *Mid-Walian*, under the heading 'Nun Drives on Water!', had only served to increase her misgivings about the modern world.

The nuns left some ten minutes later. To a casual observer, their arrival had been an act of ecumenical solidarity . . . an offer of support spiritual for a church faced with collapse temporal . . . the proof that, though professing a foreign faith, they did not wish God to flood the nave of a rival.

In fact, it was none of these things. They had come at the Commodore's request. Reason for visit was the cheap loan of several dozen plastic stacking chairs.

There were not many remarkable facts in the Commodore's long life. One was that he had the largest overdraft in the valley. The other was that he regularly managed to transfer this overdraft – and six figures would not be a wild stab – from bank to bank.

This beneficial arrangement owed much to the age of deference. The Powells were one of the oldest life forms in the valley and so occupied the top of the social ladder. The bankers being middle class, there was no known way for them to countermand the wishes of their betters. However, any reluctance of the town's bankers to take on these debts, the fruits of a lifetime's inertia, was easily alleviated by an awareness of the family's assets. Land was land was land, and the Commodore had bits of it all over the place, in the way that lesser folk have loose change down the back of their sofa. Whenever one of his many bills reached bailiff level, he would flog off another farm, tenanted and tumbledown.

But now even he – like the late Llewellyns – was finding that the unreasonableness, the *disrespectfulness*, of modern economics was chipping away at the social structures of feudalism, that mainstay of personal happiness.

Their church was but the latest family institution to slide into the mire. Their estate, their shoot, their hostelry, all were on the skids that lead from colonial grandeur to plastic stacking chairs. Had he the nous to be an enlightened landowner, to think occasionally in the future tense, he need not have lived in a home of leaks and drafts, fulfilling a folklore image of feckless gentry. But the Commodore was of the old school, and believed the blame lay with the staff, whose standards had declined steadily since the 1850s.

With much of their estate looked after by the likes of Glyn, whom even Wat Tyler would have hesitated to enlist, the returns from the world of sheep now made a long red smudge in the Powell ledger. And the world of his birds did little better. In his woodland covers, there were rarely enough to shoot, since half the pheasants were going AWOL. Apparently in Volvos. For the third year running, he had had to cull his gamekeeper. Even the returns from the estate's one hostelry, the Dragon's Head, were baffling in their shortfall. It was as if the valley had signed the pledge.

'£3.50, please.'

Her sensuous Irish accent was almost lost under the big golf umbrella. Sporadic drops of rain were falling on to the tautly stretched nylon, which amplified their pitter-patter out of all proportion to their importance. Moira pushed a yellow ticket across the little pine table. 'And raffle tickets are 50p a strip.' She added a cheesy smile, and nodded encouragingly towards the giant thermometer beside her, whose blood-red mercury showed that ecclesiastical heritage grants currently stood at £12,500.

She was seated at the entrance to the gardens, where visitors' cars left the gravel to slither into a nearby field. It was the tradition of bottled jam and home-sewn doilies that had led long-legged Moira to sit here among the rhododendrons, adding unexpected glamour to the role of ticket-girl. Whenever events took place at 'the big house', it was a much-loved feudal tradition that the local wives help out, with all those sundry little skills that women have. (And leave the husbands, like Gareth, to do the testing manly tasks, like skittle management.) So, rejecting the domestic servitude of jam, but tempted by a wider social whirl than ever populated their parlour, Moira had offered herself up for meeting and greeting and tearing of tickets.

A tenner was tossed casually on to the table.

'Aw, bejesus begorrah, Oi'll be having ten pounds' worth!' The big spender stood back and basked in his funniness.

Moira gave an empty smile and, mindful of the proprieties of the occasion, resisted her desire to propose he shove his money up his arse. 'That'll be twenty strips then,' she replied, and began counting them out.

'And what is that Oi'll be winning?' he demanded.

Moira hesitated, determined not to slip into any response that might be construed as banter, taken as the desire for conversation. She did not know who he was, but she knew she did not like him. She did not like his arrogant body language, nor the character suggested by his misjudged clothes. The brass-buttoned blazer managed to be both flash and old-fashioned, while the tennis shorts were plain buffoonish, appropriate only to an escapee from a *Carry On* film. 'The usual,' she said offhandedly.

'And what would that be being?' asked Stéfan.

Moira shrugged. 'Oh you know, Woolworths' leftovers.' She tore off his strips. 'There's your twenty. Good luck.'

'Luck? Now would that be after being the luck of the Oirish?' persisted Stéfan, unabashed.

'The luck of any nationality you want.' She gave him another cold and empty smile. '£3.50, please,' she said to the next arrival.

Stéfan turned, and took the man confidentially by the arm. 'You be nice to her,' he boomed. 'She's the only Irish woman never been kissed by the Blarney Stone!' And then he treated them both to his trademark laugh.

Beaming happily, Stéfan made his way past the house-high rhododendrons and down the arrowed path through giant and geriatric acers, into the rose garden and on to the first of two tiered lawns that held the usual selection of stalls and local societies. It was a scene familiar to anyone who had read an Agatha Christie novel. It was the Thirties incarnate. It was people impeccably polite, with lives of laudable moderation. It was a world hard to fault on moral grounds. It was a world that made the need for murder irresistible.

Stéfan saw it differently. As he crossed the croquet grass, waving to those he knew and to those he didn't, he almost felt contentment. For him, it was a ready-made community, available off the shelf, and all its people pigeonholed. It came with instant respect and built-in deference. It was quaint, it was enduring, it was his, and he only had to be here at weekends.

He scanned the browsing crowd for the Commodore. He had business with the Commodore, though the Commodore did not know it. Nor did the Commodore know him, but that was a detail.

Stéfan stopped to guess the number of beans in a jeroboam. It was 10p a go and he had ten goes. It lacked the adrenaline rush of the two grand he'd once bet on the likely colour of a stripper's pubic hair, but he was a man who could rarely resist a gamble. Beneath the jolly smile and his joke with a farmer about not wanting to win a year's free farts, he was rapidly calculating cubic capacity and the basic dimensions of a bean, for he was also a sore loser. He would not easily give up on a charity bottle of beans.

His calculations over, he picked up his ten ticket stubs and moved on down the line of fun. It was odd, though pleasing, to be nodded at by strangers, as if his Photofit had gone before him. No one actually doffed a cap, but a couple of the shepherd class tugged what in a dim light could have passed for a forelock. Not for the first time, he regretted the surrender of the archives, for he harboured a suspicion that they might give mention of obscure seigneurial powers. Stéfan did not know quite what such powers would be, though in his fantasies it usually involved the wearing of robes. And, conscious of history, he rather warmed to the idea of supplicants on a Sunday morning, queuing at his study door for the settling of grievances and the dispensing of virgins.

The grass gave way to a flagged path with laburnum arches, and the opportunities for cheery public-spiritedness continued without respite. In quick succession, he tried his hand at hoopla, block-bought the sponge cakes, and said no to joining the Bat Society. (Bats, he felt, had no place in a well-run countryside.) He was nearing the grand house, where it was rumoured the Commodore might be hiding, when he came upon the nerve centre of the day's good cause, an exhibition in an old family tent.

Stéfan looked in.

'And it's all thanks to her thighs,' said a smutty sort of voice.

It was the fat vicar. He was stood against a backdrop of grainy photographs, numbered 1 to 16 and offering inflamed close-ups of the church cracks. A wodge of leaflets in hand, he was busy explaining St Brynnach's predicament to the Traffic Warden.

Stéfan backed out. His devotion to the saving of St Brynnach's had its limits, and proximity to fat clergymen was one of them.

He paused under the tent's awning, and began wondering how to flush out the Commodore.

'Ringalongathon, sir?'

'Do what?'

It was Mrs Hartford-Stanley, owner of the wind-sensitive thighs, and she was clutching a clipboard. 'Sponsored bell-ring,' she said with matronly hauteur. 'We're aiming at twenty-four hours. On the town bells.'

'All night long? Wouldn't you make more money if you were sponsored *not* to ring? Ha-ha-ha!'

Had she not sensed the size of his wallet, Mrs Hartford-Stanley might well have stomped on by. But years of shaking tins for cat sanctuaries had given her a killer instinct and she knew where his jugular would be hidden.

'Mayoress is down for a pound an hour.'

'Put me down for two pounds.' Stéfan seized the biro and made sure his signature was the bigger. It wouldn't be *his* fault if the bells of St Brynnach's never rang again.

Satisfied, Mrs Hartford-Stanley moved on, leaving Stéfan to take stock of the Commodore's substantial house, which lay before him up a flight of weathered stone steps. Despite the flaking white paint, it was an elegant building, with a portico at the side and grand circular bays to the front, their windows looking out across the valley and the ill-behaved river below. Stéfan was pleased to see that it had just the two storeys, where Crug Caradoc technically had three. He also won on the listing, for he had checked and the Commodore's was only Grade II. And it was Queen Anne, whom King James trumped by over a century. Admittedly, the Powells had a few hundred years of ancestors, whereas the end of the line for Stéfan was Great-Aunt Ottilia, of no known address. But that was easily solved by a few lies, should the need arise.

As he was looking towards the house and the upper lawn, a straight-backed lady in her sixties came from the direction of the stable block and walked briskly along the terrace to the public address system. She moved confidently for she had an OBE. Quite why she had a flat in the stables was unknown, but was said to be connected with propriety. Though why the Commodore should be thought of as a sexual object by anyone, least of all his sister, was a puzzler. Especially as, since her earliest age, she had shown no interest in single men, only committees. The committees themselves were on a random assortment of subjects, betraying no common passion, and her strengths were widely held to be in minute taking. This, however, was enough to keep the Welsh Office happy and all her life she had risen inexorably towards an unknown goal.

She tapped the microphone. It was 3 p.m.

There was a short delay while the sound got some screeching out of its system. Stéfan took a scrunched-up yellow leaflet from his blazer pocket and looked again at its contents. It had been drawn by the Commodore, in elaborate spidery detail, the work either of a draughtsman or an autistic child. Under the words Sinking Church Fund's Musical Afternoon & Spring Fête were the interwoven outlines of the wind, brass and string sections of an orchestra, exactingly sketched in Indian ink. In each corner was a disembodied hand with a baton. If one had a criticism, it was that three days' work seemed excessive for a village fund-raising do.

Dilys got the last of the vulgar noises out of the mike and started to speak. It was a short speech, and merely informed those in the grounds that music was now available in the house. For anyone who was interested.

As Stéfan glanced over at the ground floor bay – an attractive feature that, to his chagrin, his Jacobeans had omitted – he caught a glimpse of a grey-haired old man gazing through its box-sash windows. Forgoing the chance to guess the weight of a pig, Stéfan moved to join the ranks of music-lovers who were working their way up the terrace steps.

'Hallo-o again!' He felt a hand on his arm, soft yet far from tentative. The voice was sort of Ladies' College, but overdone. Stéfan looked round and saw a woman in jodhpurs, whom he recognised but could not place. She was dressed like a Sloane who had gone blind, a woman unable to detect fashion overkill.

'The auction. You nearly knocked me over.'

'And you've come for an apology?' He remembered her now. She had been sending out sexual signals, as far as that is possible in a wet marquee.

'Oh definitely. Cringing and protracted.'

He leered. 'I'm afraid I don't do cringing.'

She tapped him lightly with her riding crop. 'I'm sure that could be arranged.'

He hesitated before he responded, wondering what age lay beneath her make-up.

'£25,000, you'd just bid £25,000.'

'Yes, yes, of course I remember you.' His eyes wandered over her welded-on jodhpurs as he tried to decide whether to invest the Stéfan charm.

'Felicity. I like to hunt,' she said huskily.

'Felicity!' He went for the big, full-on smile. 'How splendid! Been a few months but I was hoping to see those buttocks again!'

At the other end of the garden, Moira's two hours of smiling was almost up. As she watched the latecomers' cars slalom into the parking field, her normal brio was going off the boil. The nuns had made her homesick. Not that she was religious – she hadn't genuflected since she was sixteen – but a vanload of black habits going past had been a sight that stirred up warm classroom memories of Bible-reading and masturbation. And with that came the aura of Ireland – which meant for her a place of laughter and passion, where there was music and emotion. Where there was joy in the art of conversation.

Moira tidied her stubs into little piles, and started to total the money.

'Done well?'

She looked up. Silk shirts were rare in the valley, and to all but cover one with cashmere seemed ultra-cool. 'Is over a hundred good?'

'Pounds or people?'

'People.'

'Oh definitely a success then.' And the urbane face creased into a smile, its unseasonal glow hinting at the vanity of a sun-lamp. 'Though there are better ways to raise funds.'

'Oh?' She took the brand new note the man offered and started to sort his change. 'Like what?'

'Like selling a video of the church when it falls into the river.'

Moira burst out laughing, though partly from relief at finding a fellow cynic.

Pleased with the response to his wit, Mr Blake modestly ran a hand over the silver waves of his hair. He enjoyed events such as fêtes. They showed his personality to advantage. Not that he wasn't already pleased with himself. It had been an unexpectedly good week at the bank. His loans had exceeded target for the month, and he had brought much pleasure to several of his customers.

A hundred yards away, Stéfan had gained a phone number but lost sight of the Commodore. The man had retreated from the window, like some pallid heroine imprisoned in the tower of a Gothic novel. Stéfan set off up the steps.

Pink arrows cut out of card directed the music-lovers along the terrace and round to the front entrance. The porch was framed by an ancient wisteria, its greenery miraculously springing out of trunks that resembled tortured driftwood. Here politeness had led to bunching on the gravel. Ahead of him he could see the ponderous figure of Clydog, whose interviewing skills he still remembered for their power of anaesthesia, and so Stéfan briefly hung back.

He was, however, curious about the company Clydog was keeping. On one side was a rather funky young couple, at the ripped-jean end of fashion; on the other side was an inverted pyramid of a woman, whose dress designer appeared to work in the floral sack industry. Someone had granted her the copyright on conversation, and she was holding court on the subject of art.

Then the bottleneck unbunged, and the little group went into the house.

Stéfan followed a few paces behind, and was immediately

struck by the entrance hall. He had not expected the mêlée of muddy boots and the musty smell – nor the fact that no attempt had been made to tidy up for the day. A couple of fishing rods, wedged inside waders, were leaning against the lincrusta, and a handful of feathers, matted by blood, were stuck to a side table. A croquet mallet and a dog bone rested on a pair of waterproofs that lay in disarray, and on the window-sill stood a row of rifle cartridges. A huge old Oriental vase, cracked the length of its Chinamen, was stuffed with walking sticks and rolls of toilet paper; no longer an art object, it was used to anchor down a rug from Turkmenistan, stained with dog urine.

And sprinkled over these objects, like a helping of black pistachio, were bat droppings. (Only pipistrelles, the Commodore had been heard to say with disappointment.)

Stéfan was in no doubt that his own foyer beat this entrance hall hands down. And yet, although contemptuous of its tattiness, somewhere he had an uneasy envy of its lived-in quality, somewhere an insecurity created by a décor that was the accretion of generations, not the *tabla rasa* of an interior designer.

As Stéfan followed the echoing voices down the unlit hall where brown was the default colour, he listened out for the sound of music. The music of the leaflet was undefined, and the instruments depicted on it gave false clues, for they were simply those instruments that the Commodore could draw. Though the mayoress – she of the operatic bosoms – seemed to have been hoping for a charabanc outing by the Hallé, Stéfan's money was on a chamber orchestra, made proper by evening dress.

Dilys was on the door, being gracious with her hands. Even without its bay, the lounge was the largest of the reception rooms, and had in slower, grander times been waltzed over. It was a room with a view, a room that saw the day dawn and stayed in sunlight till afternoon tea. For today, though, the crinkled chesterfields had been despatched to an anteroom and the potted plants – which social historians would have recognised as aspidistras – were relegated to the recesses.

Now filling the seventeenth-century salon were stacking chairs: grey, plastic and in rows. A sense of aesthetic anticlimax was hard to hide, but the locals gamely clattered into place. There was no guest list for the fête, no winnowing of Bs and Cs, just people who had, for £3.50, come to give a nod to God and plug the gap in a damp Saturday. The concert was thus short on cognoscenti; the bums it put on the seats had familiar faces, the same faces as had been gathered in for Harvest Festival . . . and for every other do since the ox-roast and the Silver Jubilee. In neat, cramped rows sat the farmers, the farmers' wives, the vet, the eggman, the pond provider, the fence contractor, the semen salesman, the poisons adviser, the turkey breeder, the sub-postmistress, and a goodly sample of the agro-bourgeoisie, all rounded off, of course, by the valley elders, wheezy martyrs to a lifetime of agriculture.

There were just two notable absentees. One was the church's atheist surveyor, who had diagnosed the damage to St Brynnach's in such loving detail, who had ordered the digging of the dumper-loads of dirt . . . and who had now failed to attend the fund-raiser. The other was the church's godfather, the Commodore himself.

Stéfan was a restless man, who lost interest on page one of books, and he had no desire to be trapped alive in a concert. He spurned the seats and stood in the claque at the back, the better to observe and escape.

Then, from the corridor outside came a terrible squealing and grinding. And a piano, pulled by the gamekeeper, and pushed by the Commodore, made a late entrance. In a world more aware of postmodernist irony, such an entrance might have provoked a round of applause – even been seen as the performance itself – but here it only provided the trigger for a community smile of deference. Except from Stéfan.

'Heave!' he roared, having once seen the Last Night of the Proms. 'Heave!'

Heads were turned, and an embarrassed titter did the rounds. The Commodore reacted as if to incoming fire.

The piano and its recalcitrant castor was then pushed to the bay, its rosewood lid was opened, sheets of music put in place, a stool put in front, and for a brief, appalling moment the prospect of rustic male duets seemed imminent. Whereupon Dilys brought on the performers.

Isobel and Arwyn. Aged eleven and twelve.

Pianist and violinist. Grades 3 and 4. Dressed by the Fauntleroy family.

Shyly, the two youngsters gave a little bow each, to oohs and aahs from the audience. They then shook hands and turned to take up their playing positions, silhouetted against the Queen Anne windows.

'A minuet in D by Bach,' warned Dilys sternly.

Outside, the two lawns led the eye down to the water-meadows where the Welsh Blacks still munched through the rich grasses, and on to where the Norman churchtower rose above the yew trees. Indoors, the scrolled pediment and the rococo arabesques on the ceiling gave visual testament to the house's rich history. And doing the rounds of the acoustics was the tentative tuning of violin strings.

'Ah, now this,' whispered the mayoress to the six nearest seats, 'is just like Jane Austen.'

And, in a way, it was.

Young Isobel flexed her fingers on the keys of the baby grand, young Arwyn pressed the over-polished violin under his chin, then, after pausing briefly for an outbreak of farmer's lung to subside in the front row, they set to work on Bach.

Between them they had had nearly fifty months of lessons, much of it from a music teacher, although, as the children lived at opposite ends of the valley, they rarely practised together. So, while their individual notes were excellent, they moved through the music at somewhat different *tempi*. And that perhaps produced the mild artistic tension which could be detected from Arwyn's habit of beating time with his foot. But all agreed it was lovely to watch two such charming children play the classics so delightfully.

A very generous outburst of clapping greeted the end of the minuet, appreciation for a performance that had kept the rural audience in apparent rapture, and at times almost silent.

At the back, Stéfan, not to be outdone, and eager in some way to integrate, shouted 'Bravo!' More than once. Had there been a vase of flowers to hand, he would have snatched it up and hurled it stagewards. But even as Stéfan applauded, he kept a watching brief on the old Commodore, who throughout had lurked inscrutably by the open salon door.

The applause finally died away, only for Dilys to reappear – and announce a second piece. This time by another, lesser known, composer.

Stéfan listened for a minute or so more, while the violin tried very hard to be contrapuntal, but his mind was elsewhere. Time, as he so often said, was money. It certainly wasn't music.

There were some dozen people standing along the walls but he had a clear sightline of his target, and was fearful the man might vanish again.

'Pssst!' he said. 'Pssst!'

It was one of the few moments that day when the acoustics of the room did full justice to the quality of the sound. Almost everyone in the room turned round – with the exception of the Commodore.

There were two possible reasons for his failure to respond. Deafness; or the fact that no one had ever gone 'Pssst!' to a Powell before.

However, the intrusion was short-lived, for this second composition was more *forte* than *piano*, and the vigorous keywork of eleven-year-old Isobel quickly recaptured the attention of the audience. Stéfan, meanwhile, had still to capture the attention of the Commodore.

Elbowing his way through the groupies, he manoeuvred to the door. He delayed his greeting to the very last moment, laying his hand on the Commodore's shoulder at the same time.

'Stéfan. Crug Caradoc.'

The Commodore spun around, startled, like a highly strung thoroughbred faced with a firecracker. Physical touching and the use of forenames were the sort of things he had fought a war against.

The old man stared uncertainly at Stéfan. The blazer in particular foxed him, and he briefly wondered whether, in one of his less lucid moments, he had promised to hold a charity cricket match.

'Wonderful concert. And such a lovely house.' Stéfan had to shout slightly, to be heard above the noise of the young duettists.

'Oh . . . er . . .'

'And such a good cause. Brynnog is one of my favourite saints.'

Heads were now beginning to turn, the audience was growing tetchy, and Arwyn's *glissando* skills were starting to suffer. Stéfan took the Commodore by the arm and led him into his hall.

'Business proposition for you, Julian.'

He waited expectantly. In his experience, these were words that brought a flush of excitement to any man's cheeks. . . . But not apparently Julian's.

'Oh . . .' He gazed vacantly down the hall, towards the portrait of his father. 'Er . . . no . . . No, not my sort of thing . . . thank you.'

'But you don't know what it is.'

He made a fluttery sort of gesture with his hands. Eventually, if only because it was his turn to speak, he said, 'I don't know what anything is these days.'

'It's a figure with a lot of noughts on, that's what it is!'

'Oh.' If it were possible, the Commodore's gloom increased. He started to look around him. 'Have you seen Rupert?

'Rupert?'

'He needs to widdle.'

'He can widdle later. I want to buy your pub.'

'Is it for sale?'

'Well, *you* own it!'

'Oh . . . oh yes. Yes . . . I suppose I do . . .' The Commodore's head began to ache. So much conversation in one day was extremely taxing. He ruminated a while, then said, 'D'you ride?'

'Ride? What, horses? No.'

'Oh.'

The old man fell silent again, leaving Stéfan uncertain whether he was still considering his proposal, or indeed whether his brain had stopped. After a while, he realised the Commodore's slight head movement showed instead that he was listening to the music, whose strains were drifting in and out of the hall's shadows like a 78 soundtrack warped by misuse.

'I'd give you a fair price.'

'I used to hide in your attic.'

'Pardon?'

'My record was three and a half hours. Because I could keep quiet. My sister never could.'

'Crug Caradoc?'

'Tea with the Llewellyns, we used to have to come to tea. We hated the Llewellyns. All our family hated the Llewellyns.'

'Well, no dark corners to hide in now. I've spent £18,000 on paint and lights alone. And I'd be spending that sort of dosh on the pub as well.'

The Commodore did not appear impressed. Indeed, few expressions ever crossed his face apart from sadness and puzzlement. And now puzzlement seemed to have advanced from the general to the particular, from the mysteries of a baffling world to the strangeness of one inhabitant.

'Why?'

'Why what? Why do I want to buy the pub . . . ?' Stéfan struggled for an answer, sensing that temper tantrum would sound an odd motive.

The Commodore mused aloud. 'It makes no money. You'd be out of pocket. I'm out of pocket.'

'And you want to keep it?'

He shrugged, with a vagueness that gave no purchase point for a discussion, and eventually said, 'My father kept it.'

'D'you like it? D'you go to it?'

He shrugged again. 'They tell me it's a dreadful place.'

'Well, I could always reduce my offer.'

'I suppose so. You'd have to talk to my solicitors about that.'

'About what? About . . . Is that a yes?'

Applause burst from the music room, again prolonged and enthusiastic, a sign perhaps of the extended family which the two young players possessed. The Commodore, sensing a surge of people might be imminent, started to back off down the hall. 'I wanted to have tombola,' he muttered.

'Is that a yes?' Stéfan asked again, more insistently.

The old man looked flustered . . . but finally nodded agreement. Adding, 'I'm on pills, you know.'

Stéfan gave him a clenched first salute, for reasons that escaped both of them.

The Commodore continued towards his front door, querulously calling for Rupert. He was almost outside when he turned, and said, as if remembering the need for conversational niceties, 'They're all buried in my churchyard, your Llewellyns.' Then he went out, leaving Stéfan to simmer at what he assumed to be one-upmanship.

As he stood alone in the ancestral hall, Stéfan found himself taken by the urge to now buy a church of his own.

'Oh, I love *all* art!' declared the mayoress, as her entourage filed out of the concert and back down to the garden.

Rob did not reply. He had replied the first time she had announced this, and the second time, and the third time, but had now realised that the tone was *municipal declamatory*, a debased form of the oratory favoured by the Romans, and required no response other than well-timed nodding.

'My father was forty years in the male voice choir, that's where it comes from. D'you sing? I'd love to sing. I used to sing as a child.' She eased herself respectfully over the camomile and feverfew in the flagstone cracks. 'I've always been good at projecting.'

Clydog had introduced the parties as his contribution to rural networking. He had only a hazy view as to how patronage worked, but knew that Myfanwy Edwards had pull with the sister-in-law of the man who owned the launderette where art exhibitions were sometimes held.

'Welsh National Opera came to Abernant last year. Touring their celebrated production of *Rigoletto*. I went both nights. Once as mayoress, once as myself. Wonderful! Quite wonderful!' (Verdi was responsible for Clydog's only known column as opera correspondent, an experience that severely tested his prose. Especially since Abernant's status as a cultural centre meant WNO sent only two singers and a piano, a detail which – for reasons of local pride – he chose to omit from his review.) 'If this were Italy we'd have an opera house. Everywhere in Italy has an opera house. We should have one here!'

'Not a lot of votes in that,' observed Clydog. 'Hubert can't even make money out of pasta.'

'So, Robert!' said the mayoress, turning to him as the four paused at the bottom of the terrace. 'You're an artist, then. Tell me about your work. Who is your muse?'

Rob and Jane exchanged looks, a snigger not far away.

Before he could reply, Jane sighed sadly and said, 'Aah, you know the fickle world of art, Myfanwy. His muse keeps leaving him to fuck someone else. But then that's muses for you!'

Valley people had long noticed that incomers swore more often and more vividly. Some deplored this, but others attributed it to their greater sophistication; most were aware that valley language was rooted in the propriety of the Fifties, way behind the curve when it came to liberated obscenities. This had resulted in a two-speed language zone, the outsiders effing and blinding while the locals listened benignly and replied in the Queen's English. Or in their idea of the Queen's English.

A fuck would never have passed the lady mayor's lips, and not just because word might have got back to the Queen. Nonetheless, as an artistic person herself, she understood that creative types have to be free of the rules that bind ordinary mortals.

'True, very true,' she replied. 'Inspiration's never nine to five, is it?'

'He does Japanese landscapes,' said Clydog.

'Oh, I love Japan,' said the mayoress, who had once been to Cyprus. 'How big are they?'

'How big would you like them to be?' said Rob.

Everyone smiled.

'Are you familiar with the art world in Abernant?'

'Er, no, not . . . er . . . not as such, no.'

'Oh we must get you along to one of our coffee mornings. I have coffee mornings for people who are artistic. Where we all exchange ideas, cross-fertilise. We're short on painters. Got a lot of potters, though. A pot-pourri of potters, as I call them.'

This time, Rob avoided Jane's eyes, for a snigger now would be terminal.

'It's like a rural Bloomsbury set, I suppose. Rosie – she's a divorcee – her hedgehog pots go all over. Started out with just mugs, and now she's got an order from Disney. Disney! And apparently they want other animals. Not lifesize, but it's still a great achievement.' The mayoress would have continued her way through the rest of the CVs had she not caught sight of Dilys, who was bidding farewell to the vicar. It was her opportunity to display some effusive gratitude to the hostess.

She hated her hostess. Dilys was everything the mayoress wanted to be. She played in a bigger league, she had classier invitations on her mantelpiece, and every time Clydog wrote about her in the *Mid-Walian* he put OBE after her name. And her breasts didn't need stabilisers. Yet the mayoress also knew that a good word from her, a leaf of her scented notepaper, and doors might open – doors to flunkeys and medallions.

'I'll be in touch!' she said, and was off powering up the slippery terrace steps like a fell runner.

Clydog gazed after her.

'Guess it's time to go. I think the fat lady's about to sing,' he said, somewhat unexpectedly.

Rob and Jane were also ready for a quick exit, as they had promised some tea and sympathy to Bryony, who seemed in need of a hug. The day had been a good crash course in meeting neighbours but there are only so many circuits to be made of bring-and-buy stalls. In the interests of community spirit they had loaded up with doilies and jam but now the damp was starting to tell.

The parting cars crunched down the gravel drive, mud spraying from their wheel arches, and eased out into the lane. There were still several hours of daylight left, still time to check the stock and bake a cake. The families – and many had come as families – began the short, familiar journeys back home to their farms in the hills.

Watching them from the junction by the church, seated on a shiny new black motorbike with garish striping, was a biker kitted out in shiny new black leathers. On the back of his bike were two full paniers and a CYMRU sticker. His visor was closed, and although many gave him a second glance, he remained anonymous to them all.

Eryl sat in the still-spitting rain for some ten minutes, then revved hard, executed a flamboyant wheelie, and raced away down the valley, the valley that was once to have been all his.

Part Three

Chapter 17

'In a lay-by?'

'Yes.'

'A lay-by fifty yards from the caravan?'

'Yes.'

'Why would he put it there?'

'Precisely!'

Hubert pondered this information. 'And you saw it two weeks ago?' He puffed his Old Holborn over the profiteroles. 'What time?'

'On my morning round,' replied Dafydd.

'Some time between dawn and dusk, then.'

'About 9.30,' the postman retorted. Then added with animus, 'And I'm always finished by eleven these days. Well, nearly always.'

'You've no idea if the car was there all night?'

'No—'

'You didn't slip back and feel the bonnet?'

'No, of course I didn't!'

'Call yourself a postman! What use is your bloody gossip if you don't get all the details?' Hubert was enjoying himself.

'You've got enough proof. Why would the bank manager's car be parked fifty yards from her caravan? And how come she wouldn't answer the door to sign for her parcel? *Rare Breeds of Hen*, she's been waiting weeks for those magazines.'

'Oh you managed to find out what was in her parcel, then? That wasn't too much trouble?'

'I just deliver things to people. I don't kick their doors down.'

'Come on, Clydog, you're the pro here, what's your theory?'

Clydog had not so far spoken, as he had got into trouble with his Mississippi Mud Pie. For several minutes he had been leaning on the counter, trying not to choke. Attempts to speak made him go puce. Gamely, he struggled to get enough air together for a sentence.

'Well,' postulated Hubert helpfully while they waited, 'perhaps Mrs Whitelaw was overdrawn and he's killed her. Banks are getting very strict on loans these days.'

At last Clydog spoke. 'It's not far from the river. He could have gone fishing.'

'*Fishing?*' The other two men spoke almost as one as they turned to stare at him.

'Early morning. Relieving the stress of high finance on his way to work. Make a nice human interest story, that would. Sympathetic. 'S got a page seven feel.'

'Except it's bollocks!' said Dafydd.

'You don't know that.'

'I do.' The postman hesitated, glancing around the deserted delicatessen with an almost conspiratorial air.

'Well?' pressed Hubert.

'I don't know if I should say this . . .'

'Oh you can speak freely in front of Clydog,' said Hubert. 'He's like a priest. Nothing you say to him – no matter how shocking or scandalous – will ever be repeated. Certainly not in print.'

Clydog did his best to look weary at this familiar thrust.

Dafydd, meanwhile, remained circumspect – and then mysteriously lowered his voice. 'Guess where else the bank manager's car's been parked. . . . At 9.30 in the morning.'

'Hope it's not on double yellows. Council's planning to make that a hanging offence.' (Hubert was spearheading the anti-fascist campaign against new parking regulations, and this made him prone to obsessiveness.)

'Go on, guess.'

'Outside the nuns.'

'Outside the old schoolhouse. Lived in by,' the postman nodded knowingly towards the back kitchen, where sounds of angry chopping could occasionally be heard, 'your Bryony.'

'Bryony? But he's old enough to be her . . . her . . .'

'Bank manager?'

Hubert was more than shocked. He was miffed. He was only ten years older than Mr Blake, the new bank manager, and this left him wondering whether he too could have successfully tried it on with her. Assuming that it was true. That these sightings weren't mere coincidence. 'And you sure you're . . . ?'

'Being a postman,' said Dafydd, 'you get a feel for funny goings-on.'

'The man does wear silk shirts,' admitted Hubert.

'There's no proof he's up to anything,' Clydog said again. 'He could be one of these . . . these new roving bank managers—' Dafydd and Hubert found this very funny '—who do home visits.'

'Go on, then,' said Hubert. 'Tell him you want a home visit and see what happens.'

Clydog wished, not for the first time in his life, that he was witty.

'Yes, go undercover, Clydog! Say you want to try the home bonking service!' Hubert was on a roll. 'Demand customer satisfaction!'

The laughter took a while to subside, eventually quieted by the fear that Bryony might come out to investigate. Amidst all the joking the postman felt his revelation had not received the credit it deserved.

'Your editor should employ me,' he told Clydog. 'As gossip columnist. Like that Nigel Dempster.'

'Local people don't want to read tittle-tattle.'

'They want to talk it. And I hear it. At least you'd get some decent stories.'

'That's not journalism. That's muck-raking.'

'I'd have more scoops in a week than your paper has in a year.'

'Like what?'

'You'd need a *nom de plume*, Dafydd,' said Hubert. 'Can't have the mail delivered by a nark.'

'Scoops like what?' insisted Clydog. 'Cars parked in unusual places?'

'Oh, I've got better than that!' said Dafydd, riled by their mockery.

'What, the lady mayor seen belly-dancing in The Bombay Garden?' suggested Hubert. 'Or "Gwillim smiles!"?'

It was Clydog's turn to join in laughter at another's expense. And adding to the merriment, he spluttered, '"Prize pig caught in love triangle"?'

The postman could feel his status was under growing threat.

'No!' he snapped. 'The valley's got nudists!'

Chapter 18

The Highway Code does not have much to say on the subject of cows. Its writers are more exercised by horses, and their need to buy tail lights and not ride two abreast. This emphasis on the safety of horsy people, though commendable, suggests a rather class-based document, in which the needs of cows – an intellectually slower, more downmarket creature – are neglected.

There exists, however, an ancient and somewhat secret law that offers the freedom of the road to the cow. And no rights at all to the motorist.

It was the favourite law of the pub landlord.

Twice a day Gwillim would herd his cows along the lane to their milking parlour, a chore enhanced by the antisocial delight of blocking all traffic. His surly swagger was boosted by his knowledge of this arcane law, whose principle was simple. It stated that the presence of a herdsman conferred immunity on even the most bolshie of his cows. Responsibility for damage to any passing cars – or indeed any politely waiting cars – lay with their drivers.

Threatened with the loss of his lease and his livelihoods, Gwillim had little armoury at his disposal. Had he been more Mediterranean, more swarthy and scarred, he could have initiated a vendetta likely to keep Stéfan's relatives busy for several hundred years. But a wet climate is not conducive to multiple generations of bloodlust. So instead Gwillim brooded, and kept his cows primed.

From his yard he had a clear view of the valley road, a B-minus road for much of its length, as it wound down from the head-waters of the Nant. This vantage-point would, he reckoned, give him some ten minutes' warning of an advancing Stéfan. Not since the Romans held the valley had such an enthusiastic watch for incomers been mounted. But Stéfan was a man of few regular habits except excess, and his long weekends in the valley followed no routine.

It was mid-morning on a Saturday when Gwillim caught a glint of his Jaguar. The cows were already back in their field, so Gwillim had to quickly send in his collies to get them out on to the road again. As the dogs nipped and barked at their heels, Gwillim snarled and whacked at their rumps, using a holly branch to discourage any docility. By the time all fifty beasts cascaded out of the farm gate on their journey to nowhere, the car was just a few hundred yards away.

Stéfan was a Wagner fan. His pleasure came not so much from the music, or the arias, or indeed the story itself, but from the level of noise. Brünnhilde had helped to psyche him up for many a negotiation, adrenalin pumping in the wake of her high Cs. For this, his second journey to The Windowman, he had chosen the Valkyrie – and was giving them full vocal support. Stéfan was off to the mountain kingdom of Mr Griffith Barton with all decibels blazing. . . . But as back-up to Wagner he had brought the last two bottles of vintage champagne from his failed Budget speculation.

He saw the cows as he rounded the long fast curve into the village. He was passing the first tentative stakes for the executive housing development when he noticed the steam from their nostrils, and the pace of their advance. They were ambling with attitude.

Stéfan braked to a halt by the ditch and waited for them to pass. The ditch narrowed the lane at this point, and the car added to the bottleneck. As the cows, caked in mud, struggled to squeeze through, Gwillim kept up the barrage of shouts and urged his dogs to greater yapping. With signs of panic gripping some animals, several tried to mount the beast in front, bellowing loudly. The crush intensified and – to the rousing chorus of the warrior-maidens – a trapped Stéfan watched as his wing mirror snapped off. A number of the cows were in calf and, as they moved, their great bellies swung from side to side with a rhythmic and irresistible force. It was an irresistible force that did not regard the bespoke panelling of a luxury car door as an immovable object. With a series of heavy crunches, nearly half a ton of Welsh beef stove in first the front door and then the back door of Stéfan's Jaguar classic. And then one more time, for the hell of it. As the car rocked, first one bottle of Bollinger fell from the back seat, and then another. The second bottle broke upon the first. From outside the car came the heavy odour of dung, from inside came the light fragrance of bubbly.

And still the Valkyrie sang on.

Stéfan was incandescent and, when the herd had passed, hell-bent on retribution. Unfortunately, he could not open his car door. He began to yell his rage at Gwillim, who was walking blithely by. Unfortunately, he could not open his car window. He crawled across the front seats and opened his passenger door. Unfortunately, it opened on to a ditch. It took several minutes of a muddy struggle before he made it on to the cowpats of the lane.

'Hey!' he yelled after Gwillim. 'Hey!'

Gwillim kept on walking.

'Hey!' Stéfan started running to catch him up. 'Hey!'

Gwillim whistled, an apparently simple whistle. But to the two Welsh sheepdogs, attuned to the subtlest of commands, it meant 'go and bite large lumps out of that unpleasantly rude man behind us'.

Stéfan hesitated, then, faced with the advancing jaws, he turned and began to retreat . . . faster and faster as he realised he could not reach safety through his offside doors.

'See you're getting used to the countryside then,' said Mr Griffith Barton. 'Not nearly so smartly dressed any more.'

Stéfan looked down ruefully at his muddied trousers, the cowshit on his shoes, and the soaking left arm of his jacket, still rank from where he had tumbled into the ditch. He did not attempt to explain.

He held up the one remaining bottle of champagne.

'You've cut your fingers.'

Again he offered no explanation. 'Drink?'

The Windowman looked doubtful, as doubtful as a householder faced with Mormons. He showed little sign of asking him into his lean-to. 'Why, what are you celebrating?'

'Oh, end of another month. Time to wet the project's head.'

'Bollocks!' he said, then turned. 'I'll get a bandage.'

Stéfan followed him in, and he disappeared.

The kitchen was as Stéfan remembered it, except the piles of papers and unopened post seemed that little bit higher. The partly finished breezeblock wall remained partly finished. The lounge was still in semi-darkness. And as before the latest *FT* lay open on the table, grist to The Windowman's dystopia.

Stéfan rinsed the dried blood off his fingers, and watched the pink-tinged water eddy out of sight down the crockery graveyard in the sink.

'You annoy the fuck out of someone else, then?' The Windowman handed him a small air-sealed tin of Band-Aids.

Stéfan thought of being wittily offhand, and saying 'cow rage', but felt even that reflected badly on him and so he ignored the enquiry.

'I suppose champagne glasses would be out of the question?'

The Windowman hesitated, then disappeared again, returning with a pair of engraved antique flutes. He watched, stern-faced, as Stéfan opened the highly excitable Bollinger and poured him a very generous measure.

'We're not bonding, you know,' he warned Stéfan sharply, lest gratitude be inferred.

'Of course not. It's just a gesture.'

'A gesture? A gesture of what?'

'To show I'm a serious client.'

'One tax-deductible bottle of posh plonk does that?'

'How do other clients show appreciation?'

'They bugger off.'

Nonetheless, he emptied his glass, and allowed it to be refilled. A bloodied, mud-covered Stéfan was a not unsatisfying sight.

Silence settled, a silence that Stéfan would normally have colonised. But he felt low on brio, and anger kept taking his mind elsewhere. Yet he knew he needed to do the empathy thing. He had brushed up on the Hapsburgs (thanks to 2.5 yards of *Encyclopaedia Britannica*, bulk-bought to bring cultural credibility to his study), but dead people were not really his bag. And besides, he occasionally suspected himself to have been the butt of some private Hapsburgian joke.

His gaze drifted round the room's bric-à-brac in search of conversational leverage.

'Bullet holes.'

'Sorry?' said Stéfan.

'They're bullet holes.'

'What are?'

'There. Where you're looking.' The Windowman pointed to the lintel above the would-be doorway. 'Straight through the window, into the wall! Bam-bam-bam!'

'Bullet holes?' repeated Stéfan.

'Made four weeks ago.'

'They're fresh?'

As on his previous visit, the agenda was moving away from him.

Trying to conceal his doubts, Stéfan inspected the lintel. But, yes, there were holes, round holes, of what he assumed to be bullet size, and, yes, they did seem recent. He did not know what to make of this. He remembered how last time their talk had quickly turned to the violence of the world. And once again his host was dressed in military camouflage.

Stéfan looked from the wall to The Windowman, those early

177

worries about his state of mind starting to re-emerge. 'You have a gun then?'

'What? No! That's not *my* doing! *I* don't have a gun.' He spoke as if to a child.

'Oh . . . But I thought . . .' Stéfan gave up on what he thought. 'Well, so how . . . ?'

'The house was attacked. In the middle of the night.'

'What, by a dissatisfied customer?'

'No!' But The Windowman allowed himself a grin at the thought. 'No, by the army.'

'The army? Your house was attacked by the *army*? Why, had you declared war?'

Then Stéfan wondered whether it was wise to joke.

He had begun to worry whether he was in danger. No one knew he was here, he was miles from any other habitation, and The Windowman was all muscle. The extreme isolation, the anti-social behaviour, the obsessions, all was now forming a familiar profile. Stéfan already wished he'd followed Plan B today, and rung the woman from the hunt for a shag.

'The attack seems to have been a mistake. The army has apologised.' The Windowman's face had a tight smirk of triumph. 'A man with lots of stripes has been up and said sorry.'

'I don't understand. Why would the army attack your house?' Stéfan baulked at calling his future window maker a liar. Or indeed a delusional paranoid.

'SAS actually. Misread their map references. Good job we're on a bloody island! They could start a damned war with that sort of mistake!' He stretched for the last of the champagne.

'Crack soldiers misread their map references?'

'So they said. Thought this place was some target on the range. Said it looked abandoned, for God's sake!'

'The cheek! So, er, what happened to all these highly trained soldiers running amok?'

'The goat got them.'

'No, I meant—' He stopped. 'The goat got them?'

'One horn can come in very handy. Straight up the arse.'

Stéfan searched for a twinkle, a hint of a tease. He found nothing. This was not delusional. He was being made a fool of. For the second time in one morning. He geared up for some straight talking.

'And I got to keep a souvenir.' The Windowman stretched over and tossed Stéfan a snuffbox. It was full of used bullets. Wrapped in an official letter of apology from the Ministry of Defence. Stéfan abandoned the plan for straight talking.

'Biscuit?' The Windowman held out some Hobnobs.

'Please.' Enormously relieved, Stéfan suddenly felt ravenous. The events of the day had done something funny to his stomach.

They munched for a while in silence. Stéfan watched as the other man dipped his biscuits in the vintage champagne, and questioned whether he could have got away with a Reisling. After all, even dinner at the Ritz would not, he now felt, have advanced the business in hand – which so far had not been mentioned once. He had The Windowman's forbearance for just so long as he did not say the word windows.

'So . . . it's not been dull then. Anything else happened?'

'Since you last bothered me?'

Stéfan did not respond.

'They published a letter. Did you see it?' He nodded towards the mound of back *FT* issues.

'No. No, not my paper.'

'Cut it, of course. Cut the reference to the IMF as Vikings.' He rubbed at the stubble on his chin, sighing angrily. 'Sanitised, everyone wants things sanitised these days. Did you know you can get plastic goat horns now?'

'D'you send many letters?'

'Depends. If I'm angry. But send too many and they have you down as a crank.'

Stéfan saw the chance for bonding, and went for it. 'Think that's how they see me down here. A troublemaker. A maverick. Someone who speaks his mind.'

The Windowman ignored him. '*And* I got my views printed on corporate fascism. The State as a bloody pawn. That got up a few important noses! Right up!' He paused. 'So I don't think it was a mistake.' And he looked Stéfan straight in the eyes as he emphasised these last few words.

'What wasn't a mistake?'

'To attack the house.' The Windowman rattled the bullets. 'I think it was deliberate.'

Stéfan felt his heart sink.

'I think it was a warning.'

Chapter 19

'Sky?'

'Yes.'

'It doesn't look like sky.'

'It's a stylised sky.'

'Oh . . .' The old lady continued to gently fold her underwear, feeling for damp. 'What's a stylised sky?'

'It's . . . it's a sky done in a certain style. This is done in a sort of Japanese style.'

'Why?'

'Because I—'

'Are you Japanese?'

'No,' said Rob.

The old lady stared again at the picture, spinning the drum to check no garments had clung to its sides.

'My husband and I, we like Welsh skies. D'you do Welsh skies?'

'That's my interpretation of a Welsh sky.'

'He was in the war. They did terrible things to their prisoners, in those camps.'

Rob's hunch said he hadn't got a buyer. As she zipped up her laundry bag, he dropped lightly down from the spin dryer on which he was perched. Holding open the launderette door, he smiled politely at her as she left.

The exhibition was on its tenth and final day. There was not a red dot in sight. Ellie, who did the service washes in the morning, said his clouds reminded her of people's laundry swirling round and round behind the glass. She was not a buyer either.

At the age of eight Rob had declared – according to his mother – that when he grew up he was going to live in the country, and be a painter. He had no memory of saying this, nor could he even remember thinking it. Only when he announced that he had bought a hovel in the hills did she tell him it was his lifelong ambition. He did not demur for he was more than ready to leave the city. In recent years the lure of landscape art and alfresco sex had conjured up a catalogue of potent images in Rob's mind. And the chance to turn a sporadically profitable hobby into a proper living had become irresistible.

His earliest oeuvre, at age eleven, had been a dinosaur – bendy wire spine and papier mâché. It became extinct after three minutes. A design error caused its stomach to rest on the ground. This made it easy prey for the pterodactyls in the class. But his art teacher, a flamboyant man whose enthusiasm for matters retro unwisely included a handlebar moustache, had seen faint signs of promise. And had diverted him from the clutches of metalwork.

He progressed to Indian ink. His subject of choice was oak trees (winter). Not oak trees as in real life, twisting and gnarled, but symbolic oak trees – round, symmetrical and bifurcating. He was much taken by the starkness of black on white, by the simplicity of trunks that split into branches, then into branchlets, then into twigs, then into twiglets. The art hour saw him working away on bold black lines that methodically, inexorably diminished into filigree silhouette. It was an unreasonable perfectionism: in end-of-term exhibitions his work was often entered as 'Tree, Unfinished', with one side absent, as if the victim of lightning.

One tree led to another. There was a brief cypress period. And a bit of toying with bamboo. The introduction of wind was a major advance. It was the first sign of nature, and some of his trees began to lean. Leaves, though, rarely made an appearance. In his universe, it was forever winter (or possibly summer full of dead trees). But gradually the idea of trees *in situ* gained hold and he took to visiting parks.

The actual history of art never bothered him unduly. His list of influences was decidedly short. At the suggestion of Mr Moustache he had once gone on a school trip to Florence and the Uffizi, but the fun of table football in back-street cafés won out over the line drawings of Leonardo. Rob's later work showed little sign of the Renaissance.

Jane was his main influence, providing moral support and framing. She did, though, stamp hard on his sentimental dreams of garret life, always arguing that death in poverty, no matter how artistic, was an end best left to biopics. It had been her idea to exhibit now, and not wait until such time as the defunct abattoir received arts funding. The actual display also owed much to her eye, for she had once worked in PR (before majoring in acupuncture) and so knew about presentation. Nonetheless, both agreed that washing machines did not adequately contextualise his work.

Rob was on the hard news section of the *Mid-Walian*, reading the court reports of the meter unrest, when the launderette door opened again.

'D'you reckon you can get the stains off this jacket?'

Rob did not need to look up. Nor did he smile. 'Have you tried a blowtorch?' he said with feeling.

'OK, OK!' Nico eased off on the jokes. 'It'll be gone by next week. I promise. Landed gentry chap wants a birthday present for his son – kid called Trefor – mad keen on old tractors.'

Rob lowered the paper. 'Any relation of the pensioner who was nostalgic for farming in the Fifties? The sure-fire cash buyer?'

Nico gave a shrug, unabashed. 'It's a volatile market.' He turned his attention to the paintings and walked very slowly up and down the launderette, focusing with the screwed-up eyes of a connoisseur. Sion followed two paces behind, with the blank look of a philistine. Rob went back to his paper.

The Sixties launderette had a disorienting air. Its colour and smells and shabbiness had an urban anonymity that could have been Abernant or Manchester, or anywhere. And, after ten dull days, Rob found the background noise of endlessly churning clothes had come to resemble the ambient sounds of deepest space. The place made his mind feel numb, as if he too were living in a sealed tub.

'Don't they do the red dots any more?'

Rob allowed several calming seconds to pass. 'Your point?'

'I'd have thought it was fucking obvious.'

'It's not exactly an ideal venue.'

'Oh, I don't know. At least people *have* to sit here and look at the pictures.'

'If they can't afford a Hotpoint, they can hardly afford a painting.'

'And the rest? The punters? You seen the comments in the Visitors Book?'

'No.'

'Bollocks! Course you have.'

Of course he had. But denial went deep.

'Want some advice?'

'From you?' Rob did not try to hide his disdain.

'I know about art.' Disdain was an oddly ineffective weapon against Nico. His skin had grown thick in response to a lifetime's disdain. Even so, it was still hard to say whether the barbs entered the bloodstream or just bounced off him. 'And I know what people want round here.'

'And what do people want?' The question was dipped in sarcasm, but did not quite conceal a desire to know. ' "Round here?" '

Nico pulled himself up on to the dryer opposite. Sion leant silently against the soap powder machine.

'I've been twenty years in the antiques business. I go round

184

people's homes. I see what they buy. What they put on their walls and their sideboards. What plates they collect. The mugs, the jugs, the bowls, the knick-knacks. So I know their tastes, the designs they like, the patterns they choose. The pictures they want.' Nico glanced dismissively at the pictures facing him. 'I know what will sell.'

'Oh really?'

Nico nodded, displaying that cockiness which had driven Stéfan out of Sotheby's marquee and into the storm. 'Yep!'

'And . . .' Rob tried to smile patronisingly, 'what would this magic formula be?'

'Farmyard scenes.'

Rob's disdain was muted by a sudden memory of Clydog's response to his work, and he didn't immediately reply.

'No farmers. Just livestock. Well-fed pigs, and cows, and chickens and things. Bit like the Ark – but on land. And farm animals only.'

'Oh, right! All smiling and waving, I suppose,' said Rob. 'Anything else?'

'The animals have to be big. Definitely big. Bugger perspective!'

'Oh that should make it easier.'

'It's what I call the school of Animal Realism,' said Nico.

'It's what I call kitsch,' said Rob, drawing a line under the discussion. He was about to drop emphatically down to the floor when he realised that, being in charge of the exhibition, he could not exit, and would be obliged to wander vaguely about.

'Really? You think it's kitsch?' said Nico.

'A cross between kitsch and crap.'

'Oh. I think of it as more in the tradition of Rousseau.'

Rousseau? Where the hell did Rousseau come from? Rob tried to stay ahead. 'Didn't think Jean-Jacques had much to say of relevance to animals.'

'Not the philosopher Rousseau! The painter Rousseau.'

'Oh.'

'Pierre-Étienne-Théodore Rousseau? 1812 to 1867?' The pleasure in Nico's voice was palpable.

'Oh, Théodore!' said Rob unconvincingly.

'Yes, the Barbizon school? Of landscape painting?' Nico's teeth were not to be that easily prised off Rob's metaphorical leg. 'Man who did the big tigers . . . ?'

'Yes, yes.' He had not got the reference but the prompt really bugged him. 'It's on an Athena poster.'

'I wouldn't know about posters,' said Nico with a straight face.

'Did big stripy tigers. In a bright green jungle. Like cardboard cutouts.'

'That's the one, you've got it. Still going strong, that picture. Very popular. Now, forget the tigers, forget the jungle. But hang on to the idea of cardboard cutouts.'

'What, of livestock?'

'Yes, standing in front of barns.'

'This is your idea of a rural scene?'

'The punters' idea.'

'And who on Earth are the punters who'd buy paintings of . . . outsize, one-dimensional farmyard animals?'

'Farmers.'

Rob did not know it, but Nico had long believed there to be a gap in the farmyard animal sector of the art world. Domestic animals were well catered for, being smaller and often coming with their own cushion. But bigger beasts could be stroppy and muddy, and unwilling to hold the same position for hours. Nonetheless, they were much loved by their owners, who were often sentimental and easily parted from their money.

'But it's not just the paintings,' continued Nico. 'It's the merchandising.'

'What merchandising?'

'Donald Duck isn't just a cartoon character,' he replied. 'You paint Ferdie the Bull right and you'll have an icon. Probably a tea-towel as well. And a coaster.'

'Is that in the Rousseau tradition and all?'

'Every artist belongs to his time.'

'This isn't art, it's business.'

'This is art that makes money. Art with hundreds of red dots.'

It was a nasty thrust, and Rob shifted uneasily on his dryer.

'Women like red dots,' said Nico softly.

'And I like painting sky and trees.'

'Lovely hobby.'

'I don't know the first thing about farmyard animals. I certainly wouldn't know how to "merchandise" them.'

'That's why you need an agent.'

Chapter 20

'Thigh bone,' said the Commodore.

Startled to see him materialise by the yew tree, Gareth twitched upright in a feudal reflex, abandoning his rest against the gravestone. His mind was elsewhere, wondering whether a hobby would make him more interesting. It was not far short of dusk, and he'd thought that he and his sheep had the churchyard to themselves.

The Speckled Beulahs had been nibbling round the graves, enjoying a softer grass than covered the hilltops, since soon after matins; with night coming on they were quietly setting up camp beside the lychgate and the giant thermometer saying £18,000. Not even the errant chimes of the church clock disturbed the animals' Zen-like calm, and the need for his shepherding skills appeared distinctly less urgent than he had led Moira to believe.

'Last time it was a shin bone.' The Commodore gave a rare crinkle of a smile.

Rupert had now slavered into view, and was bearing the bone in question. He dropped it on Gareth's wellington boots, and then lay down, his ancient labrador instincts no longer certain what happened next.

The two men suffered a similar uncertainty, and stood like ill-made statues while the darkening air filled with the cries of the rooks above.

Gareth knew his duty was courteous deference but his

thoughts were elsewhere, for his unease about his wife's legs had spread to other parts of her body, like her brain. The Commodore found it equally hard to focus on cemetery protocol, for his thoughts were on the dinner party that he had escaped from. Yet he also felt obliged to grant the farmer a few moments of his presence, in unspoken acknowledgement of the sheep, so kindly offered in St Brynnach's hour of need.

(The surveyor's insistence on ever more excavations had caused access problems for the mower, and this required a fresh approach to the Tidy Churchyard Scheme, where rampant grass always lost points. The community council had voted eight to one in the sheep's favour, the dissenting voice being the church-warden, Mr Lugley, who stood to lose £15 a fortnight from his mowing stipend. This failure to think flexibly was to cost him dear at the next parish elections.)

Gareth flicked the sticky and unexpectedly heavy bone off his feet, back to Rupert. He wondered about evening classes, but had heard the choices were usually martial arts or dried-flower arrangements, neither of them an obvious way to create an improved bond with Moira.

'That's why he always likes his number ones. Usually finds something,' said the Commodore.

Lately she had started humming to herself, in a happy sort of way and for no apparent reason. This puzzled him. He had little experience of sustained smiling. He was of course glad to see her happy, since her enthusiasm for the vegetable garden had been waning and for a while she'd seemed bored. None-theless, he felt excluded. Humming was not an activity for couples.

'It's male,' said the Commodore.

She also read books. Gareth did not object in principle, but found this strange after he'd been to the trouble of renting a 24-inch television. Apparently, the Irish were the most well-read people in Europe. She had not taken kindly to his surprise at this fact. She had recently even gone as far as joining the library, and was often out hours choosing just the right book. Occasionally, he wondered if he would enjoy books.

'It's a Llewellyn, you know,' said the Commodore.

Gareth took comfort from the fact that the Commodore did not expect two-way conversations. Even the old boy's sister, blessed with the OBE, had been heard admitting that her brother sometimes made little sense. But then a parallel emerged from the muddle of Gareth's thoughts, and he realised how few two-way conversations there were in his marriage. Lately there was even a shortage of one-way conversations. Cul-de-sac conversations! He warmed to this use of traffic language. But then he tried to extend such analysis of his relationship to roundabouts and indicators, and realised he had stumbled into an intellectual minefield.

'He got a whole hand once.'

Rupert put the bone back on Gareth's boots.

'A hand?' said Gareth, the Commodore's words finally breaking through. 'A human hand?'

'Of course all the rings had gone. Looted years ago.'

Gareth looked down at the dog's bone resting on his boots, and hurriedly kicked it away into a trench.

As if in answer to a question, the Commodore pointed through the fading light to the rusting, broken railings of the Llewellyn's Victorian vault. Inside, broken and upturned slabs, their inscriptions mossed beyond recognition, lay in a giant jumble.

'Dozens of the buggers!' he cried delightedly. For a moment, he became almost animated at the idea of his ancestral rivals being dispersed so liberally around the churchyard. 'Go, boy! Fetch!' He urged Rupert on towards the vault, and slowly, arthritically, the old dog set off to cannibalise some more Llewellyns.

'Does the vicar . . . ?' But some sixth sense of discretion left the enquiry hanging in the air.

The Commodore gestured to Gareth to accompany him, and the pair followed the retired gun dog across the neatly nibbled grass.

The mysterious supply of bones had begun some months earlier, when the Commodore had been avoiding a New Year's Eve Masked Ball in aid of a charity for dry-stone walls. Unable to bear the thought of hours of unbroken bonhomie, he had slipped away with the dog and a bottle of Pimm's and seen out the old year on a gravestone. Amidst all that night's number ones, Rupert had, with much snuffling, managed to assemble sufficient skeletal remains for a modest crime scene.

The two men peered down into the murk, where the ivy fought for survival with the bramble.

'My sister says they were parvenus,' sniffed the Commodore. Only to slightly weaken his position by adding, 'Sixteenth-century parvenus.'

There was little obvious sign of recent desecration. The stone memorial obelisk had some carved initials of lovers, most of them ancient enough to also now be bones, but the damage of the looting seemed to belong to an earlier era. From a time, perhaps, when Llewellyns had been buried with undue ostentation, flaunting their deaths in the face of their neighbours.

What was new, though, was a collapse in the side wall, some ten feet down. The earth had tumbled away, and taken with it several rotting coffins and their contents. The once whole occupants had burst through the wet blackened wood and come to a new last resting-place, but in a more informal arrangement of bones. It was from this *ad hoc* charnel house that Rupert was obtaining the regular supply of marrow that now helped sustain his own final years.

'Doggie heaven!' said the Commodore, who also seemed revivified.

Gareth, the more fleet of the two, made his way along the railings and found a fissure in the earth. It led towards the river end of the church.

As he came round the back of St Brynnach's, the cause was immediately apparent. Euan, the indefatigable diocesan surveyor and closet atheist, was now taking his inspiration from the

Somme. In his search for bedrock, he had left no mud unturned. Out of sight from the road, his zeal to underpin the declining church had created a battlefield, zigzagged by trenches that could have hidden a tank company.

Chapter 21

'Oh don't lie down! Please! Get up! I want you to look at me!'

Rob's entreaties had little effect, for she was sulking. His emollient tones had failed to move her; his physical caresses had been ignored by her; she had even refused to acknowledge his offer of potato peelings. Tinkerbell was not a happy pig.

It was the dog collar she had taken exception to. And the dog lead that attached her to the gate post. Like any sensitive domestic pig, Tinkerbell liked to have a positive self-image: she saw herself as a born-free pig, with roaming in her blood. The idea of portraiture did not come easy.

Rob had been inking her in since dawn. He had left her snout till last, for it had a quizzical quality, a porcine ambiguity, that he found difficult to capture. Doing the body itself had been a doddle, for the Vietnamese pot-bellied pig is a creature of simple, if eccentric, layout – albeit in the queerest of colour schemes. With every inch of the beast being black – like nature's idea of a Model-T Ford – its oddball looks seem more fitting for a fairy tale than a farmyard.

Tinkerbell herself was still a juvenile, her belly almost spherical. To see her whizz around the garden was to watch a cannonball with legs. Prodding her drum of a stomach added weight to such imagery, for her rind had no more give than a boxer's diaphragm. But unlike most cannonballs she had the soft baby bristles of a nascent Desperate Dan. And as Rob's thick nib filled out her bulk and gave her character, his mind filled with yet another image. He kept seeing her as a barrage balloon, tethered in the sky above the barn. For Tinkerbell had a nimbleness that made her seem weightless, that made one believe pigs really could fly.

The Indian ink, that once laboured over bifurcating oaks, now spread like a giant blot across the cartridge paper. As a primer in animal portraits, as a precursor to posing a hot-blooded bull, Tinkerbell was the perfect candidate for Rob.

Then, as he struggled to realign her snout, she suddenly nuzzled him with the sort of sloppy, slimy kiss that set her apart from your normal life models.

'Sorry, am I interrupting something?' said the postman, appearing at the gate.

Distracted by art, Rob had for once not heard the hyperactive engine of the mail van, revved into the red as it struggled up the last few yards of sodden track.

'No, just creativity,' replied Rob with a grin, pushing himself back on to his feet.

Dafydd looked at the work-in-progress on the easel, cocking his head slightly to one side, in that manner which laypersons believe appropriate to artistic appreciation. 'So it's true then?'

'What's true?'

'You doing animals.'

'Who told you that?'

'Mrs Whitelaw.'

'Who's Mrs Whitelaw?'

'Buff Orpington eggs?' This detail did not aid Rob's understanding. 'Now her hens would look good, all lined up outside her caravan.'

'Oh well, I suppose I should be grateful for the way news travels.'

If Rob was philosophical about abandoning his ambitions as an artist, it was because he was essentially a romantic. He was in love with the romance of being a painter, with the romance of the painterly life. He had no artistic demons driving him, no inner urges dictating what he put on canvas. What he liked was the lifestyle, the image and the aura of the artist. If surviving in the valley meant a bit of Animal Realism, then Animal Realism it would be.

'Of course, black isn't a very popular colour,' commented the postman, his head now at a new angle.

'Is that so?' said Rob crisply. Despite his art having no inner urges, there were limits to criticism.

'Farmers are very particular in this valley.'

'I might have guessed.'

'They like their pigs to be pink.'

'And on a plate,' said Rob. 'Never mind. I'll give her some red spots. Call it "Pig with Measles". A postmodern pig.'

'Should be a queue for that!'

'Well, it's only a try-out, this one, anyway. 'S not for sale.'

'Oh, right! Looks good, though,' said the postman, back-tracking. 'Very . . . er, piglike.'

'Thank you.'

Daffyd felt the need for safer ground and turned his attention to the mail. He held out a brown foolscap envelope. 'So who d'you know in Aberystwyth, then?'

'Aberystwyth?' Rob shared his puzzlement. 'No one.' He shook the envelope, felt its weight. 'Bumf, I think.' He slid his finger into an unstuck corner and ripped the envelope open, leaving a jagged, black-smudged tear.

Inside the envelope were several Photostatted sheets, with pictures of a wind-pump from sexy angles. The address meant nothing. And then he remembered Nico. Who had said he knew a man who knew a man who . . . Rob instinctively turned away to read the pages, aware his putative pump was source of much mockery.

'Can I do a bit?'

Rob looked round at the postman, unsure what he meant.

'Black the rest of your pig in. I used to like art at school.'

'If you want.' The postman reached for the ink. 'The arse is a bit patchy. And you can fill in a leg.'

'Right.'

Rob looked more closely at the photos, and at the diagrams of blades and bolts, and at the accompanying graphs and arrows and numbers. Rob was not a natural technician, and as he skimmed across the tech specs he sensed confirmation that this was not a DIY project. He could only 'sense' it because he could not actually read the text. The text was in a language unknown to him. He assumed it was Welsh, but it was short on double 'l's and did not look very lyrical.

Reluctantly, Rob turned to the postman, who was inking away with vigour, and showed him a section of the text.

'Can you translate that, Dafydd? Is it Welsh?'

Dafydd peered at the paper for several minutes, then admitted defeat. 'Don't know what it is. Looks a bit like German, but it's not. What's it on about?'

'Wind-pumps.'

'Wind-pumps?'

But before either could say more, Gareth had squelched into the farmyard.

This was unusual. A distant wave of the shotgun was the usual limit of his sociability. His daily check on his sheep was done with eyes well averted from humans. Rob had once joined him in celebrating – if celebrating be the *mot juste* for sharing a thermos of day-old Bovril – the rather messy birth of lamb triplets. But even then few words had been exchanged. Jane's theory was that Gareth wanted to talk – or at least his subconscious was keen to – but he didn't know the rules of conversation.

'Got any mail for me?'

A plausible question, but a pretext. An evening in the company of corpses had left even him feeling the need of a few convivial grunts. He had observed Rob from a distance, but didn't know what to say to a man who kept a pig on a lead. Then, when at the far end of the field, he had heard the van. After a lifetime of post he felt comfortable with Dafydd.

Yet a secret part of him wanted to talk to Rob. Especially as he knew Jane was out. He had seen how they were when together, how they touched and played the fool. And it gave him pain, an emotional ache he could not articulate. It was their laughter that most upset him, the sound of merriment wafting through the morning mist as he checked for sheep pox. He longed to know the key to such levity, to know how that pleasure could be his.

'What d'you reckon?' said Dafydd, stepping back from the almost completed pig.

Gareth moved closer and stared hard at the picture. And then thought and stared some more. 'Could do with a bit of tractor behind it.'

'Right,' said Rob.

'And a sheep would look better.'

'Right,' said Rob.

'And maybe some rain.'

'Rob's branching out,' said Dafydd. 'Farm animals.'

'I know,' replied Gareth. He wondered whether telling Moira about the postman helping paint the pig would make her laugh.

'Oh,' said Dafydd, slightly deflated by his answer. 'Did you know about the Dragon's Head?' he asked, by way of revenge. 'That odd bloke's trying to buy it.'

'*Bought* it!'

'Bought it?'

'Had surveyors in. They told him it'd got dry rot. He told them to sod off. And he bought it anyway.'

Gareth mulled over the news. He'd lived through some changes in his lifetime, but this was one of the biggest. 'D'you reckon he'll allow a dartboard?'

'Topless barmaids, I've heard.'

Gareth failed to spot a wind-up, and his heart raced disconcertingly fast for several moments. But then Dafydd reluctantly admitted he had no details; and the pair fell to speculating about themed Irish pubs and fruit machines. It was broadly agreed that a bar with more than one brand of beer – and probably still on sale after children's bedtime – would be an improvement. As would service without abuse. As would crisps. Even plain. And yet somehow Gareth could not shake off a lingering melancholy. It was as if a stranger had bought his living room.

Meanwhile, Rob's mind had drifted off the conversation and was on its way to Aberystwyth. In his dreams he was already an eco-pioneer, and fit subject for another Clydog profile. He was eager to tell his news to Jane, but her acupuncture exams were coming and she was down at the old schoolhouse practising on Bryony. He was also eager to hear Jane's news, for she had plans to see if Bryony wished to take friendship to a more intimate level than just oils and needles.

The friendship had begun with a shared interest in organic vegetables; during the early days of the vegetable patch, when the hoe kept hitting the leftovers of the lounge, Hubert's delicatessen had been the sole source of life's rarer vitamins. The pair had first met her on the day of the Mayoral Cash Point Opening, when Bryony had advised against the shop's nuts – for some reason they were warm to the touch – and this radical approach to shopkeeping had created a political empathy. (On later visits, Bryony would sometimes ignore Hubert's pricing regime and behave as if trained by KwikSave.) Some days they would see her on the road and give her a lift home, where she would entertain them with the follies of the valley, and occasionally a folksong. Bryony was outside the mainstream, in a sweet-natured if wild-child way, and this was unusual in the land of the Nant. Both Rob and Jane found much to their liking in her freewheeling approach, her eco-friendly habits, her warm-hearted nature. And her lightly concealed breasts.

'I said what d'you reckon, Rob?' repeated the postman.

'Sorry. Reckon to what?'

'I've heard there might be call for some sort of artwork down the new pub. You be interested?'

'Artwork?' Rob laughed. 'They'll have to speak to my agent!'

Dafydd laughed as well, aware the answer was yes. He put the round, dip-pen nib back on the easel, and ruffled Tinkerbell's pliant ears. He felt pleased with himself, and wondered if there was a value to be put on his networking skills. As he nodded farewell he even forgot to ask, as he always mockingly asked, how long before Rob and Jane could afford to repair their track. And with the wheelspin of a rally driver he was gone.

'Can you give one as a present?'

Rob was caught unawares and he looked blankly at the farmer.

'Can you give one as a present? A painting?' Gareth asked again.

'Of course you can,' said Rob, baffled by the question.

'It wouldn't be odd?'

'It wouldn't be odd at all. It would be a nice thing to do.'

'Right. I just wondered.'

And with that, Gareth too was off down the field.

Gareth and Dafydd were barely out of sight, and Rob was still trying to align Tinkerbell's snout, when Jane returned up the hill. Pleased to be alone for her return, Rob gave her a big hug and swung her in the air, holding the letter aloft in his hand.

And yet they were not alone for her return. Glyn, as always, had secretly noted her pass through the bottom gate, and he was watching, hidden, in the trees beyond the gully.

'Got some great news,' cried Rob. 'I've hunted down a wind-pump!'

Jane smiled at him, feigning composure to hide her heady excitement.

'I've got some news too,' she said, pressing her hand hard against his groin. 'I think she's up for it.'

Chapter 22

'Wildebeest?' said Hubert incredulously.

Stéfan sighed, trying to hide his exasperation. 'That was just a for instance,' he said, irritated at the man's failure to grasp the bigger picture. 'It could be, I don't know, water buffalo, or bison, or gazelles.'

The President of the Chamber of Commerce toyed with his pipe, avoiding Stéfan's eyes. 'We don't get a lot of demand for water buffalo.'

'You don't get a lot of supply either. That's my point.'

He was making little headway. Even the delicatessen, which had led the county in aubergine, struggled to cater for Stéfan's vaulting ambitions. His latest idea, for a game park and abattoir in his grounds, was everywhere running into the swamp of small minds.

Where Rob blew with the wind, and adapted to the valley in the hope he might survive, Stéfan blew back at the wind, and strove to bend the valley to his will. This was the age-old choice of strategies for incomers, as ever lured on by the chimera of social acceptance. But in the Nant Valley the only true path to acceptance was to be fourth generation. And Stéfan had scarcely patience to be first generation.

So far he had a pub with dry rot and no beer, and a large collection of scaffolding poles with a house attached. He had decided to open a third front, and it was wildebeest. Or water buffalo. Or whatever. The estate had for some time been a thornbush in his side. As planned, he had enhanced his land-owner's status with a pair of Rhodesian ridgebacks – but in the absence of local lions they had twice breakfasted on sheep and cows, and a magistrate had judged this unneighbourly. His plan for fifteen marble deities had also hit the buffers: the quote required the profligacy of ancient Rome, prohibitive even if he had forsaken the 38DD version and gone for smaller-busted deities. And, albeit on a less grand scale, the floodlighting of scaffolding seemed an ill-advised vanity.

For a while, his fickle attention span had alighted on rare breeds. They had a recherché status, and it was rumoured that royals – no doubt a distant cousin – were sympathetic to their cause. But Stéfan could never quite grasp the point of rare breeds, nor see the need for endless minor variants on goats and sheep and pigs. Apart from some quirks of nature, like a kink in the tail or a toe too many, they all looked the same – and equally dull – as their more successful counterparts. He was all in favour of speeding their way to extinction.

It was the Pick Your Own fields of strawberries – in more enterprising England – that had given him the idea for a game park. Initially, the concept was Longleat with a difference – various exotic animals roaming his swards, and large placards by the roadside saying Shoot Your Own, with family barbecue sites in a compound. Petty legal minds had sabotaged this idea and now he was exploring more practical options.

'Don't get a lot of supply? I should bloody hope not!' snorted Hubert in response. 'I've not got much room for water buffalo! Would they be sliced ready for sandwiches?'

'You slice venison for sandwiches,' Stéfan replied, skewering his objection. 'What's the difference?'

'Have you researched the water-buffalo market?'

'Look, forget water buffalo. That's just a for instance—'

'Another one?'

'I'm talking exotic meats. The top end of the market. Eating like you're on safari.'

'But my customers aren't top end of the market,' retorted Hubert. 'It took three years to interest them in pepperoni.' He grimaced. 'Several thought it was a large worm.'

'That's just a question of marketing.'

'And how are you going to market wildebeest? Get David Attenborough behind the counter?'

Stéfan was a broad-brushstrokes man and offered no view on the subject.

The agent provocateur surfaced in Hubert. 'Now if it came with mint sauce . . .'

Which is just how Mrs Grotichley would serve it up, thought Stéfan, beginning to weary of the conversation. His vision had not carried. He needed firmer, more detailed proposals, maybe a visit to the zoo. The basic idea was sound, of that he was sure. Ever since childhood he had thought there were not enough big things in the countryside.

The irony of the exchanges was that Hubert too viewed himself as an adventurous entrepreneur, forever pushing back the boundaries of the Abernantian palate. A proto-Stéfan. And in truth Hubert rather took to Stéfan, whom, until an hour before, he had only known as a customer, if a rather noisy one, and the only one ever to have bulk-bought his quails' eggs. For where Hubert liked to wield a nonconformist stiletto, Stéfan laid about him with a nonconformist cudgel. Hubert was tempted to ask if he felt strongly about the proposed car-parking charges, since volunteers were needed for the next round of direct action.

Instead, having deftly derailed the plan to bring the veldt to the valley, he said, 'Have you thought about olives?'

Stéfan, who had a sexually active afternoon ahead of him, and was eager to leave Hubert's smoky backroom office, sank down again in his chair, unable to hide his surprise. 'Olives?' he repeated.

Hubert smiled, as befitted a man blessed with the trump card of a special discount.

'You could still make history,' he said. 'First pub in the area with olives.'

It was raining heavily when Stéfan arrived at the pub – now his pub – for the second of his three appointments that day. The watery mud that swirled down the road from the farmyard lay dammed and ankle-deep outside the door, a token of Gwillim's response to his terms of notice. The 200-year-old pub was locked and in gloom, almost as if pining for trade. Sheltering in its tiny porch was Rob.

Rob and Stéfan had never quite met. Stéfan had once forced his car off the road when on the way to The Windowman. Rob had once seen him weighed down with charity sponge cakes at the Commodore's. And the postman had kept each abreast of the other's odder doings. It was not a perfect basis for friendship.

'Fucking weather!' said Stéfan, shoulder-charging the jammed door after finally getting the key to turn.

Inside, the flagstones gave off damp and the air smelt unhealthy. Stéfan switched the lights on at the fuse box. The Formica tops were still stained with slops. Behind the bar, the few crates were full of empties; the only sign of alcoholic life was three elderly bottles of tonic in the fridge, probable result of some long-forgotten error in ordering.

'All going to be gutted!' said Stéfan. 'With sensitivity.'

Rob had not been inside since he and Jane had failed to order pasta, on their very first day in the valley. He looked around at the brown, smoke-stained walls, only now aware of the dismal decay of the place.

'Secret ambition, was it? Own a pub?'

'No, bought it because I like a drink. And if I own it, I can't be thrown out of it.'

'Can't fault that logic,' said Rob. 'Perhaps I should buy one.'

Their voices echoed as the dominoes once had.

'Going to have a restaurant. Pub and restaurant. Something a bit special.'

Rob looked around the walls a second time. A few uplighters in the alcoves, and his stylised nimbuses and windswept hills would look almost homely.

'Teg and Ben with ties, eh? That'll be worth seeing.'

'Yeah, well, I'll have to hide the locals. Extend the snug into the farmyard.' He laughed. 'Or encourage them to go and drink somewhere else! Up on the moors!'

Rob glanced across at Stéfan as he boomed with laughter, only to realise he was about 10 per cent joking and 90 per cent serious. Rob went with the 10 per cent, and sniggered uneasily in his wake.

'So. The walls, you having a neutral colour scheme?'

'Ah, all that's still under wraps. But I've told the designer, "Golden rule of décor – no fucking chintz!"'

'Should be a British first, then,' said Rob.

'What it will be is classy. We're having silverware that'll test your biceps. Plus live music, no pissy tapes. And if Clydog does the restaurant review, he'll have a coronary!'

This time Rob laughed without guilt.

'Now, the mayoress tells me you're a painter.'

'Yes, skyscapes and—'

'Gather you had an exhibition, full of lifelike pictures of washing machines!' Stéfan burst into laughter at his own wit.

Rob smiled thinly. 'Yes. A collection of my local work, the valley in all weathers.'

'Uh-huh.'

'As a group of paintings, I think they'd create a good atmosphere in here.'

Stéfan's brow furrowed. 'In here?'

'Yes, colourwise they've got a—'

'I don't want any of your paintings!' Stéfan said.

'You . . . you don't? Oh.' Rob paused. 'But I thought the postman said—'

'No.' Stéfan took him by the arm and led him back through the bar and out into the rain.

He pointed upwards. 'I want a new pub sign.'

Blinking in the downpour, Rob stared up at the paint flaking off the dragon.

'Can you do that?'

'Well . . . er, yes . . . I suppose so.'

'Good.'

'Though I've never done a dragon before.'

'I don't want another fucking dragon!' Rob spread his hands wide in a gesture of confusion. 'I want a picture of *me*!'

'. . . Of you?' The rain ran in rivulets down Rob's face as he pondered on this latest unexpected development. 'Of you?'

'Yes.'

'Outside the pub?'

'Yes.'

'On a sign?'

'Yes.'

'Oh . . . Oh I see . . .'

'Is there a problem?'

Rob wondered how to explain to Stéfan that this was not a British tradition. Unless he were both landlord and king. Which of course he might have plans to be.

Rob was also wondering how best to advise him of the belly laughs that would ensue. Yet at the same time, he was keen to observe the rules of the painter/patron relationship.

'You can do portraits?' demanded Stéfan rudely. His final rendezvous of the day was at home in under ten minutes, and he was growing impatient. He was now both late and wet – neither of which is good for a first date. Especially with a predatory horsewoman.

But then again, thought Rob, being a laughing-stock is *his* problem. And the commission would help pay for heating their bathwater in an environmentally responsible way.

'Yes, I can do portraits,' he replied.

'Good. I'll send you some photos. My best side. Both of

them!' Then Stéfan sealed the deal with a hurried handshake, his mind on haste and lust, and dragged the pub door shut.

A curt farewell, and Stéfan started running back towards his car. He had felt constrained to leave it in the farthest corner of the car park for fear of another outbreak of cow rage.

'Oh, hang on!' Rob called after him. 'There is a problem!'

Stéfan squelched to a stop. 'What?'

'Won't it look odd to have "The Dragon's Head" written across your face?'

'Oh sorry!' Stéfan had the grace to grin. Then he shouted through the rain, 'I forgot to say. There's been a change of name.'

'Oh? What's the pub called now?'

'The Stéfan Arms.'

Chapter 23

Felicity warmed her damp buttocks against the study fire. From auction marquee to hearth-rug had taken her longer than she planned, even though she specialised in collecting country toffs. Her last encounter with Stéfan had been in the spring. She had engaged him in libidinous eye contact by the hoopla stand, and tried some foreplay with her crop, yet in the absence of further fêtes their weekend worlds had failed to collide. While she went point-to-point, Stéfan's quality time was occupied by estate management and issuing death threats to workmen. But, as hunt secretary, Felicity knew how to run a quarry to earth. And by leaving ansaphone messages that laid coded stress on her love of bareback riding she had at last won a place in his diary.

Felicity was not of the county set, and was acutely conscious that her bloodline was less impressive than that of her horse. This insecurity had led her into a life of overcompensation, overdoing her vowels, her Sloane accessories, her lipstick and her willingness to drop her jodhpurs. As groupie to the gentry, as lackey to the hunt, she had a haughtiness worthy of Royal Warrant. Yet still her stock did not pass muster, and the best hope for her future lay with moneyed men who could not tell a fake.

Felicity stretched herself full length along the rug, loosened another button, and let out a languorous sigh as she waited for the macaroons and her new man. Mrs Grotichley had that morning been given two commands: to produce some assorted *petits fours*, and to bugger off. She had adequately done the latter, and Stéfan was now busy in the kitchen, arranging her eight macaroons in a semblance of artistry upon a plate.

Stéfan's attitude to sex was not complicated. He was, after all, a busy man and angst was for losers. Nor was his approach to it sophisticated: his technique was best described as noisy. He did not seduce women so much as overwhelm them, and they usually surrendered in the hope that he could not speak and screw at the same time. Nonetheless, as a practical man he was not a complete slave to his emotions. Wherever possible he liked to combine sex with an ulterior motive, making it the sort of dual-purpose activity so highly recommended by time-and-motion studies.

So even as he prepared to charm the jodhpurs off Felicity – the first local woman to lie on his rug – his motives were no more exclusively carnal than hers. Where her inner desires were for high-quality stabling, he had set his heart on the hunt. And membership thereof. Certainly he had nothing equine in mind, and no desire to fall in hedges, but the social cachet of hunt ball circles was a nut he wished to crack. For this way lay contacts and contracts, this way lay funny handshakes and old money.

'Macaroons and Bolly!' he announced at the study door, his tone aiming to suggest a delicacy savoured in the private chambers of the Queen Mother.

Felicity had undone another button. As she always did when in doubt.

Stéfan laid the tray on the floor and sat down beside her, leaning against the dark green leather of his chesterfield. As he looked at her reclining in the firelight, he realised for the first time that she had a halfway decent body, apart from the usual horse damage to her bottom.

'So,' she said, in what she believed to be seductive tones, 'Stay-fan. What sort of a name is Stay-fan?'

'Georgian.'

'Georgian . . . ?'

'From Georgia.'

'Oh.'

He could tell that, as he'd expected, she was none the wiser. He rarely offered information on his background, but he felt sure any secrets would be safe with her, safeguarded by her incomprehension.

'Near Azerbaijan . . . ?' he added, as if helpfully.

'Oh . . .'

'Nagorno-Karabakh . . . ?'

She shook her head.

'Armenia . . . ?'

She shook it again.

'How about the Caucasus? . . . You familiar with the Caucasus?'

'Not really,' she replied.

'Well anyway, that's where I come from. It's where Stalin came from.'

'Oh. Did you know him?'

'Not closely, no.' He poured her a glass of champagne. 'Georgians are famous for being very wild, and poetic, and passionate!'

'Super,' said Felicity.

Outside, the afternoon rain was easing off, the steady patter on the windowpanes giving away to a silence made homely by the crackling of the firewood.

Stéfan made his move. He slid down alongside her on the floor, and murmured (as far it was possible for him to ever murmur), 'D'you want to drink the Bolly or have it poured over your nipples?'

She giggled, but in the manner of someone who found this a fairly routine choice. 'And what are you going to do with my macaroon?'

He took this as a yes to sex, pausing only to leer and say, 'Oh I'm sure I'll find a place to put it,' before he set to work on her remaining buttons.

Her breasts tumbled easily out, not up to deity size, but a more than adequate amount of flesh for him to try and pummel into arousal. The jodhpurs (which she wore with or without horse) were a trickier proposition, a more advanced obstacle to seduction. Being an old-fashioned sort of man, he felt it was his responsibility to rip a woman's clothing off, but the heavy-duty material cleaved to her limbs like an equestrian wetsuit. It defeated his ripping techniques and he had to call for assistance.

But they still made good time and Felicity was down to a small pair of frilly red things in approximately one minute forty-five seconds by his grandfather clock.

She wrapped her legs around his neck and the pair tussled in erotic mayhem for several moments. These were legs that won rosettes for dressage, restraining stallions from their urge to bolt, and Stéfan soon found his head pinned between her calves as if by railings. This was not his erotic position of choice, but the whelps of pleasure from Felicity gave a bawdy hint of unconventional tastes to come.

They disentangled to undress further.

She liked his bulk, and warmed to his arrogance. It turned her on that he showed no sign of inhibitions, and owned an endless number of rooms in which to prove it. Yet there was also a puppy dog chaos to his advances that, with her love of animals, she found engaging. She wondered if there were other Georgians in the area. Felicity judged it likely that the night would score an eight. Already, only minutes into the rendezvous, she was raring for the ravaging.

Stéfan dragged her on to her back, plunged face forwards between her legs, and tugged down the last of her lingerie. Her pudendum didn't disappoint – and startled even in its lack of orthodoxy. From the closest of quarters, he could see that her pubic hair was partly shaved, though, as with all her fashion statements, the effect was a little overdone. She appeared to have a vagina with a Hitler moustache. As if offering the choice of whether to suck it or salute it. But then she grabbed his head and all restraint was gone. Felicity began to utter noises that made him glad he had no neighbours for nearly an acre. Convulsively she arched her body into the air, and he was frenziedly kicking off the last of his clothing when there was a tap at the window.

Stéfan looked up over the sofa. The clouds had started to lift and a watery sun was shining on the rain-streaked glass. On the far side of it stood Mr Griffith Barton, The Windowman. Waving a tape measure.

Immediately, Stéfan's heart began to pound.

The Windowman tapped again.

'What the fuck is that?' cried Felicity from underneath her Georgian.

'He's come at last!' cried Stéfan.

'He's what? Who has?'

'The Windowman! He's come to do the windows!'

'Well, tell him to fuck off!'

'I can't!' cried Stéfan, 'I can't!' He scrabbled for his trousers in high excitement. 'I've waited nine months for this!'

'So have I, you cunt!' she screamed. Although used to rejection, she had never before lost out to a man with a ladder and khaki camouflage.

But Stéfan ignored her. And, still struggling with his zip, he rushed from the room to go and greet his tradesman.

Mr Griffith Barton, meanwhile, stayed outside, watching through the old windows as the naked huntswoman scraped her macaroons across the chesterfield in a temper tantrum.

Chapter 24

Rob went down into town from the Dragon's Head. Sex was on his agenda too. He had a suggestive smile to give to Bryony, and some possible dates for her evening assignation at Pantglas.

But first he wanted a language lesson from Nico, and some explanation of the mystery letter.

Rob always felt uneasy when he met Nico. He found him too plausible. Nico knew too many facts and had too much charm. It was a phoney charm, and some of the facts felt false, but Rob had yet to find a way to derail him. How Nico had become his agent still remained unclear to Rob, though his advice so far seemed sound. But Rob had a feeling he was not a good person to annoy.

Nico's antiques shop was on a side street, just narrow enough to be blocked whenever he parked his Volvo. It was blocked now. He did not have grand premises, but they stood on the corner of an eighteenth-century alley, and offered the poky promise of an Aladdin's cave. Nico knew how to dress a shop window with just the right balance of bric-à-brac and treasure trove, of tat and promise.

Rob had passed the shop before, in forlorn attempts to find an off-the-beaten-track quartier of Abernant, but had never gone in. Overpriced *objets d'art* were low on Pantglas's priorities, and he had no wish to trigger Nico's sales technique. But now the need to know about Aberystwythian wind-pumps overcame that kind of cavil.

The door had a set of tinkling glass chimes, that aural pot-pourri for sad pseudo-mystics of the Sixties. Inside, the shop was a clutter of farmers' cast-offs, as if a hundred Farmer Matthews had just died. On every side, some glassware, some porcelain, some records, some bookcases, some more bookcases, even some books. Plus several of that traditional standby, the Welsh dresser, always the first item for the elbow when time comes for that retirement bungaloid by the byre.

Nico was on his own with his back to Rob, and was negotiating hard with an attractive woman in her thirties, notable for a shock of frizzed auburn hair. She was carrying a large raffia bag and had laid out its contents on a battered gateleg table. Alerted by the tinkling, Nico glanced round, and was a little surprised to see Rob. He made a quick holding apology and hurried over.

'I've got a rock-solid buyer this time,' he said in a confident whisper. 'Vintage tractor dealer in East Anglia. He just needs to clear time to collect it.'

'Oh, damn!' said Rob. 'I'd rather hoped to hang on to it a little longer.'

'You do? Whatever for?'

'Artistic backdrop. Bit of agricultural history behind the animals. In a nice red. Got some definite interest in that idea.'

'Oh. Yes, I can see why . . . could be a good gimmick. OK.'

'. . . OK? But what about your buyer?'

'Oh, I was lying.'

And with that, Nico hurried back to his customer, and resumed examination of her items. As Rob wandered round the shop, idly checking out the prices, he could hear snatches of their conversation: Nico, professionally sad, sighing and regretful, the woman, insistent, needy and argumentative. He watched as a carriage clock and an early American flag (thirteen stars) changed hands. There followed a disagreement over the value of a lava lamp. Several objects, including a garlic crusher, remained unsold. The woman put these back in her bag somewhat disconsolately and threaded her way out of the shop, the door opened and closed by an unctuous Nico.

'Never get divorced!' declared Nico, in worldly summary. 'She's from up your way, that one. Part-time teacher. D'you know her?'

Rob shook his head.

'Lives in a caravan now. Whitelaw, Mrs Whitelaw.'

'Oh, the Buff Orpingtons!'

Nico looked at him as if he were mad, then went on, 'Bank's turned nasty for some reason. Wants its loan back. That's when they all come in here, bank trouble.' He refocused. 'So, people showing interest, you say?'

'In my paintings? Yes. Yes, a few farmers starting to come out the woodwork. Seem to want a family group, most of them. Daddy bull, mummy cow, baby heifers and a duck thrown in! Even Gareth's making noises.'

'Grunts, I should think. Well, the sooner you start to make your name, the sooner we can get into the spin-offs. You paint 'em cute enough and we can start thinking posters and T-shirts, and – who knows? – mugs, and teapots, and playing cards . . . maybe even those little pegs that fit on wellingtons!'

Even for Rob, now an ex-artist, their pact was veering too far to the Faustian. But before he could plead integrity, the irritating chimes tinkled again and a middle-aged couple – a touch too stylish to be local – came into the shop. He let the issue drop. 'What do you know about Aberystwyth?'

'Let me know if I can help you,' Nico called to the couple, his accent upgraded a notch. He turned back to Rob. 'Er, town on the west coast. Rain tastes of salt. Where university students go to die of boredom. Anything else?'

Rob held up the letter. 'Why do they speak Swedish there?'

Nico glanced at it. 'Aaah. They don't. It's Dutch.'

'Dutch? OK, why do they speak Dutch?'

'They don't. That's from head office – in Holland.'

'So why am I getting a letter from Holland?

'Lot of wind in Holland.'

'True.'

'And this contact of mine – the one who's into eco-things – he knows a firm sells their wind-pumps in Aberystwyth. So, as a favour, I passed on your name.' (The word 'commission' hovered over that sentence like a ghost at the party.)

'Sounds promising,' Rob confessed.

'Antiques isn't just antiques. It's contacts.' Nico's eyes kept darting away from Rob, following the new customers around the shop like an undercover agent's, sensitive to every nuance that might mean money.

'Guess I'd better get over to Aberystwyth,' said Rob. 'You know, I've spent the best part of a year looking for someone that makes wind-pumps!'

'Oh they don't actually *make* wind-pumps in Aberystwyth.'

'But I thought—'

'No, the firm just sells them. Supplies them. They come from Holland.'

'So why—'

'Look, I'd better attend to this pair.' Nico's interest in wind-pumps was waning. 'I'm on my own here.' Nico turned and squeezed past a six-foot wooden hayfork, a much sought-after item in parts of London. 'Sion's left me in the lurch.'

'What, that lad who never spoke? With the suntan?'

'That's the one.' Nico pulled a face. 'Supposed adult. Just disappeared last week, not a word of warning. Like he'd been abducted by aliens. Now, you'll have to excuse me a moment. Money calls.'

Rob was not in the mood to wait, and set off to see Bryony.

Part Four

Chapter 25

The summer was just about over, its arrival and departure noticed only by the calendar, its one seasonal concession the warmth of its rain. Now was the time of year when incomers had second thoughts.

Dafydd was more aware than most of the cusp of autumn. This was the season of mists and heavy removal vans, when 'Please Forward' was the leitmotif of letters. To him, a postman, the cycle of life meant the urban idyll-seekers returning like salmon to spawn in the city. For some incomers, the process took one year, for others, it took five. For some, the cause was the absence of street lighting, for others, it was the failure to grow sprouts.

Dafydd claimed to have a nose for those whose dreams would die. Sometimes it was their words: the wish to 'commune with nature' provides an early hint of trouble. Sometimes it was their actions: strangling a neighbour's cockerel bodes ill for integration. And sometimes it was their attitude: a belief that 'good morning' can be said in under five minutes reveals the irredeemably urban.

Which is why, as the postman drove back down the valley on that last Saturday of summer, fresh from his deliveries to Crug Caradoc and Pantglas, he was pondering on the prospects for their owners. In his twenty-odd years of Royal Mail service, he had consoled many a pining exile. However, there had as yet been no call for a sympathetic shoulder from either Stéfan or

Rob. Each had had their little local difficulties – many of them difficulties with locals – and each had seen their best-laid plans go bottom-up. Yet their unorthodoxy had given them resilience, and their battles with the valley were going the distance. Indeed, they were even making headway, albeit eccentrically, as he had witnessed that very morning.

Yet to be a gossip is usually to be a cynic, dependent on the worst in others. So Dafydd and his hunches quietly took the long view, and he stayed host to the thought that their dreams could still end in disaster.

'Is this scaffolding safe?' asked The Windowman.

'Surprised you believe in scaffolding,' retorted Stéfan. 'Thought you'd take the purist approach. Hang by a rope from the gutter.' Now that Stéfan had a pick-up truck full of finished windows in his drive, he felt less constrained in his manner.

If anything, it seemed The Windowman was flattered. He gave a vestige of a smile as he put his foot upon the sill and prepared to climb out the bedroom window, or rather, out the space awaiting a window. He did not hurry. The ground floor now done, this was his tenth new window of the week, and the work had put him in reflective mood.

'Tell me something.' He paused to flick spilt snuff off the cushions on the window-seat, and then he looked at Stéfan and said, 'I've met a few crowned heads in my time . . .'

Stéfan, who was about to object to the effect of army boots on his freshly painted window-sill, elected to wait for the completion of the sentence.

'Well, pretenders to crowns, mainly. Kings-in-exile, that sort of thing. Your Zogs. Your descendants of Louis. They used to exchange postcards with my wife. Her being Hapsburg. Well, lapsed, of course.'

Stéfan's attention was no longer focused on his army boots.

'And in the old days – when we were first married – we'd take trips, and visit some of these royal pretenders at home. Provide a bit of company for them. Because it's a lonely business, waiting for the call to come from your people. It can sometimes take a lifetime to get your throne back.'

For some reason, Stéfan found it hard not to nod.

'So Helga and I, we were able to see how they lived, these monarchs-in-waiting.' The Windowman pulled himself up on the sill, one hand upon a scaffolding pole, then turned and looked down on to Stéfan.

'And, by and large, they had fewer windows.'

The wind gusted through his legs from the parkland and Stéfan shivered as he gazed at Mr Griffith Barton's knees.

'So tell me. You're a single man. Why do you need a house this size?'

It was an obvious question but Stéfan showed no signs of a ready answer. Not because he had no answer, but because he was struggling to understand why anyone would ask the question.

In the end, he said, 'To keep you in business!'

It was a good answer, and they both laughed. And the moment of human contact was over. The Windowman manoeuvred himself out on to the planks of the scaffolding, and checked the frame was millimetre perfect in its new home. Stéfan watched from within, running his fingers along the beautifully grained wood of the new window, which rested at a coquettish angle against his giant circular bed.

'By next spring, they'll be profiling this place in *Country Life*! Hire a few debs with pearls, and I'll be Squire of the Month. Now that's worth splashing out on!'

'If you want to be burgled,' said The Windowman gloomily. 'And I'd be grateful if you said the windows were from MFI. I have quite enough prats turning up, thank you.'

Over the months, The Windowman had discovered one of the few pleasures in working for Stéfan was that his ego made him almost impervious to insults, and The Windowman was able to indulge his innate misanthropy to gratifying lengths.

Not that Stéfan was entirely immune to pique. What did stick in his craw, what he regarded as almost insufferable lese-majesty, was to be the employer of a workman who might, had history turned out differently, have inherited Hungary.

This galling thought gave Stéfan the urge to go up himself on the scaffolding, for there he could bask in the therapeutic vista of his own estate. He gripped the pole, squeezed past The Window-man, and pulled himself out. The summer rain was pattering gently on his trout lakes, and in the oak woodland the first leaves were giving up their green. He carefully promenaded along the planks and past the bedrooms, looking in a great arc from east to west. Though still short on statuary and beasts of the jungle, he took much pride in his acreage. He was master of all he surveyed for nearly as far as the pub, and a warm glow of vainglory enveloped him.

But most of all Stéfan gloried in the ancient house, whose creepered walls were at last being punctuated by windows worthy of the name. Single-handed, give or take a craftsman, he was now reversing the neglect of decades. And from this he gained a real – and rare – sense of achievement.

'Don't paint lamb chops, do you, mate? Because I'd buy that!' laughed the first wind-pump man, struggling past Rob's easel with a lethal-looking rotor blade.

'Yeah, make mine a leg steak!' laughed the second wind-pump man, following him out of the barn with a spaghetti-coil of wire over his shoulder.

'I'd, er . . . I'd like the middle sheep to have a bit of a smile,' said Gareth, who was nervously observing Rob's brushwork from the barn door.

It was not just the sheep that was short of a smile. These were not ideal circumstances for an artist to carry out his first commissioned painting of rural life.

Rob had told Gareth that he considered it best to paint generalised sheep, sheep typical of their kind, the common sheep. But Gareth had it in his head to commit to posterity his favourite sheep, sheep whose character marked them out, whose features had meaning for him and Moira. To this end, he had herded three of his finest up from his lowland fields, and proposed their arrangement in a tableau.

At approximately the same moment, the two burly wind-pump men had arrived without warning – and with a multitude of wind-pump parts – after setting off before breakfast from the far side of the Cambrian Mountains, from the land where the rain tastes of salt.

There being a financial nexus between these two events, Rob felt unable to spurn either party.

And now all were busy in the barn, away from the late summer rain. Art was at one end, wind-pump assembly at the other. One and a half sheep had taken bodily form, and a steel mast was firmly fixed to his chimney.

'Give it a smile . . . ?' repeated Rob. 'Is it a smiley sort of sheep, that one?' Even as he spoke, his attention was being distracted by an extension ladder quivering in the vicinity of his chimney pots, an eighteenth-century feature which had figured prominently in the house negotiations.

'I want her to look homely. Women like homely things, don't they?'

There came a clang, and a shout of 'Steady there!'

'I suppose so,' said Rob, who had never counted homeliness among Jane's virtues. The ladder wobbled under the weight of the man who had the rotor blade, now struggling up the chimney to begin the bolting-on.

'I think of the middle one as mother,' said Gareth, a surprising sentimentality in someone who had so recently removed unsightly dung and snagged hawthorn twigs from her fleece.

'Mother?' said Rob, echoing on autopilot. Out of the corner of his eye he could see the man who had the wire, now examining several component parts with the tentative approach of a bomb disposal officer.

'Mother and family. Not real family, obviously. Because

223

they've gone to the abattoir. But make-believe family.' Rarely had Gareth spoken so much.

Rarely had Rob listened so little. 'Everything all right?' he called.

'Fine!' cried the first wind-pump man.

'Fine!' cried the second wind-pump man.

Rob wondered about their grasp of Dutch. He turned back to his painting. 'D'you want the sheepdog in as well?'

'Umm . . . Not sure,' said Gareth. 'You're the expert. What d'you reckon?'

'Umm . . .' Rob stepped back in the way artists do when they want a better perspective.

With years of shepherding skills at his disposal, Gareth had arranged his three sheep in what art critics at the Royal Welsh might describe as an agricultural triptych: two sheep sitting, the middle one ('Smiler') standing. Given the barn setting, this had oddly biblical overtones, and with Rob's gawky new animal primitivism the half-complete painting suggested how the Nativity would have been portrayed by Stubbs. Except that in the background of the picture, where one might have expected to see a little Lord Jesus, there was a bright red combine harvester (one which Rob had prepared earlier).

'Homely,' Rob declared. 'The dog would look homely.'

He reserved a spot for the dog and then went back to fleshing out his three lifelike sheep. It was his style to give them a bulky quality, the muscular armature of sheep wearing a fleece two sizes too big. Were it not for the smile they could have been mistaken for gangster sheep. Rob was finishing off mother when the wireman wandered over from the parts department.

'Not come across a wiring diagram, have you?'

'No, sorry. Is it important?'

'No, no, nothing to worry about.' The wireman was looking over Rob's shoulder at the painting. 'Those animals, should they be that size?'

'It's primitivism.'

'Oh. But aren't sheep normally smaller than tractors?'

'Bloody hell, it was wet and windy on that chimney!' said the rotor-blade man, bursting into the barn to join them.

'You done up there, then?' asked Rob.

'Yeah. It's solid as a rock. Well, solid as glass fibre reinforced polyester.'

'Don't they make pullovers out of polyester?' asked Gareth.

'Just got to connect all the bits together now. The bits that give you light and heat.'

'Not a day too soon either. Be glad to get shot of my old generator!'

'I'm not surprised. It's a ropey model, that one. I can hear it from here.'

The wind-pump men began to rummage through the various parts that now lay across the floor of the barn. They were large chaps with hefty hands, who would have made light work of Rob's rock garden.

The barn's gaping entrance gave Rob a clear view of his virgin turbine, a glistening addition to the skyline. Its profile had elegance and simplicity, like a silver bow tie that was born for the wind. It stood, still tethered to the mast for safety, as if waiting for a giant finger to spin it into action. It had the aura of science fiction, the quiet arrogance that it was the future.

'Don't know what an inverter looks like, do you, mate?' asked the wireman.

'A what?' said Rob.

'An inverter.'

'An "inverter"? No idea. Why ask me? What's it do?'

'God knows! Just thought, you being one of these green sorts—'

'You don't know what it does?'

'Not really. I think it must sort of—'

'Hang on! Hang on! How come you don't know what it does? *Or* what it looks like?'

'Don't get aerated! There's a lot of bits here, mate.'

'A barnful!' said the rotor-blade man rather mournfully.

'OK, and you're supposed to be able to put them together!' snapped Rob.

'I know. And we will. We will. It's just it's the first wind-pump we've done.'

'What if we had a ram in it?' mused Gareth, who had moved further into the barn for a better look at his first commissioned work.

'*The first one you've done?*' said Rob.

'Well, it's the first one we've sold.'

Rob was not normally an angry person, but on this occasion he was prepared to make an exception. Unfortunately, he was angry at Nico, and Nico was not there. Rob felt all interest in art ebbing and he clenched his fists and glowered at the ground. He moved away from the painting and paced up and down a couple of times, but taking care to avoid the heating coil, the control unit, the permanent magnet, the brushless generator, the galvanic steel units, and the other lo-tech bric-à-brac which now lay strewn across his flagstoned floor. Then he went to the barn door and stood in the rain like an outcast smoker.

The two men waited patiently for him to calm down. The rotor-blade man thrust his cold hands deep into his overalls and wandered over to have a look at the sheep triptych. His partner had another go at connecting the wire that would turn wind into water.

'Should they be that size, those sheep?'

'It's primitivism,' said the wireman.

'So if,' said Rob, returning with improved composure, 'if you don't do wind-pumps, what do you do?'

'It's not we *don't* do them,' said the rotor-blade man, 'it's more that we're diversifying into them.'

'. . . I see. So what do you normally do? I mean, what's your normal line of work?'

'Oh, that'd be agricultural hardware.'

'Yes, firm's been doing agricultural hardware over twenty years now.'

'What, farm generators and things?'

'Not exactly,' said the rotor-blade man.

'More sort of . . .' The wireman hesitated.

'Milk churns.'

Chapter 26

Two weeks had passed, and Gareth was a happy man, even an excited man. He had just auctioned six heifers at a profit, he was on his fifth pint in the Market Tavern, and at noon the picture framer would be finished. In less than an hour, Moira would be the proud owner of the first framed painting of stock in the family's history. *And* he'd managed to keep it a surprise.

Such was his enthusiasm – Gareth was a man of few enthusiasms, none visible to the naked eye – that he was even ending his drinking early. The all-day licence of market day, the saloon-bar crush of noisy farmers, the post-mortem minutiae of meat sales, this was normally the high point of his week, a heady mix for a man who so often stood alone in wet fields. Usually he would totter out as the empty livestock pens were being hosed down, and go home with early evening coming on. But today he was on a mission.

As he left behind the roar of the bar and the dank Barbour odours, he came across Dafydd, also on his way out.

'You off early too?'

'I wish!' said Dafydd.

'I'm collecting a framed painting of my sheep.'

'All 500 of them?' said the postman, mischievously obtuse.

'No, no, just three. For the wife.'

'She'll think Christmas has come early.'

'You're not married, are you?'

'I have my moments. That little red van's a turn-on for some women!'

On a less momentous day, Gareth might have asked for details. After a few more pints, Dafydd might have offered them. The one unsung Royal Mail perk was the privacy to be found at the end of long tracks, where the wait for a second delivery had been known to drive some women wild with excitement.

'You're lucky,' said Gareth. 'Don't think a tractor ever turned anyone on.'

They went down the alley that led into town. Behind them, a cow mooed with panic as it was corralled towards the auction ring. Ahead of them, the grey slate roofs managed to look aesthetic and depressing at the same time. Storm-clouds were forming over the mountains, and a strong wind was beginning to gust litter into the air.

'It's looking a bit rough,' said Dafydd.

'I've shot moles in worse.'

They walked down along the High Street, navigating around the farmers' wives bursting to spend the cash from the carcasses of market day. It was no longer a high street where spending was easy, for of late, despite the best efforts of the Chamber of Commerce, almost every second shop had become a charity shop. Nor indeed was the navigating easy, for of late, despite the best efforts of Hubert, its President, works were in their final throes for the county's first parking meters. The blight of modernity was gaining ground.

In the distance, they spotted Clydog as he struggled to doff his hat in the wind.

'You going for a gossip at the deli?' Gareth asked the postman, almost garrulous amidst the slew of new emotions he was coming across.

'Maybe later. I'm just off to be "appraised".'

'Oh, I was appraised last year. Gave me the all-clear, apart from cold sores.'

'No. No, not the Well Man Clinic. My boss.'

'Oh, I see. Glad I don't have a boss.'

'If I owned a gun I wouldn't have! Know his latest bloody idea?' The postman was on to his hobbyhorse. 'Annual "performance monitoring and assessment". Annual bollocks, more like! "Did my method of letter delivery bring happiness into your life?"'

For a brief moment, Gareth thought he was expected to answer this question, and fell to ruminating. Dafydd too seemed surprised by the vigour of his outburst and he said no more. And then they reached the crossroads and went their separate ways.

It was just fifty yards to the picture-framing shop, a shop whose existence Gareth had never known of until a week before. Tucked in the alley opposite Nico's antiques, it was run by a Jehovah's Witness, a tight-lipped man who kept little texts under glass to offset art with ethics. His worldly skill was carpentry and ten years ago he had been called to the area to build a meeting hall. He was now awaiting another call, to go any place in the world where further carpentry work for Witnesses might be needed. All this, Gareth had learnt while they agreed that 48 inches × 30 inches was the optimum frame size.

The picture was ready for him, leaning against the wall alongside black-and-white photographs of the mountains and drawings of small hairy dogs in baskets. Had he been more confident socially, Gareth would have confessed that this was the type of dog he usually shot for sheep-worrying. There seemed to him an artistic appropriateness to have the pictures lying side by side.

He hoped the owner would pass approving comment on his picture, but he said nothing apart from offering to wrap it. Gareth refused his offer. He had in his head this image of walking into their farmhouse and holding the picture up in front of his face. He did, however, accept the suggestion of temporary brown paper, for he still felt uneasy about walking the streets with artwork.

It was five minutes of unsteady walk to his empty cattle truck and fifteen minutes of low gear work to his farm. The farm and its outbuildings stood quite high on the eastern side of the valley, with an unappreciated view of the river and the church below. Above him on the ridge lay Pantglas and Rob's studio-barn. Downstream, Abernant was hidden from sight by the curve of the hills, though at night a glow in the sky told where it might be found.

On each side of the potholed farm-track stood a row of poplars planted by his father, the result not of commitment to conservation but of greed for grant-aid. The poplars now had some thirty years of girth, but provided a sorry, gap-toothed approach to the farm, as their taproots made them vulnerable to gales and to Gareth's weaving late-night returns from the Dragon's Head. For the trees still standing, the going of Gwillim had been a godsend, since the absence of an alehouse had left Gareth confined to his fireside for over a month. This had perhaps been less of a godsend for Moira.

Gareth drove the cattle truck slowly into the farmyard, around his Land Rover, and parked in the large barn between the winter stock of hay and his portable skittle alley. Skittles were the nearest he had to a hobby. He took his skittle alley to all the agricultural shows, and one of his happiest memories was the day of the fête, when he had raised £88.50 for the church and Moira had helped tear the tickets.

Gareth clambered out of the driver's cab, handling his painting like china as he muttered his way through a short speech. Then he slipped softly round to the back of the farm, to the farmhouse kitchen where Moira spent her days. He crouched low as he passed the window and, easing the latch with his bottom, he burst in backwards, spun round and held the painting aloft.

To his surprise she was not there. Her apron was there, and the early stages of the stew were there. But of her there was no sign.

Gareth had choreographed this moment for several weeks and now felt cheated of his triumph. A triumph with no back-up plan. He wondered whether to down a sixth beer while he waited for her to return from his parents, from their bungalow just across the yard. . . . And then he heard the tell-tale creak of floorboards above his head. And he suddenly realised the truth. Had he known Moira better, he would have realised it immediately. For him, Friday was market day, but for her, it was the day she changed the sheets.

He set off up the stairs, torn between the desire to run and the need to be silent. The treads were cracked and creaky, and he moved on tiptoe from safe step to safe step. Held in outstretched arms, the picture was taken upstairs with more care than Nico had accorded his corpse.

Fortunately, the bedroom door was ajar. Gareth counted silently to three, like the armed response groups he had seen on TV, barged open the door, and burst in, the huge painting clutched to his upper body.

Mr Blake's orgasm suffered an immediate setback. One moment, the bank manager had been lying face down examining Moira's privates, the next, he was looking at three giant sheep sharing a joke in a Bethlehem tractor-shed. Moira's description of her husband as odd now made perfect sense. Few cuckolds express their anger with an art exhibition.

Arguably, however, Gareth Richards suffered the greater shock. But it wasn't just the infidelity. It was the originality of the sexual position. What is more, he simply hadn't expected his first-ever encounter with oral sex would involve a third party from the world of banking, and certainly not from a local branch. So shocked was Gareth that initially he forgot to lower the painting, and continued to peer over the top like a visiting voyeur.

Moira, whose head was buried between the manager's thighs, had still not actually seen her husband, but felt it reasonable to assume his presence given the size to which the bank manager's penis had been reduced. She decided not to emerge for the moment. Conversation with her husband was difficult at the best of times.

There were two aspects to the betrayal that Gareth found

particularly hurtful. One was Mr Blake's height (approximately six foot one), and the other was that he hadn't bothered to take his socks off.

And still no one spoke. Denial seemed, in the circumstances, to be a lost cause. But recrimination required a level of fluency to which Gareth could not rise. He felt he would be verbally outmanoeuvred by a bank manager, as he had been the last time he asked for a loan. And he was a foot too short for a fight. He continued to stare, angry, confused, betrayed, helpless, violent.

Not knowing where he was going, he left.

Not knowing what he was doing, he took Rob's picture with him.

He clattered back down the stairs, through the house, and out into the yard. He leaned against his Land Rover, struggling to regain his thoughts. Then an impulse took him. He walked ten yards out from the house, and threw the painting down in the deepest mud. He got into the 4×4, started up – and drove over the painting. Then he reversed over it, went forward over it, reversed again, went forward again, and continued back and forth, back and forth, until its all-terrain tyres had crushed the last piece of canvas from sight.

After that he rested his head upon the steering wheel and slumped in unmanly despair.

Around Gareth the quiet determined patter of the coming storm began to grow in volume, and gusts of wind scuffed the puddles in the yard.

Finally a new impulse overtook him. With mud spraying out behind, he pressed the accelerator to the floor, scattered the remnants of the frame to fragments, and roared out up the track and back towards town.

Chapter 27

At around the same time, Stéfan was driving over the mountains on the last lap of his weekly journey. Waiting for him was a completed Crug Caradoc, the battle of the windows won, the facemask of scaffolding finally peeled away. Tomorrow, almost a year to the day since the auction, he would be celebrating in the Stéfan Arms, where the last blobs of emulsion were even now being stippled fashionably into place.

No expense had been spared – the talk of the valley was of inside toilets – and the Stéfan taste had been stamped throughout. The pub now had a décor that belonged to few brewery chains, indeed to few, if any, buildings west of Offa's Dyke. *And* he had created a culinary first for the area: a menu without lamb! The actual cuisine was still a secret. Rumour held it to be exotic and spicy, since Stéfan kept saying – with his usual mocking laugh – that he liked his food to have a kick in it.

The only detail yet to be sorted – apart from the bills – was Gwillim. He still kept cattle on the Commodore's land, but the flat above the pub was his farmhouse home, and the Notice to Quit would shortly see him evicted. Few things in life made Gwillim happy, and one of these was bearing a grudge – ideally of the Albanian format, which endures for generations and fills the cemeteries. As a heavyweight malcontent, his way with cows still caused Stéfan's car engine to miss a beat whenever they rounded a bend. So Stéfan had proposed a meet, and was trying hard to think of offers that Gwillim couldn't refuse.

But first came the bills. Stéfan was a cash man. In his world of import-export (and still the locals could not say if this were cashew nuts or cocaine, guano or guns) it was cash that paid the bills. And his pub bills were no exception. So, despite the worsening weather, Stéfan decided to stop off in Abernant, at the cash point immortalised by the mayoress.

It was not easy to park. A new parking regime was to start the following day; the meters wore hoods like a gang of embarrassed outlaws, the department of tape had run amok, and the white-line men were out in force. But illegality was a trifle that rarely troubled Stéfan, and he crowbarred his resprayed Jaguar into the end of a disabled bay.

Declaring a cash point open is the easy part. Keeping it stocked with money is what takes the years of training. And every week the demands of market day proved beyond the wit of mortal clerks. Stéfan pressed every button in sight but the cash flow was a no-show.

Inside, the bank was almost as full of farmers as the Market Tavern, all paying in their wads and filling out their stubs. On such days the place had the feel of a gossip exchange, like London's early coffee-houses, but without the coffee. There were four queues, and it was all hands to the tills, including those of the senior lady cashier.

So Stéfan reluctantly waited in line, even though he was a man who felt he should have a doctor's note excusing him, explaining that to queue was not in his nature.

It was an old-world, old-style bank, built at a time when moneymen believed in cornice work. Its double doors opened on to a marble floor of generous proportions, with space that served no financial purpose, and its high ceilings had an echo that added dignity to a cough. Known in its formative years as a banking-hall, the building spoke of an age when a starched collar was the prerequisite for an overdraft. Even the wainscoting had survived, here escaping its destiny as an archaic noun.

It took some ten minutes for Stéfan to reach the counter, ten minutes of waiting while each transaction was subjected to enquiries re the next of kin, and their health. And the name of their new baby. And anyone recently dead.

The senior cashier was a matronly figure, ten years short of retirement, and, it seemed, a blood relative of all her customers. But she had a brisk efficiency where cash was concerned, and breezed through Stéfan's five-figure request. Like the bank itself, she had an old-fashioned quality, a concern that things be proper, a respect for the niceties.

Mrs Plimpton was counting out the last few hundred pounds when the armed man came in.

It was almost a low-key entrance, a few people moving to make room, the odd raised voice. It was when he started to push his way to the front of the queue that the mood in the bank changed. Stéfan sensed some sort of mêlée behind him and turned around. And there, in his dingy cap and dungy Barbour, with his shotgun under his arm, was Gareth. Walking like a man who had come via the Market Tavern.

Gareth stopped a couple of yards from the screen-free, customer-friendly counter.

He held himself steady to address the staff beyond it.

Then he yelled, 'Your manager's screwing my wife!'

He now had the full attention of the bank.

There was no immediate response to his cry. Indeed, it was hard to see what kind of response there could be. Some of the staff exchanged looks, but no one wished to provoke him by saying anything. Some of the farmers exchanged smirks, but none of them wished to go on record. The only person deriving satisfaction from the drama (apart possibly from Gareth) was Mrs Plimpton, the senior cashier. She was now feeling a warm glow of vindication for her long-held view that Mr Blake was a rogue and a wrong 'un. But she said nothing, well schooled by a lifetime's training in customer confidentiality.

The silence that greeted his news did not please Gareth, as he wanted understanding of his plight.

He yelled again, this time turning around to address the bank's customer base, 'Their manager's screwing my wife!'

It was hard not to be moved by his pain, yet hard not to laugh at his folly. Life in the fields had jammed his tongue for so many years that it no longer serviced his brain. All the rights and wrongs of his marriage had clogged into this moment of madness. He no longer knew how or where to receive relief. But finally he wished his suffering to be shared.

The assembly of customers – and many had known him since childhood – avoided his eye and hid from his pain. They too had wives, they too had fields. Had she died, they had a ready repertoire of words. But a wife in another's arms? They had only sidelong glances. And a queasy fear that he would go the way of Hefin, but not quietly, and not in a lonely barn. Stéfan meanwhile breathed again, sensing his money was safe.

Still yearning desperately for some impossible dream of redress, Gareth raised his gun above his head. To a female chorus of gasps, he fired both barrels into the ceiling.

And then he yelled one more time, 'YOUR MANAGER'S SCREWING MY WIFE!'

The only immediate consequence of his action was that a section of elaborate stucco fell from the ceiling and unfortunately concussed Mr Probert, the estate agent, who until a few moments earlier had been enjoying a rather successful day as auctioneer.

Seeing the man's body crumple to the floor, Gareth realised his folly had gone too far. All that remained to him was a chance for dignity.

He stepped towards the counter and, with the over-elaborate precision of a drunk, he uncocked the shotgun that had done for so many moles and laid it carefully along the counter, its barrel pointing away from the staff. In a flurry of melodrama, a first-aid box and a fire extinguisher were rushed to resuscitate the auctioneer.

Then with much conscious effort to display composure, and brushing a little loose plaster from his shoulders, Gareth addressed the senior cashier.

'Excuse me,' he said, with the courtesy that is the hallmark of the valley.

'Yes, Mr Richards?' Mrs Plimpton decided to make no mention of the waiting queue.

'I wish to close my account, please.'

Chapter 28

Bryony was more than a little nervous as she waited for Jane to pick her up from the old schoolhouse. She was glad that the day's events at the bank – retold in detail to the deli by all but the town-crier – had given her enough hot gossip to bridge any early awkwardness at the night's multiple tryst. Not that she was a reluctant party. Especially as even the bog-standard two-person date had failed to figure in her love life of late.

After Eryl the heir there had not even been the masochistic mistake of a rebound. The valley males did not inspire. Blockish, blokish, with a chat-up art from the ark, they moved seamlessly from the Young Farmers' Club to middle age, pausing briefly to fondle a rugby ball. It did not encourage a girl to mark her dance-card.

Choosing what to wear for Pantglas had not been easy. To go for the erotic effect of next to nothing on? Or to go for the erotic effect of something sexy to be taken off? And what was a turn-on for *both* sexes? Hardly a question to ask in Brenda's Boutique, where there were still memories of the whalebone corset.

And then there was the choice of essential oils, which ranged from bergamot to vetiver, from clary sage to thyme. Did she want to smell of the East, or whiff of the West, or take the noses of her lovers back to ancient Egypt? Did she want it applied by bath or massage, by fragrancing or compresses? Over the last few months her grasp of oils was, despite an inability to spell any but pine and rosemary, beginning to suggest a vocation.

Bryony had finally elected to go out in something short, tight, and easily unzipped – and clinging to a body deeply redolent of eucalyptus – when the Morris 1000 whined nasally into the playground.

'What a foul night!' Jane shouted as Bryony scampered out past the swings, a coat draped over her head.

The lift had been a last-minute thing. Bryony had intended to take a taxi – only to learn that the one minicab firm in town now employed the moonlighting Traffic Warden. Who was no doubt researching vol. 17 of *Kinky Kab Rides*. The thought of ending up the subject of his porny prose, having previously refused to transcribe it, was an irony rich in poetic layers, none of which she wished to explore.

'Thanks for coming to get me,' said Bryony, her gratitude marked by some goodies and an offering of home-made elderberry wine, fermented from a vintage crop of her hedge.

She was glad to save the fare. The bank manager had quickly tired of using Bryony's body as collateral. The Eighties' recession had provided many near-bankrupts and in a competitive market he had soon moved on to other women. In consequence, the terms and conditions of her overdraft had, like Mrs Whitelaw's loan, been unfavourably reviewed. So, despite her sacrifice, she had not got as many bucks for her bang as she hoped, and the news of his disgrace made this a good night to celebrate.

'Sorry about the feathers,' said Jane.

'Looks as if you've had a shoot in here!' Bryony's two attempts to slam the car door shut had created a swirling Winter Wonderland.

'Rob's bloody ducks got in!'

'Pretty colours.'

'Thank Christ they didn't nest! Hard enough driving this car without having to worry about giant eggs rolling around.'

As if to prove the point, the car heeled first to left, then to right, as Jane wrenched it round the old dog-leg, humpback bridge. Below its stone arch, the rising river was the colour of turbulent tea as the first storm of winter sluiced tons of alluvial sludge towards the sea.

'Oh, and by the way,' said Jane with coquettish modesty, 'I can legally stick needles in you now.'

'You've passed? Oh well done. Well done!' Bryony reached over and squeezed her knee, letting her hand linger just a little longer than was normal for congratulations on an acupuncture diploma. But just long enough to let it be known there was full understanding of the evening's intent.

'So that's another reason to celebrate,' said Jane.

'Another?'

'Oh, there are several!'

'Like what?'

'Ah. It's a secret. Wait till we get there.'

'Fuck secrets! Like what?'

Jane just laughed. 'Why don't I tell you about the twelve basic meridians instead?'

'No!' Bryony started to laugh as well. 'Secrets! I want secrets!'

'How about the first six points of the yin lung meridian? Would you like to know about them?'

'No! Secrets! I want secrets!' she began to chant, in an endearingly silly voice that often came upon her after a joint.

Jane was fond of teasing her. True, they had similar views on all the cosmic issues of life, on herbicides and hunting and battery hens, but still she teased her, for intellectually Jane had the edge. In the pecking order of knowledge, acupuncture will always outrank aromatherapy.

'What, tell you and spoil your surprise?' Jane glanced across to choose a knee area for a return squeeze – and almost failed to see a fallen branch. It lay hidden in the half-light and she had to swerve at the very last moment, leaving brown skidmarks along the grass bank.

'Jeez! That wasn't down ten minutes ago,' she said, switching to full beam and dropping her speed.

They both fell quiet as the car moved on to steeper gradients and climbed up through the woodland. Although the little engine was loud, loudest of all were the wipers, clicking hypnotically at the end of each sweep, smearing to the rhythm of a metronome. Through the bleary screen came vision after vision of autumn leaves jerking manically at their leashes of twig as the wind gusted to gale force.

'I guess you forgot wellies?'

'Why?'

'I'm not sure this heap will make it back up our track. Not tonight.'

A few minutes later the headlights lit up the turning space at the end of the lane. The end of the line. Ahead lay the two gates, one leading down to hermit Glyn and his hovel, the other leading up to Pantglas. The last of the light was fading, an hour ahead of time, as Jane got out to check beyond her gate.

To show willing – and drawn by the drama of the storm – Bryony forced back her troublesome door and struggled out after her. The dark sheen of the tarmac was ever so quietly rippling with the run-off from the hills, sinister shivers convulsing the false surface wherever the wind let rip. A few yards beyond, Jane was stomping on the puddly ruts of her track, trying to guess at the adhesive grip of her mud.

'Evening, ladies,' said Glyn.

It was a paranormal gift, Rob always said. Several paranormal gifts, in fact. Glyn the Troll (this, the nickname chosen by his new neighbours) had a rare form of ESP: he was able to detect the presence of the second sex from half a mile away under all circumstances, *and* he could then beam himself up and rematerialise at their exact grid reference. This was a sensitivity to pheromones that even *Star Trek* had never perfected.

'Evening, Glyn,' said Jane.

'Evening,' said Bryony.

'Wild old night,' said Glyn.

'End of summer,' said Jane.

'Start of winter,' said Bryony.

'Wild old night,' said Glyn.

Before either woman could comment further, Twm, his ageing sheepdog, had wriggled through the rotting bars of Glyn's gate and was advancing unhygienically towards them. Twm was a softie, and had none of the reclusive qualities of his owner. Jane was a particular favourite, possibly the first person ever to pat him. But on this night he ignored her, and made straight for Bryony, his tongue at full stretch.

Bryony proffered a hand for a lick, but Twm was after a more thorough sloppiness. Wet and smelly, with a nose bored by sheep, he was a collie clearly glad of company. Bryony did her best to fend off his affections, but neither she nor the rain nor Glyn's two-toothed whistles managed to dampen the old dog's ardour.

Trying to keep his muddy paws at bay with fancy footwork, Bryony was forced back and back, and into the full beam of the headlights. As she manoeuvred to resist the slobbery advances, her grip on her flapping raincoat slipped and it briefly slid from her shoulders – revealing in floodlit detail her short, tight and easily unzipped little number.

'Bad boy!' said Jane, her scolding undercut by her laughter as she helped drag the mutt back to its equally dilapidated owner, as Glyn had now lost all interest in dog control.

'Animals always like me,' said Bryony apologetically, and oblivious to the difference between loving doggy urges and the power of eucalyptus oil as a canine aphrodisiac.

'Hope you like shanks's pony,' said Jane. 'We're walking from here.'

The dog safely behind five bars, and its tail held by Glyn, Jane came back and turned off the headlights. She took out a torch, and the two women set off up the track.

'Wild old night,' called Glyn, still leaning on his gate.

For the first hundred yards or so the trees offered shelter from the wind and the worst of the rain. The joshing died down as they concentrated on where best to put their feet, on which brick and which stone gave the best impersonation of dry land. They passed the slalom section, and the lichen that Rob had so loved on his first day, and the tree that florid Clydog had leant against when he thought his time had come. Then they reached the tree-line, and their first view of the ridge.

On it stood the long-house, all lit up against the incoming night.

'There!' said Jane, pointing. 'There, that's one of your surprises.'

'Pantglas?' said Bryony, puzzled.

'No. New Pantglas! *Eco*-Pantglas. With light, and heat, and water! *We have wind power!*'

'It's working?'

'It's working. Listen!'

And as Jane and Bryony stood and listened in the gusting rain, they could faintly hear the whirring of the wind-pump.

'Wow!' said Bryony. 'That's certainly worth celebrating!'

'It certainly is.' Jane paused, and then, allowing herself a touch of drama, she added, 'And that's not all!'

Bryony sensed that she was supposed to guess, but could think of nothing and shook her head.

'Rob has sold his first painting!'

'Wow!' said Bryony again. 'That's great!'

'Yes. Took best part of a year, but he's cracked it,' said Jane proudly.

'And it won't be long before the rest of the valley knows!'

'Oh yes, Dafydd'll see to that! Soon they'll all know there's a Rob original over a mantelpiece!'

'Was it hot enough?' asked Rob.

'It was wonderful,' said Bryony.

'Did it last long enough?' asked Jane.

'Best I've had in ages.'

Bryony smiled with contentment as she reached for a fig.

The mud had been an ideal ice-breaker. Splattered up her legs and on to her clothes, it had provided perfect logic for the easy and early unzipping of her short, tight dress. The muddy clothes removed, her inaugural guest test of the shower had been like the subtlest of foreplay, offering her a natural segue into eco-sensitive nudity and appreciation of their new power supply.

Now washed all over and wrapped in Rob's white woollen bathrobe, Bryony was stretched out upon their sofa, helping herself to the delicacies she had stolen earlier in the week.

In front of her, Jane was squatting on an old leather pouffe, warming her bare feet by a vigorous log fire as she nibbled on a date. Her head rested between Rob's knees as he leant back in a battered armchair. The room was a patchwork of hand-me-downs and bargains, in no particular style except old and rustic and vaguely tasteful. Two of the walls were the original brick, the others were plastered and painted off-white. The much-trodden flagstones were almost black with wear, their coldness remedied by an array of rugs. It was a room that looked its best in subdued light, as now, when the mismatches and threadbare patches merged into yellow mellow harmony.

'Anyone like more elderberry?' asked Bryony.

She reached down for the bottle with care, ensuring that her bathrobe was sufficiently loose to provide a clear and accidental view of one or more breasts. As she filled the glasses, the wind boomed down the chimney and the flames leapt about in abandon.

'Aphrodisiac, is it?' enquired Rob, teasing her as he slowly swished its blood-red stain around his glass.

'Only if you put oysters in it,' replied Bryony.

'Oh, I don't think I need an aphrodisiac,' said Jane softly, and tipped her head back until it nuzzled his groin. 'But then I never do.' And she stretched out a bare foot and ran her toes gently up Bryony's leg until they started to part her bathrobe.

'It's an Elton John song, isn't it? "Elderberry Wine"?' persisted Rob, who found an erotic charge in remaining cool even as his erection grew.

'I'm not sad enough to know!' laughed Jane. In the background, her Sade album was spreading her idea of sensuality through the room, its words 'Hang On To Your Love' rich in poignant counterpoint.

Bryony undid the cord on her bathrobe as Rob leaned forward to pull Jane's T-shirt over her head.

At that same moment, a giant gust rattled all the windowpanes in their sockets, and overhead the whirring of the rotor blades seemed briefly to go up an octave.

'Wild old night!' said Jane, and she and Bryony burst into giggles.

Outside, in the dark of the barn, a figure strained for a better view.

'"*You were a wife of mine/You aimed to please me/Cooked black-eyed peas-me/Made elderberry wine*",' quoted Rob, a touch smug at his powers of recall, as he watched Bryony slide down on to the thick-pile fireside rug and unhook Jane's bra.

'Oh God, I'm going to be sucked off to poetry!' cried Jane in a tone of mock-despair.

She let Rob grip her hands to render her passive as Bryony knelt and wrestled with her tight jeans, the borrowed robe constantly, tantalisingly falling open before their eyes. The Levi's resisted a seamless seduction, so Bryony raised Jane's thighs and tugged, and Jane fell softly from the pouffe to the floor, her bottom upturning the fruit bowl. The jeans came off and now she lay almost naked in the firelight, her feet resting in Bryony's lap, her hair gently stroked by Rob.

There was a moment of sexual uncertainty, a moment when their frolic could still be but a joke.

'Would you like anything done with the grapes?' giggled Bryony, thrusting a bunch suggestively towards her.

'Oh, you shop-girls, you're all the same!' Rob said camply. 'Always thinking of new ways to promote the produce!'

All three collapsed with the giggles, overdone, overlong giggles that put them at their ease, that helped them to bond, that gave them licence. As the giggling died away, Jane arched her back, raised her leg, and her toes toyed again with Bryony's robe, except this time she let the sole of her foot brush against her nipples.

Outside, hidden in the barn, Glyn was growing desperate. His sight-line from the barn to the bodies had been ruined by their descent to the floor. He could see little more than a bobbing head. The chance to see his first-ever bottom and his first-ever breast had come to nothing.

Blind to the risk, ignoring the storm, he crept into the yard.

' "*Drunk all the time/Feeling fine on elderberry wine/Those were the days/We'd lay in the haze*",' crooned Rob, undoing a shirt button at the end of each line.

'You must excuse him, Bryony. He sang in a band when he was little,' said Jane.

'Bloody good band too. We played in many a fine public bar.' He pulled his shirt off and dropped it gently over Jane's head. Patiently she removed it. She knew his game of nonchalance, she knew that a casual matter-of-factness in the midst of debauchery was what most aroused him. What most aroused her was to be the centre of attention.

'I used to be a groupie,' said Bryony, who knew little of music.

Jane's toes had now eased the bathrobe down to Bryony's waist, and Bryony was sat like a Buddha, patiently letting her heavy tear-drop breasts hang in waiting. Bryony was an un-complicated woman. She liked cuddles. And for Bryony, cuddles with two people was simply cuddles squared.

Jane lay in the warmth of the fire and gazed at Bryony's body, squeezing Rob's hand for the added thrill of the shared moment. Yet even as she luxuriated in a wash of emotions, Jane's mind did not abandon the practical, and she was quietly constructing a wish list from the erotic optional extras. For her, a priority turn-on was to be first to nudity, front-runner in any night of excess.

So Jane rose to her feet, and stood between them in little more than a grandiose thong.

Then invited them jointly to remove it.

As if to mark the moment, another dramatic gust hit the curtainless windows. Even amid the heat of the hearth, she felt a draught upon her shoulders, while overhead the endlessly whirring wind-pump gave an unprofessional rattle as it rotated – as though it, too, were aroused.

Rob and Bryony knelt either side of Jane's slender body and gently slipped down her last piece of clothing.

Outside, Glyn crouched astride the drainage channel, at the limit of the shadows, and strained for sights of sex. He no more felt the lashing rain than he had felt the scratching brambles on his stumbling run through the woods. Never would he be nearer to the facts of fornication. Over all the long, lonely years he had known nothing of women save the passing crotch at the gate. By day, he roamed priapic across the hills; by night, he slept in a grandfather chair beside the range, his decaying parlour full of smoke and fevered dreams and phantasmal wives.

Ever since his first sight of Jane, smiling with Mr Probert, he knew that she did it. Knew that she thought about it. Knew that she laughed about it. Knew that she liked it.

Overwhelmed by dark and desperate thoughts, Glyn began to tear at the buttons on his trousers.

Jane sank back down upon the pouffe, its crinkled old leather warm to her skin. Without a word, Bryony then rose from her knees, smiled, and took her turn in the middle. Together, Rob and Jane gave just the lightest of tweaks to her undone robe, and it collapsed around her ankles. Bryony gave a twirl, the unneeded proof that she too was nude.

Jane gently clasped her hands around Bryony's waist.

' "*How can I ever get it together/Without a wife in line/To pick the crop and get me hot/On elderberry wine*",' sang Rob provocatively, in his best Elton John.

'Could you stop that?' said Jane. 'Some of us are trying to have sex here!' And with that, another fit of giggles hit them all.

They collapsed upon the floor, their formal, almost choreographed, middle-class approach to troilism giving way to the more traditional scrimmage, in which they all rolled around and groped and tickled and Jane kept crying, 'Get his trousers off!'

Amidst such a riotous free-for-all, no one heard the whirring rotor blades subtly change their tone.

Nor, at first, amid the tumult of nature, did Glyn. His bailer twine loose, his self-control gone, he was panting hard and grunting, his hand working like a piston, his legs trembling on the concrete ground. Lost in his private red mist, just yards from his neighbours' window, he was oblivious to the world about him, oblivious to discovery, to embarrassment, to ostracism, to shame. Even to damnation. Never would this chance come again, this chance to be part of life, part of loving, part of feeling, part of being human.

'Woo-woo-woo-woo-woo-woo-woo-woo-woo-woo-woo.'

Like an Indian war cry it came, like a mighty ululation across the plain, like a deadly vibration in the brain.

'Woo-woo-woo-woo-woo-woo-woo-woo-woo-woo-woo.'

And still Glyn's lonely, horny hand kept pounding.

Rob's Y-fronts were on their way down, eased tenderly from his groin by multiple ministering fingers. With erotic reciprocity, he was fondling every inch of buttock within his reach. The giggling was giving way to heavy breathing. The intertwining of limbs would soon be upon them, the promised land of synchronised orgasms no longer a distant dream.

But then they heard it too.

'Woo-woo-woo-woo-woo-woo-woo-woo-woo-woo-woo.'

And then it ceased.

And it ceased with a crack like the crack of doom. Out went the lamps. Off went the Sade. Alone in the room was the sound of the storm. Then the storm was made trite by a cacophonous crashing.

And a hideous feral scream from the farmyard.

Fornication had never seemed more frivolous.

'Oh my God!' cried Rob. 'Tinkerbell!'

He tried to stand, but his trousers tangled in his trainers, his Y-fronts twisted round his ankles, and the elderberry wine went toxic in his head. Rob fell back on to the pouffe, his penis redundant.

Jane raced to the door in panic with Bryony close behind. They ran outside, bending low against the rain that howled around the long-house, shining the torch into the black of the night.

The wind-pump parts were spread across the yard, as they had been on the day of assembly. One seven-foot rotor blade was upright in the pond, like a giant spear hurled by the God of Wind from the roof above. The other rotor blade lay almost flat upon the yard, resting on a bundle of old clothes.

Glyn groaned. The giant blade lay across his chest, crushing his ribs like a judgement of guilt. The wet and the cold and the shock added to his trauma, and he found it hard to breathe. The world was going hazy. As he lay inert, waiting for the final trumpet, he heard the sound of voices, and someone crying, 'Heave!'

The weight of wind power was lifted from his chest and he looked up to the heavens and saw two naked women disposing of a rotor blade. These naked women came and knelt beside him. These naked women told him not to move. One naked woman wiped the rain from his face. The other naked woman held his hand.

He died a happy man.

Chapter 29

At first, Stéfan could not tell why he had awoken. Indeed, for a second he could not tell where he had awoken. And then he realised he was on the chesterfield in his study.

He had dropped into the study for a late-night Armagnac, to wind down beside the fire. The study had an intimacy his other rooms lacked; it also had a temperature his other rooms lacked, for in his battle with the boiler he was still coming second. In olden days, the place would have been a den, the hidey-hole of the husband, the home of the stuffed owl. It irked him to think this, but, despite his grand designs elsewhere, the features of his favourite room were not so much Imperial Domestic as Suburban Cosy.

He had needed the brandy as reward for his day. After the tedium of the drive and the drama in the bank had come the drudgery at the pub – where last-minute crises were available on draught. 'Finishing touches' were words he never wished to hear again in the Nant Valley, unless spoken by builders willing to take lie-detector tests twice daily. At last, though, after much late stippling and ad hoc plumbing, the Stéfan Arms was more or less ready to open. Even the live music had finally been booked. *And* he had come to a working arrangement with Gwillim.

Several minutes passed as Stéfan lay yawning on the sofa. He was almost sure that something had woken him. But what it was, he could not tell. He looked across at his grandfather clock. It was well gone midnight, even allowing for its erratic pendulum. He decided against another brandy, for tomorrow would be a busy, boozy day. And then he heard it. Quiet but distinct. Low-key but important. Steady but insistent.

Dripping.

The noise of the rain had masked the sound. The house faced south-west, and was taking the force of the wind on its Jacobean chin. The sudden squalls would hit the windows like handfuls of gravel hurled from a sling. Yet, for Stéfan, to hear the lashing rain was not unwelcome, as it said the scaffolding had finally gone, the work on the house completed. The elements could huff and puff and Crug Caradoc's owner could ignore them . . . But the noise of the rain had misled him, had noisily merged with the dripping. Except for one small detail that had jarred upon the ear. One small detail that betrayed the dreadful truth.

The dripping was on the inside.

Stéfan leapt from the chesterfield. Not since his coitus had been interrupted by The Windowman had Stéfan leapt so fast. He rushed to the window, looking for the dripping. He soon found it. It was not just one drip. When drips come, they come not singly but with fellow drips. Evenly spread and forming little puddles. Pouring from the frame and down the wall. Pouring from the floor above and down the frame. Pouring from God knows where and laying at your feet.

Stéfan hurried to the library, and there too he found drips in mass attendance. He hurried to the lounge, to the salon, to the dining room; to the reception room, to the second reception room, to the third reception room, and to a room he had as yet no name for. The scene was the same, give or take some hundred drips. He hurried upstairs, to bedrooms 1–7, and to the room where he and The Windowman had had their epiphany. Everywhere, the unhurried, undiscriminating drip, a chilling remorseless sound, the advance guard of terminal wet rot.

Hours and hours of driving rain had breached millimetre gaps in the frames' hand-tooled defences. Defying gravity, the driven rain had gone up and along and about and around to hunt down the Achilles' heels of carpentry. These water-packed raindrops had, like programmed mice, squeezed their way through a hundred hairbreadth holes, only to end their journey on Stéfan's carpets. Which now squelched beneath his feet.

It was at this moment that he recalled Nico's mocking smile on auction day. It had transcended the mere sparring over lots. It had been a smile not of transient venom, but of malign certainty that the fates were against him. It was the smirk of experience, the smirk that said he, an outsider, was doomed to fail. Such was Stéfan's temper tantrum that day, he had stormed from the tent. And had determined to succeed.

A year of valley habits had modified this outlook. He had learned that the forces of class and feudalism, of history and apathy, were ranged against him. He also had complaints about the local laws of economics and the biased behaviour of the bench. And the unenterprising approach towards big game. But only tonight did he fully understand why Nico had such confidence in the forces of reaction. Only now did Stéfan realise that the climate itself was aligned with the enemy, that the seventy-five inches of annual rain were strictly personal.

And then his thoughts turned to Mr Griffith Barton. And what he would say to him (were he not ex-directory). And what he would do to him (were he not miles away in the woods). It was a thorough plan. Apart from the violence, he would personally take The Windowman on a grand tour of the house, now, at one o'clock in the morning. And he would show him every last drip. And every last drop. Every pitter-patter, every splish-splosh, every plip-plop, every plink-plonk, that he could possibly find. Several times over.

Then it struck Stéfan that his plight could have been worse. If he had let The Windowman have his way, he wouldn't even had windows – he would have had sacking.

Chapter 30

'Oooh!' cried the little group in unison.

A gargoyle had fallen off, breaking an angel into several parts.

'An architecturally duff gargoyle,' said the surveyor unfeelingly.

Attention switched to the weather vane, which had already had a heavy night of oscillating, and was looking iffy.

'My great-great-grandfather did the gargoyles,' said the Commodore, speaking to himself as usual.

There were seven people standing on the humpback bridge, possibly a record for 3 a.m. It was the vicar, on his way home from a Boy Scouts' drinks party, who had noticed that St Brynnach's was inching itself into the river. It is rare that a man sees a third of his income sliding into a river and he was naturally distraught. The crisis was much too serious for prayer and he had rushed at once to the Commodore's.

'Oooh!' came another cry from the bridge as ominous crunching was heard.

'Just a voussoir,' said the surveyor, who took no prisoners when it came to ecclesiastical architecture.

The Commodore had not reacted well to the landslide news; it was this sort of upset that had led him to leave the war early. But his sister was not an OBE for nothing and knew to reach straight for the phone. The 999 call had initially produced an administrative uncertainty as to which service was most appropriate to assist a terminal church, but in time a policeman, two fire officers and a water official were sent.

All were now peering across the river at the church's progress through the graveyard.

'At least it's stopped raining,' said the vicar, who was wishing he belonged to one of those religions that gave you worry beads.

'Too late,' said the surveyor, with suppressed satisfaction. His elaborate trench-work now resembled a miniature Venice, and the river's highest surge had yet to pass through.

'He's got a plaque,' said the Commodore wistfully. 'A shiny plaque. 1822–1876.'

Another yard of river bank collapsed. Undercut from below, the earth and stones slithered from sight with the ponderous drama of a hippopotamus deciding on a swim. The Nant was a greedy river, at its greediest in spate. Even darkness could not hide its ceaseless scouring of the muddy meadow banks that ordained its course.

With the waters burrowing away beneath the church like a monster vole, the body of the nave had begun to slightly tilt. The Hartford-Stanley crack was widening, groaning, and letting in enough wind to blow off a corset. Pressure was growing on the tower to say goodbye to the nave, to begin a new life as a ruin.

'*I*'d like a plaque when I'm dead,' said the Commodore.

Suspecting this to be more an interior monologue than a conversation, the vicar did not respond. Instead, he continued to lean upon the parapet of the bridge, a little dizzy from mixing the evening's alcohol with air, and gaze glumly towards his vanishing church. He had mutterings of his own to give vent to. 'Great recommendation, eh? "*Reason for redundancy: Act of God.*" That should be a first for a vicar's CV.' He added a self-pitying sigh.

'We live in interesting times,' replied the church surveyor, 'when insurance companies are the only people left who believe in God.'

'Did you know the bishop said I was too fat?'

'Did you deny it?'

'He's a bishop.'

A yard or two away, the men in uniform were monitoring the situation – by means of looking in the direction of the church and standing around with authoritative posture. At one point, the senior fire officer spoke into his walkie-talkie, updating headquarters on the status of the incident, and the words 'big splash' were heard. But for these people the drama had no personal importance, no deep significance.

'I do find life is odd,' mused the Commodore sadly. 'Very odd. When I was young I used to have dreams that our house would fall into a great big pit. Dug by the clergy. And now this . . .' He gestured haplessly downstream.

The vicar struggled with the imagery. '. . . You were worried about falling down into hell?'

'No, no, no, no, no,' said the Commodore. 'Into the gold mines. Under our sitting room.' He had always found the vicar to be slow on the uptake. 'My sister was forever warning me. "The Church are coming!" she'd shout. "With their shovels."' The childhood memory was vivid in his eyes. 'It's a large house. I never knew which room the vicars would be digging under. All mining away with their cassocks on. Hunting for the gold.'

This was a view of church history with which the Reverend Oliver was not familiar.

It was the surveyor who understood.

'House was first a rectory,' he said *sotto voce* to the vicar. 'And the church likes to keep the mining rights under its old property. Just in case. After all, heaven's still on the gold standard. Souls are just a sideline.'

The dead thud of a bellyflop signalled that the first headstone had hit the water. Now the end of a coffin poked from the bank. Last in to the cemetery, first out, poor Hefin's body was about to move on from the daisies to the fishes. The retaining wall of the graveyard, the last line of defence, was now just token stones.

Waiting to be taken by the flood. The vicar looked to heaven. The surveyor smiled.

The departing church meant more than merely matters spiritual. For the Commodore it meant hundreds of years of history; for the vicar it meant hundreds of pounds of salary; for the surveyor it meant a job well done. It was a job Euan loved, bringing pain to the clergy; repair bills to the bishopric; demolition orders to the archdiocese. It was the perfect revenge for his schooldays – although he had as yet to see a flying buttress fall on a nun. As boarder at a religious school in the hills, his lessons had come from Christians whose teaching aids were leather belts. Euan's one-man programme of church deconstruction had its roots in five formative years of weals and welts – the syllabus according to Sister Philomena of the Plastic Chairs.

Bits of a moon were appearing. A couple of clouds were fraying at the edges. The storm was exhausted.

But still the water was on its way up. And the river end of the nave was on its way down. The scissor trusses supporting the roof were beginning to buckle. Beneath them, the mosaic friezes on the walls were popping their tiles like podded peas; the water in the font was at an angle; and the reverential approach to the altar was best done at a light downhill trot. The decline of the Church in Wales was ready to be made flesh.

Reality and the Commodore appeared to continue on their parallel paths even as the air crackled with the noise of snapping slates. Then the old man slowly raised his arthritic hands to his mouth.

'Oh dear me, the bones!' he moaned. 'The bones! The Powell bones!'

The Powell bones were in the Powell crypt, and there was no Rupert to fetch them, no faithful dogservant to lay two centuries of ossified history at his feet. Military men and farmers, bankers and clerics, here all the family were kept on file in their coffins, stacked in racks in waiting. Here, the Powells could remain a dynasty even in death, offering skeletons as Earthly proof of past pomp.

'If you're lucky they'll probably just swish about a bit,' said the surveyor, in what was meant as comfort. 'You shouldn't lose that many.'

This seemed of little consolation to the Commodore.

'I don't care if I *lose* them,' he muttered irritably. He watched as a rolling, twisting tree trunk slalomed its way through the giant eddies beyond the bridge. 'What I can't bear is the thought of our own bones . . . all mixed up with Llewellyn bones.'

As if in response to such lack of Christian charity, St Brynnach's shivered with a violent spasm, like a building afflicted with a fatal *grand mal*. The church's final schism was under way.

The crack which began life as a rare erotic frisson for a stout-legged lady was now renting asunder with the power of Samson. Beside the round-headed doorway with the voussoirs, the crack had become a chasm. At the end of the nave, the chancel had genuflected to the river. The early vegetable offerings for Harvest Festival rolled waywardly down the aisle. As God gave precedence to gravity, the altar and the choir stalls stood at an angle incompatible with prayer or song. The stained-glass pictures of Jesus and his Beulah lambs slid from their lead moorings and shattered into shards.

In the tower, the stays were cracked and the bells had begun to compose their own peal. On the bridge, their jangling fought for ear space with the grinding of ancient stones and the roaring of the water.

And above, the moon was finally freed of cloud. It shone upon a river in hyperdrive, upon a graveyard in turmoil, upon a spray that rose high in the sky as the land hurled its consecrated debris into the muddy depths.

The surveyor could not restrain a slight smug smile as he murmured beneath his breath, 'Hardly one church indivisible, I think.'

The broken-backed building gathered momentum, eased as if by God's grease over the edge of the meadow bank. As the nave broke from the tower, it took on the form of an errant railway carriage, decoupled and on end in a pile-up. The vicar knew there was now no chance to reach the collection box. Then the Victorian nave slid in almost stately slow-motion into the River Nant. An entire church on its way to baptism. The chamfered plinths, the angle buttresses, the stone dressings, the masons' craftwork, all conferred a sad defiant dignity on the crumbling nave – and the long remains of the church entered the dark waters like a rare breed of ecclesiastical liner, launched upon a doomed final voyage.

The Commodore was sombre, the Powell stiff lip almost gone. 'Black mark, losing a church,' he said. 'No one in my family's ever lost a church before.'

And then, amid the bells and the spume and the crashing of tombs, he started to mumble about the war.

Chapter 31

'With his trousers round his ankles?' repeated Hubert, astonished.

'So the police said,' insisted Clydog.

'Hefin had his trousers round his ankles too,' remarked Dafydd.

'Perhaps it's a centre for satanic ritual,' suggested Auberon.

It was not normal deli practice to gather for gossip on a Saturday, but events of the last twenty-four hours had left a gossip overload that would take weeks to clear.

'What sort of satanic ritual leaves you with a soppy smile on your face?' retorted Clydog, irritated by the silliness of his young photographer.

'Glyn was smiling?' said the postman in disbelief. 'Twenty years and I've never seen him smile. Leer, yes, but *smile* . . . ?'

'That's what the police said,' insisted Clydog. 'From ear to ear. And still up there, because the hearse is stuck.'

'Why would you smile with a rotor blade across your chest?' asked Hubert.

'Perhaps it's like a devil's cross, some kind of satanic symbol?' suggested Auberon, the news of a violent death having suddenly ended his eighteen years of inarticulacy.

'It blew down off the damn chimney,' snapped Clydog.

' "Said the police," ' added Dafydd pre-emptively. He was piqued that he had no insider's input, no exclusive angle, for

Pantglas had been sealed off by tape at the bottom of the track, and even claiming an urgent need to deliver the latest edition of *Acupuncture in Medicine* had cut no ice with the officer guarding the gate. But Dafydd was also nurturing a deeper malaise, for these last twenty-four hours had dealt him a bitter blow too.

'I don't understand why he didn't take his trousers down in his own farmyard,' muttered Hubert, who had also had a morning of shocks. Not often on one's walk to work does one see a crucified Christ surfing the weir.

'Why did it blow off the chimney?' asked Auberon.

'Wind-power's a funny thing,' said Clydog, in the tone of a man with a scoop. 'Creates unexpected centrifugal forces.'

'Did the police say that as well?' asked Dafydd.

'No. I rang Holland.'

This was the greatest shock so far, and was greeted with a well-deserved silence. Clydog's use of telephones had previously been unknown, and to ring abroad, to a foreign country, was an initiative smacking of Fleet Street.

'Why?' asked Hubert.

'You get a nose,' said Clydog. Which was news in itself. 'There was a label on the blade, in Dutch. It was—'

'I was right about the bank manager, then,' interposed Dafydd, bidding for his share of the limelight. 'He's coughed to fifteen other women. Seems you could get five per cent off your loan for a legover. *That*'s not on their posters!'

Deep down, though, Dafydd wanted to talk about his own news, his personal news . . . and yet he knew it could not compete on a day which had sex and violence and religion and death.

'It was a Dutch wind-pump,' persisted Clydog. 'Made for Dutch wind. That's why it blew down. Wrong sort of wind.'

'Wrong sort of wind?' said Hubert, incredulously. 'You're saying Glyn was killed because—'

'Welsh wind's no good. All gusty and nasty, my contact in Rotterdam said. Invalidates the warranty. Whereas Dutch wind—'

'Bollocks!' said Dafydd.

'Whereas Dutch wind is solid and reliable. Like their clogs.'

'Well, you certainly don't hear of Dutch churches being blown down,' admitted Hubert, who had had a scary night. 'Did you see the river this morning? It's full of pews!'

'They'll be for sale in Nico's by tomorrow,' said Dafydd.

' "One owner. Careful kneeler",' added Hubert. He rotated slowly in his office chair. 'I saw Christ go by. Before I knew the church had collapsed. Steady four knots he was doing, with weed round his beard. Hell of a shock at seven a.m. I almost converted.'

'It's not the wind did it, it's the water,' said Clydog, always a stickler for facts. 'Church surveyor blames it all on farmers, and their new drainage schemes. I think we'll have to censor that.'

'Nico can't resell coffins, can he?' asked Auberon. 'Because I saw a coffin float under the bridge in the High Street.'

'With or without corpse?' asked Hubert. 'He'll charge extra for a corpse.'

'Got a great photo of it for page one,' Auberon added.

Clydog groaned. 'Poor lad's still not got the hang of his aunt's paper,' he said to the other two. 'Auberon, we don't do coffins, on any page.'

'Or anything that might upset somebody still living,' added Dafydd.

'There's a churchload of stuff in that river, though,' Hubert went on. 'Hymn books, lecterns, everything except the vicar. I'd have thought he'd have floated by, size of his gut. Guess it must have been a wild old night up the valley.'

'Easy to see why Bryony's not come in,' said Dafydd. 'Could spoil your orange juice, waking up to find the church opposite has vanished. And not know whether you've slept through the end of the world.'

'Bryony's not religious,' snapped Hubert, who was feeling less sympathetic.

Her absence irked him, as in ten minutes he had to leave the shop. As President of the Chamber of Commerce he had yet again to stand and watch the mayoress perform her public duties, with Wagnerian flourishes and Dolly Parton embonpoint. Yet again he had to stand in public view alongside the council and watch Myfanwy Edwards unveil another milestone in Abernant's march to modernity. But today was an occasion he was dreading more than usual. Today was an occasion that would test him.

'I think we might find the bank manager is absent from today's little ceremony,' murmured Clydog, who had noticed Hubert check the clock. Clydog gave a rare, if lugubrious, smile.

'Apparently it was his socks that did for him,' interposed Dafydd.

'His socks?' said the others. With gratifying astonishment.

'Yes. Didn't bother to take his socks off when he bonked Gareth's wife. Ultimate insult to a sheep farmer, apparently. Socks on for sex. If it were wellingtons, I could understand Gareth being cross. That's plain bad hygiene. But socks . . . ? Could have been the pattern, of course. Or some funky slogan.'

'Like "Sod Gareth!"' suggested Auberon, and was ignored by the postman.

'Except that man goes for fashion . . . silk . . . cashmere. Not exactly inappropriate items for adultery. But . . . just seems to have been the wrong socks in the wrong place at the wrong time. And the sight of them simply tipped Gareth over the edge.'

'These socks,' said Clydog suspiciously. 'How do we know about them?'

'Oh, the police said,' replied Dafydd insouciantly, not bothering to elaborate that the police station was on his Saturday round. And was responsible not just for his facts but for most of his fanciful speculations.

'Admittedly, he's not making a lot of sense. Wants a law passed declaring it illegal for bank managers to be over five foot six. And wants a refund on some picture. But he's not in a strong bargaining position. He's going to be charged with firearms offences and criminal damage. Only bank ceiling ever to be victim of a *crime passionnel*!'

'Any other news?' enquired Clydog drily.

'Oh, apparently he's asked after Glyn's dog. Wanted to know if there were any takers.'

'Well . . . !' said an impressed Hubert. 'That was all top-grade information. I loved the socks detail.'

'Thank you,' said Dafydd, gratified. 'Nice to go out on a high note.'

'What's that supposed to mean?'

Dafydd sighed bitterly, and expressively. 'Means the bloody end, that's what.' His tone made them take notice. 'Means I was "appraised" yesterday. Annually appraised. It's a management word. Typical two-faced management word! Seven letters spell praised. And the "a, p" bit means fuck off, you're sacked.'

'Sacked?' said Clydog and Hubert together.

'What for?' asked Hubert.

Even at a moment this bleak, Dafydd was aware that he had his audience in the palm of his hand, and he did not disappoint.

'Oh, a long list of offences. Crimes against efficiency. First was looking after Hefin after he died. Then it was stopping that yob Eryl from cutting your Bryony's house in half. Then it was for helping paint a bit of Tinkerbell, one time up at Rob's with Gareth. And so on and so on. My boss had a long dossier of things like that. Inappropriate use of Royal Mail time, he calls it.'

'But how would he know?' asked Clydog.

'How indeed? Is my van bugged, I ask?'

'So who else knew?'

'Who *could* know?' said Dafydd.

'Lionel Blake,' Hubert said quietly. 'That's who. And, of course, the rest of the Chamber of Commerce. Including the Royal Mail representatives. Very entertaining man, the bank manager, especially about you and the pig.'

'Oh my God! But how—'

'Pillow talk, I guess. Via Bryony. And via Moira via Gareth.'

The postman did not need to act dumbfounded. At the last count, the bank manager had slept with thirteen of Dafydd's customers. Who knew every last detail of Dafydd's deliveries. Indeed, in exchange for three eggs he had even shown hard-up Mrs Whitelaw how best to remove unfranked stamps.

The ruin of his career was now moving beyond melodrama, and the postman felt sick at heart. 'That's the trouble with this valley,' he said angrily. 'People just don't realise the harm that idle gossip can do.'

'I know,' said Hubert sympathetically. 'It's very unfair. I wish I could do something to help.' He spun his chair round one last time, and stood up. 'Look, I'm sorry, Dafydd, it's nearly time, we've got to go. The mayoress awaits.'

Clydog eased his bottom off the desk, and wiped the last of the Wicked Chocolate Fudge Cake from his chin. He gave Dafydd an awkward, repressed pat on the back. Young Auberon did the same, his camera swinging dangerously loose as he leant across.

Hubert delayed them a second while he reached under his desk and pulled out a rather heavy holdall to take with him.

'So what's she doing this time?' asked Dafydd. 'Our Lady of Good Works.'

'Unveiling the new parking meters,' said Clydog.

'The new unwanted parking meters,' said Hubert, with his Chamber of Commerce hat on.

'Oh, yes, the infamous High Street meters,' said Dafydd, trying to raise a smile.

'The very same,' said Clydog. 'So we can't be late. Can't miss this one. It'll be our big lead story of the week.'

Chapter 32

Eryl revved down and eased the big black motorbike off the bypass and into the roundabout. He turned at the sign for Abernant and soon saw the grey slate roofs below him in the late afternoon sun. He pulled into the first lay-by and pushed up his goggles. He laid his heavy black gauntlets along the jazzy red stripe of the fuel tank and rubbed at his tired eyes. Then he stretched out his legs and looked almost fondly at the view ahead.

'There!' he said to his wife. 'Home! Abernant! That's where it all happens!'

'Yes,' said Irina.

'No,' said Eryl. 'A joke. Nothing ever happens there.'

'Yes,' said Irina.

'And beyond,' he said, pointing, 'is the Nant Valley. Where nothing ever changes.'

'Yes,' said Irina.

Eryl pulled down his goggles and tugged his gloves back on. The mileometer registered 24,736 miles. Dank and lonely though the memories were, he already felt nostalgic for a pint at the Dragon's Head.

He rode slowly in through the outskirts, his wilder wheelie urges sated by endless hours of foreign tarmac, and pointed out the few Abernantian items of interest. Irina seemed impressed, for where she came from there were no outskirts. Eryl pointed out the Elim Tabernacle, the new car-wash, the monkey puzzle tree in the Pensioners' Memorial Garden, the stuffed-animals shop that was always closed. All was as before, apart from an unexpected mini-roundabout, and little had prepared him to see an altar lodged under the bridge at the end of the High Street.

Eryl pointed it out to Irina, a practising Catholic, but could think of no convincing explanation. He also lacked the language skills to convey that submerged altars were not a standard cultural feature of the mid-Wales landscape. Or that the crowd on the bridge were not worshippers. But Irina seemed unfazed and continued to cling trustingly to his expensive leathers as he rode on past, the road too narrow to stop.

The High Street was busier than usual and he kept the revs low, looking for friends to wave to, looking for friends – and indeed merest acquaintances – to whom he could introduce his beautiful foreign wife. Abernant on a Saturday is hub of the local universe, and it was not long before he spotted a familiar face. Normally he and Gareth sat glumly on bar stools, bemoaning their lot and their love lives; Eryl knew him as a man who rarely strayed far from a field. The sight of him being led handcuffed from the police station to a waiting squad car was therefore hard for Eryl to fathom. He did think of waving in moral support but diminished funds meant his de luxe bike was no longer taxed. Eryl watched as Gareth's head was pressed down to enter the police car, and he rode on past.

All that is important in Abernant is in its hundred yards of high street. Food, finance, fashion, TV rental, all of life's support systems are within a short pub crawl. Eryl had pointed out the KwikSave, the Woolworths, the Short Cuts hair salon, the cinema where *Beau Geste* had changed Sion's life, and was about to thrill Irina with the deli when he caught sight of the bank.

The blue and white tape of police movies was festooned across its pillared porch. Fluttering and fluorescent, it proclaimed 'Crime Scene' to the world. Two chunky men in uniform stood guard outside, barring entry to all but those in white coats. Even the historic cash machine was out of bounds. In a region where almost all crimes were animal related, armed bank robbery represented an historic first. Eryl was by now at a bit of a loss, and he rode on past.

Until he saw the meters. And the crowd ahead.

He slowed the bike to walking pace. Rows of taped-off parking meters stretched ahead of him on either side of the High Street. Polished and shiny, their slots at the ready, they stood like symbols of lost innocence. In the distance on a dais, stood the mayoress, awaiting the town's official scissors.

To Eryl, this was yet another unplanned event that defied his phrase book.

To his Romanian bride, this was yet another thread of the rich capitalist tapestry she had dreamed of so often while under communism.

Ever since Eryl, the man of mystery, had ridden into Irina's remote and primitive farm collective, she knew that he offered salvation. Her father knew it too. Never had they seen such a bike, so powerful, so expensive, so stylish. Never had they seen such bikewear, so lavish, so airtight, so imperiously black. Never had they seen such a biker, so aristocratic in his Austro-Hungarian moustache. As Eryl, the knight in shining leather, rode into sight past their midden, trailing wealth from his mighty exhaust, Irina's peasant father had said to her, 'This is a man sent by the gods. He will bring us fortune and happiness.'

Irina was a prized and lovely virgin. She sprang from the tradition of dutiful, adoring (and silent) women whom Eryl had sought in vain. Encouraged by the family, he paused for a few days' pit-stop. While he engaged the daughter with his ragged playboy charms, he impressed the father with his capacity for toasts in *tzuica*, the national plum brandy. Neither his Romanian nor her English allowed for the interchange of seminal thoughts (of which he had few), but the language of signs helped to create a bond. In Eryl's sign language he spoke constantly of a great estate far away. Although the finer points were hazy, there was a house that had many rooms and much land and big lakes.

The romance was whirlwind; the brandy was constant; the betrothal was a blur; and the marriage was a red-letter day for the village. And thus was Irina granted her entrée to the wonders of the West, to an unknown land of Celtic milk and honey.

'Parking meter ceremony,' said Eryl, by way of explanation.

'Yes,' said Irina. And watched dutifully.

The Traffic Warden, the authority in whom parking was vested, carried forward the velvet pouffe bearing the ceremonial scissors and a 10p coin. (The mayoress had suggested he walk backwards, but the modernising wing of the council had vetoed the idea.) The mayoral car stood perfectly aligned in the parking bay, waiting for its fifteen minutes of fame. The mayoress waved to the crowd, adjusted her centre of gravity, and aimed the scissors at the tape.

'I declare these parking meters—'

'A monstrosity!'

Hubert burst into view, followed by the Free Trade faction, and advanced upon the mayoral dais. To a shaky chant of 'Meters Out!', the parking extremists moved through the crowd handing out protest leaflets. Irina puzzled silently over hers. A cartoon depicted meters as metallic triffids, lashing out at family cars and strangling the town's traders to death. The accompanying text forecast the bankruptcy of Abernant, as blood and pound notes drained away in the bottom right-hand corner. A retired local architect wrote of the visual vandalism to the historic high street vista.

Hubert reached Myfanwy, opened up his holdall, and pulled out several lengths of chain. He and his followers then spent several minutes working out how to handcuff themselves to a row of meters. Once secured, Hubert declared himself available for interviews and Clydog – whose nose for news had given him no warning – moved in with his pad and pencil. To keep it professional, he began by asking Hubert's name.

The climax to the protest, which had been several months in the planning, was for Hubert, President of the Chamber of

Commerce, to be very publicly arrested. Unfortunately, the only police on duty were busy guarding a loose piece of stucco at the bank. Equally unfortunately, Auberon had used up all his film on shots of a coffin and had had to return to Boots. And the only authority with statutory powers was the Traffic Warden, whose history of blackmailing traders for gifts rendered him prone to be thumped.

This left Hubert chained to the meters without an exit strategy – and, thanks to an unwise touch of melodrama involving a drain, without a padlock key. The pro-meter faction of the council, who since the parking schism always appeared separately in public, then crossed the road to pass the time of day in an abusive manner. The crowd, who rarely got to see street theatre, tore down the tapes in their excitement, and declared the meters open without the use of scissors. Whereupon the mayoress fled in the mayoral car, fearful that news of the imbroglio might reach the ears of an honours committee.

Eryl judged it was time to move on from the town.

The valley road that led to the moors began urbanely with bungalows, last wheezing place of farmers as they downsized from cows to cats. From draughty farms to stuffy boxes. Eager to retain a rural toehold to the end, the owners allowed little latitude for names: River Bank, River View, River Side, was all it ever said in the carved wooden signs by their gates. In this landscape, the one bit of sward was a bowling green, the ultimate suburbanisation of grass.

And then the buildings ceased. Planning permission over. They were in the limbo land between town and country, passing a scrubby field with a horse, an electricity substation, and a scout hut. And graffiti that claimed the vicar was a wanker, a sentiment that was perhaps not entirely gratuitous.

Soon the Nant could be glimpsed through the wind-torn canopy of a municipal copse. The roar had gone, the surge had subsided, and just a dirty tidemark was left, soiling the ground with tree litter. A lone man was walking his dog, spoilt for choice of sticks to throw.

Eryl was nearing the town limits and the freedom of the valley lay ahead. The 'No Limit' sign came into view.

And then a 'Road Closed' sign.

Eryl did think of stopping, but it did not seem a guy thing to do. So he steered around the sign. He was puzzled, not for the first time that day. Only snow ever closed the valley road and it was not snowing. But the cause had to be an accident and a bike could always steer around an accident.

He also had the strong motive of thirst, and it was near opening time – or would be if the pub was under new ownership. Eryl had given few thoughts to the Nant Valley on his travels, but usually they had been about the chequebook which Stéfan had slammed down amid the slops on the bar. Had money talked? Had the pub with almost no beer come off the wagon?

'Pub,' said Eryl, pointing to the hills.

'Yes,' said Irina.

The familiar field patterns of mid-Wales now filled the view. Small and irregular, unprofitable and wet, and always bordered by hawthorn hedges, these were the grazing lands that made lamb lean. Here at least, nothing ever changed. The farm animals lay scattered Lowry-like, as static as props. In the sky circled a buzzard, with its usual pretensions to be a vulture. And by the field gates the green of Fisons had started churning to brown as early winter waterlogged the land.

A ferret ran jerkily in front of Eryl, from one verge to the other. It was the first ferret he had seen since he left. As a gangly youth, he had kept a ferret, raced it down pipes, even pushed it up his trouser leg for a joke and a bet. He had given the ferret a name – Joshua, not a particularly ferrety name – and kept it in a large box and treated it with adolescent reverence. Ferrets were more human than most people realise.

Sometimes, at dusk, you could see a badger crossing this stretch of road on its way down to the river. Sometimes, though, you couldn't see it, and next morning it would be crumpled by the verge, a hit-and-run candidate for the taxidermist. And sometimes, when rolling home at first light from parties, you would catch sight of a fox, whose timetable of secrecy had not catered for drunks.

Like Sion before him, he had tired of abroad. Like Nico before him, he had felt the need to come home. With the passing of countries, the ebbing of money, Eryl had come to feel there was more comfort in failure at home than failure overseas. And even the memory of failure had dimmed as the months went by, for eating up the miles gave off the false odour of achievement, and made him feel almost competent.

Ahead of him, Eryl was surprised to see a Volvo, exiting the little lane that came down from Pantglas. It was the first car he had seen since leaving town and it caught his attention because it had a body on the roof.

The Volvo was familiar and as it passed he recognised the driver was Nico. He did not recognise the corpse.

Irina pointed.

'Yes,' said Eryl.

Just for a second he felt like a stranger in his own land. Ever since leaving the bypass he had felt his cultural reference points had all been subtly changed, although Eryl would probably have not expressed it in that manner had he been asked.

He was still trying to make sense of his feeling that something was odd with the world when he saw the giant crane blocking the road.

And then he saw half the church was missing. The more useful half.

In what used to be the bit with the pews, demolition men in shiny yellow coats stood directing a killer cannonball to and fro amidst the ruined walls. Eryl almost left the road with shock as a sandstone window arch was hit for six and thundered to the ground in a storm of yellow dust.

Ignoring the shouts, he steered his bike up on the verge and round the crane, and halted on the corner of the lane just beyond. This was where he had sat on the day he left the valley six months before. Here, with his visor down and engine running, he had watched the parish parting for home, serene in the belief that a musical afternoon had saved the church.

He and Irina paused beneath the overhanging yews, and stared across at the brutal last rites. Leaning against the lychgate, toppled by the storm, was the mighty thermometer, its mock-mercury stuck at £20,000. Beyond, the men in hard hats crunched through glass where people once had knelt. Around them rose the last of the buttresses, true to the spirit of Victorian ruins. And above them, like a monstrous metronome, swung the relentless wrecking ball, helping to make the church safe from reckless worshippers.

Eryl glanced over the bridge at the schoolhouse, which he had last left with such acrimony. He had long wanted, for the most immature of motives, to introduce Bryony to his beautiful bride. He had wanted her to see just how well he had done. But now the odd events of the valley gave added purpose to a visit, gave a long list of questions to which he wanted answers. And, as always, Eryl had the motive of mischief: the fun of telling Bryony that her boss was lying in a gutter chained to a parking meter being abused by a mob.

The visit would, however, have to be another day. For a reason he could not explain, there was a police car parked by the swings.

He turned to kiss Irina – she was a girl who needed regular kissing – before they set off on the final few miles. As they clinched, a beat-up saloon came down the valley road, from the direction of the moors.

'We're lost,' said the driver. 'D'you know a Marjorie?'

Inside the car were three bullet-headed squaddies, that breed of men who were the nemesis of The Windowman. They rarely strayed from the moor and their barracks beyond. World War Three was their business, and it did not make for social mixing.

'The teacher?' asked Eryl.

273

'Teacher?' said the driver.

'Tart in a caravan,' said a passenger.

'Oh,' said Eryl, shocked. 'Over the bridge and up the hill. Follow the hens.'

He watched them go up the lane till they vanished from sight, the car's wheels crackling across the heavy fall of twigs from the night before.

Eryl slipped the bike in gear and Irina clasped him tightly round the waist. He rode ever more slowly up the last lap home, for there was trust in those arms and it worried him. It worried him as never before. Eryl had a recess in his brain where he stored those parts of life that he wanted to forget. It was now very full. For weeks he had stored his marriage there, refusing to contemplate the future, refusing to admit to a problem with the past. He was living his life in denial, and he was planning his life in fantasy, if he was planning his life at all. The plum brandy had said that marriage in a foreign language didn't count. But now he had a wife on the back of a bike. And a bike and a wife was all that he had. Plus the price of a couple of rounds. Very soon he would have to explain all this, and to a woman who only said yes.

Beyond the bend, above the hedge, the pub came into sight. It was not the pub as he remembered it.

A lopsided sign hung unhappily from a single hook, victim of nasty, gusty Welsh winds. At the bottom of the sign, in lettering which aimed for the Gothic and achieved Hammer Horror, were the words:

THE STÉFAN ARMS

Above this was the new landlord, his teeth bared in a rictus of welcome. The paint had run overnight, and his brass-buttoned blazer had smeared his white flannels. The primitive school of art had not been kind to Stéfan. His head was disproportionately large. In his outsize left hand he held a bottle of champagne, in his outsize right hand, he held a glass. And his medium-size body rested above overlong legs that stood rigidly apart, as if he might wish to pee.

Underneath the sign, beside the blackboard that read '*Welcome to Grand Opening!*', a row was raging. Teg and Ben the molemen were raising their fists to Gwillim, and Gwillim was roaring 'Bugger off!'

Even from a distance, Eryl could see that Gwillim too was not as he remembered him. Although always surly and eccentric, Gwillim had never before dressed as a medieval brigand in black baggy knickerbockers, red gaiters and a fur hat.

'Bugger off and go to Dolly's!'

Ben threw a mole at him, a spare that he had in his trouser pocket.

'What's wrong with how we're dressed?' demanded Teg.

'It's not smart casual. Got to be smart casual.'

'You're not smart casual.'

'I'm a Georgian.'

Eryl parked out of range. Despite the Grand Opening, he was spoilt for space in the newly surfaced, newly lined car park. The crane was as effective as a curfew in cutting the pub off from the town.

He took Irina's hand and walked towards the pub's newly enlarged porch, past the pub's newly rendered front wall. He would have preferred Irina to have met other friends first, though admittedly the choice was limited.

'Hello, Gwillim!'

'No bikers!' said Gwillim, pleased at his speed of thought.

'But I'm Eryl,' said Eryl.

Gwillim gave no hint of recognition, and his body stayed barring the entrance.

'. . . And this is Irina, my wife.'

'Yes,' said Irina.

'And no women-bikers. No bikers, no molers.' He paused, like a slow learner trying to master lines. Then, somehow managing to be both robotic and self-satisfied, he went on, 'No trainers, no jeans, no T-shirts.'

Eryl pointed at the blackboard. 'What happened to "Welcome"?'

Gwillim flicked some imaginary dust off his antique knickerbockers and smirked.

As he smirked, strange sounds drifted through the porch – a rumbling, growling hum intercut with the noise of a wild cry and the stamping of feet. Looking beyond Gwillim to what was once the snug, Eryl could detect a poster on the door, which read 'The First Georgian Pub in Wales'. Irina slipped away to look through the pub window.

'Or is this a foreign welcome?'

'I'm not paid to do welcomes,' said Gwillim gruffly. 'I'm paid to do dress code. And it's no deviants, no dossers.' He spoke with the tone of a man who considered these categories to embrace most of the human race. And still he did not move.

'But you know us!' said Teg, who had wiped his boots and returned to the fray.

Gwillim allowed himself another smirk. It seemed he had been in training all his life for a job such as this. Had he himself written the job description, in which to be anti-social was essential, he could scarcely have bettered the duties of bouncer.

'You've known us for years, you bastard!' said Ben.

'You must take any complaints up with the management.'

The management creaked overhead as the hook bore his weight. The blotchy champagne bottle seemed to have taken on a derisive air, and the rictus had a subtext of sneer. In the flesh, the bloated pinky flesh, here was a person who really might piss on them from a great height. Eryl suddenly felt a great urge to take on Stéfan, this man who lived the life that should be his.

'Right! We'll talk to him!' he said.

'You can't,' replied Gwillim. 'He's gone.'

And this was said in a voice of triumph, to the tune of checkmate.

It was followed by a long and puzzled silence.

'Gone?' repeated Eryl.

'For his Grand Opening?' said Teg.

'Gone where?'

'Gone away. Disappeared. Given up. Buggered off. In the middle of the night.' A broad smile modelled on his master's rictus crossed Gwillim's face.

Then, as they each tried to absorb his revelation, there came a weird, otherworldly sound. Throbbing, polyphonic, alien, like a Gregorian chant on speed, from the depths of the throat rose the cry '*Yahlagaragoraraaahlaralagor*'. Irina beckoned him urgently to the pub window. The opening night was gathering force.

Inside the Stéfan Arms, a troupe of folk singers and dancers were stomping up a storm. Weird hybrid banjos soared up and down the scale as high-booted long-skirted peasant women slapped their embroidered thighs and moved in purple waves. A line of mountain men in multi-coloured waistcoats clapped hands and kicked their legs high, gyrating their bodies into folkloric frenzy. A tragic descant of age-old emotions filled the ears. Then slowly the attention turned to a wild, searing ululation by two shawled women wailing at some desolate primeval loss in a far-off land. And finally culminated in a moving death scene at the far end of the subtly uplit new bar.

The performance was greeted by silence. There was no audience. The pub was empty. No one had got past Gwillim.

Eryl and Irina returned to the others on the forecourt.

Gwillim was glowing. After a lifetime as an embittered feudal tenant, he had found the perfect job. He was being paid to bar people from the pub. Whoever they were. For whatever reason took his fancy. In perpetuity. He even had a uniform to give him authority, though he did not realise that the costumiers in Cardiff had been defeated by Stéfan's demand for authentic Georgian bouncerwear. So it was as a Shakespearean jester cum Transylvanian coachman that burly Gwillim, the proud cowhand, stood guard outside the smartest newest nightspot in mid-Wales. And cried 'Bugger off!' to the valley.

An impasse had been reached and the sun was setting. Gwillim remained defiantly on the forecourt, his arms still crossed, barring all entrance to the pub's Grand Opening. Inside, the Stéfan Arms remained deserted, apart from the vigorous Georgian folk troupe who were booked until midnight. The owner remained absent, destination and date of return unknown. And the customers – two muddy molecatchers well past retirement and a penniless playboy biker with a non-speaking and baffled Romanian wife – remained waiting in vain for a drink.

Eventually Teg broke the silence.

'Well, I guess it's off up to Dolly's then.'

Ben nodded reluctantly. Three miles to the moors was a long walk for a pint, especially when it was full of froth.

'You two coming?'

Eryl shook his head. He was not a fan of Dolly's. He did not fancy drinking in the front room of a little old lady in a nightdress. Or sharing his evening with a small white dog that pretended to play Grieg's Piano Concerto on the bar. It was not the glamour he had toasted in Romania, nor the high life he had promised his wife.

'Goodnight, then.'

Ben and Teg set slowly off into the fading light, the drear brown of their moling clothes gradually merging with the hedgerows.

The new bride and groom were left to stand in silence, alone with their fragile dreams and hopes. Irina looked at Eryl expectantly, tenderly, trustingly, waiting for her rich husband finally to make sense of her day.

Eryl was gazing into the distance, beyond the two old men. As he stared across Stéfan's land towards Crug Caradoc, an idea was beginning to form in his head. A twenty-eight-room idea. A homecoming with truth and justice on its side. An heir restored.

The rightful squire in place. And good sense too, for big old houses need to be occupied or they grow damp.

As he was pondering on their future and the practicality of such plans, Irina suddenly tugged him by the arm and pointed into the distant meadows, the veldt of Stéfan's dreams.

He looked where she was looking.

Something had moved in the dark.

'Yes?' said Irina.

Eryl screwed up his eyes and took a second look.

It was hard to believe, but there seemed little doubt. He did not know how best to explain it to her. The day had already been long and difficult, yet Eryl still had one more surprise in store for her.

Eryl turned to face her.

'Yes?' repeated Irina.

He held her hand to reassure her . . . and then he replied.

'Ostriches.'

ACKNOWLEDGEMENTS

My thanks go to Alistair Beaton for his invaluable comments and constant support, to Louise Greenberg for her expert advice and unbounded enthusiasm, to Mike Jones for his critical insights, to Martin Noble for his encouragement, and to Jan for always believing that I would actually finish the book.